The Fear of Flying Club

ANGELA ROBERTS

Published by

Pillar International Publishing Ltd

www.IndiePillar.com

Cover by Design For Writers

Images © Shutterstock

Book Design by Lotte Bender

ISBN: 978-1-911303-03-9

DEDICATION

For Tim, for your unwavering belief in me.
And for Louise and Connell, for gifting me with Rachel.

ACKNOWLEDGMENTS

This book would not have made it off the ground without the help of a lot of people.

Chief thanks must go to Mark Lloyd and the team at Pillar Publishing for seeing a glimmer of potential in the original manuscript and for working patiently with me to turn it into the piece of work it is today. For taking a chance on a debut author and for all of your editorial advice I am eternally grateful.

I am indebted also to John and Emma Quirk, and all the team at Manx Litfest for organising the Writers' Day where I met Mark Lloyd. For all of your help with the launch, and for taking me under the Litfest wing, I thank you.

Special thanks must go to Louise Tebay for gifting me with the character of Rachel. From advising me on all of the medical information I needed to create a character with Dravet Syndrome, to allowing me insight into some of the most difficult times any parent could experience. But also for the laughs along the way, which we must treasure. I would give anything to be able to re-write your ending. Your strength is inspirational.

And to Connell Tebay, to whose memory this book is dedicated. A beautiful boy, with the most wonderful sense of humour, who in twelve short years managed to make the lives of those he met all the richer. There will always be a part of you in Poppy, and for that I thank you. Sleep tight sweetheart.

To my loyal team of early readers for their brutally honest

but also wildly encouraging feedback which helped to shape the manuscript into something that was fit to submit. Sharon Nobbs, Sharon Suwinski, Lisa Quilliam, Ellen McGirr, Claire Pullen, Katherine Rich and Vanessa Roberts, I salute you all. To everyone else who offered to read and give feedback, your offers were much appreciated.

Thanks to Joanne Surridge whose advice as an ambulance technician came in really handy for the hospital scenes. If there are any errors in this area they are mine and mine alone. Thanks also to fellow writer Ian Wilsdon who encouraged me every day at the school gate to go home and write.

Big thanks to Bob Jones at Killer Bytes for the wonderful work on the website and for your all round creative thinking.

Last but certainly not least, this book would never have been possible without the support of my family. To my husband Tim and our daughters Katie and Grace. For your unwavering support and belief in me (when at times my self-belief had gone) I thank you with all my heart. You have encouraged me every step of the way and you truly are the most amazing family anyone could wish for. To the rest of the Quilliam and Roberts clans for all of the gems that you have given me along the way. I'm sure you will all find parts of yourselves in the book.

FLIGHT DAY MINUS 4 WEEKS

Hugh was disappointed with the turnout to his first-ever Fear of Flying class. He had generated about fifty enquiries from adverts placed in the local free newspaper and some strategic marketing in *Caravan Holidays UK*. Nineteen had gone so far as to send the £40 deposit, but nine of those must have changed their mind. Ten measly aerophobes in the whole of Manchester! With the payment he had to fork out for the hire of the room in the community college, he would be lucky to make enough money to pay for next year's membership at the golf club, never mind the two week golf break in Marbella he had set his sights on. Still, at least the PhD student he had roped in to help hadn't cost him anything. And the touchy-feely woman was the cheapest he could find to do all the meditation bollocks.

'As you know, I am a former commercial airline pilot. I'll be explaining to you how planes stay in the air; what all of those funny noises you hear *actually* are—they *are*, thankfully, far more boring than some of you imagine—as well as explaining what we are trained to do in the highly unlikely event of an emergency. I've also got Will here to help you. Will is currently doing a PhD in phobias at Salford University. He will help you understand the mechanics of your fear, so to speak. And finally, we have Petal.' Hugh gave a nervous cough and gestured at the hippyish-looking woman who was sitting poker-straight on a chair to his left. 'Petal is an expert in calming and meditational techniques and she is here to help you cope with any pre-flight nerves.'

'Are you in charge of dishing out the vodka then, love?' piped up Frannie, one of the terrified-looking students.

Petal gave a thin smile before Hugh resumed his introduction, leading them through the structure of the four-week course. Special attention was given to the final week which none of the assembled group even wanted to contemplate, the climax of the course: the short flight around the North West of England.

At this point Frannie tuned out. He didn't need to know about this as he wouldn't actually be taking the test flight. He just wanted to be prepared for when he was asked to travel for work.

McKenzie had tuned out too. He wasn't stupid enough to risk going on a flight for no actual reason. He just wanted to be ready for the flights he'd have to take with his band now that they were about to hit the big time.

Eighteen-year-old Jalil spent this part of the seminar humming the latest Fazer track. The next time he would be getting on a plane would be to go to Kavos with his mates. He needed to prepare mentally for that shit, but was not going to jump willingly on some pleasure flight round Manchester.

Rachel wondered how Charlie was getting on with the kids. Poppy was due her medication. She fought the urge to pop out of class to give her husband a quick call to remind him. She closed her eyes and focused on the trip to Disneyland she hoped to take in October. Poppy's face would be a picture. There was no way she was taking this test flight though. If she died, how would Charlie cope?

Hugh clapped his hands together. 'So, that's what we have in store for you over the next few weeks. I think you've all heard enough of my voice for the moment. What I'm going to ask you all to do now is to introduce yourselves to the rest of the group, and, if you *can*, tell us all exactly what you're frightened of. That way, Will, Petal and I can address your concerns specifically, and hopefully begin to set your minds at rest about some of your worries.' He smiled at Frannie, who had grouped himself with the other men, and held an outstretched arm indicating that he should begin.

Frannie nodded and self-consciously straightened his tie before beginning. 'I'm Frannie. I'm here because I want to apply for a promotion at work, but I know that if I get it I'll have to travel regularly to the head office in Spain.'

'Thank you, Frannie. A good reason to try to conquer your fear!' Hugh smiled jovially. 'And what part of flying is it that worries you? Claustrophobia? Heights?'

'No, nothing like that.' He shook his head definitively. 'I'm scared of some sort of mechanical failure. Of a small part not being made properly, because the lads in the factory have been out on the beer the night before or something like that, and, you know, not checked the machines properly.'

Hugh cut in. 'A very *specific* fear there, Frannie. But I can assure you, that all reputable airlines have regular quality control checks on all of their suppliers. In addition to that, the Civil Aviation Authority regulates the airlines in terms of safety to an exceptionally high standard, so there is very little danger of any supplier being allowed to get away with shoddy workmanship.' He smiled. 'I'm sure that by the end of this course we'll get you your promotion at…where was it?'

'Manchester Aerospace Engineering.'

The rest of the group gave a nervous laugh. McKenzie, who was sitting next to Frannie uttered, 'bloody hell!' then stifled a nervous giggle.

Hugh only faltered momentarily before moving on to McKenzie. The young man spoke confidently yet said little, concurring that he also needed to conquer his fear for work purposes. His Marks and Spencer's cashmere casual attire seemed at odds with his urban dialect.

'And may I ask what it is exactly that you are afraid of? McKenzie, isn't it?'

'Yeah. Well, I was on this flight, coming back from Jamaica this one time, when suddenly there was this massive bang, right, and then a bit of turbulence, and then the whole plane dropped about a thousand feet or more in, like, four seconds, yeah. Two of the air-hostesses fell over. There was all this shit falling out of the lockers and everything. The gas mask thingies fell down. It was like something from a horror film, man…'

Hugh interjected, sensing that this was not the best story for the other attendees to hear. 'The problem of turbulence is a very common one. All commercial pilots will have been fully trained in handling the plane through severe turbulence, and the cabin-crew are also trained to manage the cabin in situations such as this.'

McKenzie laughed. 'The air-hostess was crying, man—actually sobbing. Her friend was too busy sorting her out to deal with us.'

'Holy Mary!' spluttered Rachel, her face ashen. 'I don't know about you, but I always look at the cabin-crew when I'm scared on a plane. If they look calm then it makes me feel a bit better. I would have freaked out at that point.'

The others agreed with her, nodding emphatically.

Hugh, desperate to calm down the group, raised his voice slightly to get their attention. 'It sounds as though the experience you had, McKenzie, was due to a form of turbulence called a wind shear. That can cause a plane to lose altitude of up to 1000 feet at a time.'

'Bloody hell, I thought he was exaggerating with his 1000 feet.' Frannie blew a short puff of air before turning to McKenzie and adding, 'no offence like, mate.'

McKenzie held a fist out to Frannie and waited for him to reciprocate. 'None taken, man.'

'So, does this happen often then, Hugh?' said Frannie, who was now shuffling uncomfortably in his chair, sweat appearing on his forehead. 'I mean, was the lad here just really unlucky with that flight?'

'Well…' Hugh stalled, mentally calculating whether it would do his class numbers any good for next Wednesday if he told them the truth of the matter, which was that most commercial pilots would have experienced altitude loss at some point, to a greater or lesser degree. '…he was unlucky to have experienced such a severe case. Nowadays, airlines are equipped with wind shear detectors, so pilots can prepare for such an event or, ideally, avoid them altogether. Obviously there will be places where wind shears are more common than others—mountainous regions for example, or areas prone to thunderstorms.'

Rachel grabbed onto the arm of the lady sitting next to her, to whom she had not even officially introduced herself. 'Ohmigod! They get thunderstorms and hurricanes and all that in America don't they? I've promised Poppy we'll go and see Mickey Mouse!'

Hugh, once again, appealed for calm. 'As I mentioned, loss of altitude can be quite common and all pilots are trained to deal with such an eventuality. Really, wind shears and other environmental factors accounted for only two per cent of fatal air crashes between 1997 and 2006.'

'What was the biggest factor then, Hugh?' asked Frannie.

Reluctant to dwell on the topic of fatal accidents, Hugh whined. 'Well, it's the same as with anything really—the main problems come from human error.'

'Oh marvellous!' cried Frannie. 'So unless the pilot is a robot, then we've all got a good chance of being in a plane crash?'

'No, no, not at all.' Hugh's first lesson was not going well. Instead of calming them down, he seemed to be fuelling their fears.

'What about me?' protested Rachel, ignoring Hugh's pleas for calm. 'I'm off to America. I've got to be flown by a human and get attacked by those wind shear buggers!'

Hugh tried to shush the class with his hands. He was used to his wife not taking any notice of him, but he was a bit miffed that these people weren't even giving him a chance to cure them.

'As I was saying. We will address all of your concerns individually throughout the course. This session is just for me to get an idea of your worries so that I can reassure you all. The main thing I want you to think about in the meantime is that for every million flights flown, there is less than one fatal crash. Only 0.79, according to the Civil Aviation Authority.' He held a finger up to prevent further interruption. 'And, that includes all of your not so reputable airlines in places like Africa and South America. You've basically got more chance of winning the lottery.'

McKenzie bobbed his forefinger and thumb up and down above Frannie's head. 'It could be yoooou,' he teased in a deep, spooky voice, before clapping his knee in a fit of giggles and receiving a playful whack on the head from Frannie.

Hugh needed to rescue his lesson. The foot of the horseshoe table arrangement to his right seemed to be the more sensible end, so he skipped across to an attractive, blonde-haired lady who had yet to say anything. 'What about you? Would you like to tell us all why you are here?'

The attractive blonde lady gave a shy wave to the rest of the group. 'Well, lots of things really, but I'm at my worst at take-off and landing. Do you remember the Concorde crash?' The group all nodded gravely. 'They believe that was caused by birds flying into the jets don't they? Now, I know this sounds stupid, but, when I get on the plane, I spend the whole time from take-off until we get into the air desperately trying to spot any birds out of the window. And when I see any, I'm convinced that they are going to get into the engines and the plane will come down.'

'Ohmigod, I'd never even thought of that!' gasped Rachel.

'It's horrible. I just can't get it out of my head, and then I start crying and I can't calm myself down until we get to cruising altitude.' The poor woman's cheeks burned at the memory of the last flight she had taken.

'And you've got that big park just a couple of miles away from Manchester airport,' frowned Rachel. 'Is it Wythenshawe Park? The one with all the football pitches and the crazy golf. I bet there are loads of bloody birds living there.' She shuddered.

As the woman continued listing her main fears, finishing off with a gust of wind blowing one wing of the plane upwards upon landing which would flip the plane over, the others mentally added 'bird strike' to their original list of worries. Hugh sighed and moved on to Rachel.

'And what about you, Rachel was it?'

'Well I *was* worried about terrorists, but now I've got birds and wind and bloody humans to worry about!'

'Let's concentrate on your main worry, shall we?' said Hugh, feeling distinctly irritable now.

'Alright, well, I've been a bit funny about getting on planes since 9/11. It starts when I get to the airport. I see potential terrorists everywhere. Anyone who looks remotely non-Christian freaks me out big time.' She glanced at McKenzie and Jalil with their pale-brown and dark-toned skin. 'No offence, boys.'

'None taken,' shrugged Jalil, who had been christened at the age of five months, but had no idea what flavour he was. As far as he was concerned all churches were the same—dull as fuck.

McKenzie, who was also faithless, laughed.

Hugh was beginning to think that no golfing trip to Marbella was worth this—even if Margueritte *had* promised to sneak out there to join him for a bit of illicit hole-in-one activity. He pressed on. 'Now, hijacking is an interesting one. Lots of people are frightened of this, however, if you take away the 9/11 tragedy, there have been less than twenty confirmed aircraft hijackings worldwide over the last thirteen years. And only one of those incidents resulted in the death of a passenger.' He reiterated. 'Just one single passenger.'

McKenzie waved his lottery finger at Frannie again, mouthing 'it could be you.' Being back in the classroom environment had regressed him six years to when he would muck about in his GCSEs. In all of the subjects apart from music, that was. He didn't want to giggle like a schoolkid, but he was finding it very hard to control himself. It was partly the nerves.

Hugh listened to the ridiculous fears of a few more of his subjects and struggled to stop his eyes rolling in disbelief. He was glad when it was time to question his final student and bring to an end the disastrous audience participation part of his lesson. 'And, finally?'

Jalil, at eighteen years, was the youngest member of the class, and seemed uncomfortable in the group. He shuffled in his seat. 'Yeah, well, I'm here because I wanna go away with all my mates this summer. They all went to Majorca last year and had a wicked time, and I missed out cos I'm too chicken to fly.' He looked desperately sorry for himself. Rachel, who was seated to his left, stroked his arm maternally.

'Well Jalil, you have come to the right place. By the end of this course you'll be packing your bags and looking forward to a good old boys' holiday.' As soon as the words had left his mouth, even Hugh could see that they weighed heavy with false promise. Was there anything he could do for this bunch? He was beginning to realise he might have been foolish. This wasn't going to be the easy money-spinner he had imagined. 'What part of flying scares you the most, Jalil?'

'Err…' He was reluctant to tell the truth which was that he had been traumatised by a disaster film he had watched at the age of eight whilst spending the weekend with his dad. 'I suppose I'm worried about *not* being killed in a plane crash.' The rest of the group looked at him quizzically. It was no use. He was going to have to elaborate now that he had started his point. 'I mean, there are some people who survive the actual crash, but then die by, I dunno, drowning, or being burned in a fire, or,' he hesitated, 'by never being found.'

Rachel continued to rub his arm, her face furrowed with concern. 'Like that one from a few years back? Or the poor buggers in that film—the ones who had to eat each other to stay alive?'

Frannie patted his more than adequate belly. 'Don't be

looking at me, son,' he joked. 'Anyway, my wife's got me on some weight watchers' starvation diet at the moment. In a few weeks' time you'll be lucky to get a few chipolatas off me, never mind some prime steak.'

Hugh briefly closed his eyes, put his hand to his forehead and took a deep breath. He had been expecting questions about take-off, landing, turbulence and claustrophobia. He had a catalogue of responses to these concerns. Instead, his first lesson had turned into a discussion on cannibalism. He handed over to Will for a few moments whilst he contemplated the test flight in four weeks' time. Unless he could hire a robot to fly the plane; cull all birds and fell all mountains within a sixty mile radius *and* convince Rachel that not all non-Caucasian people were terrorists by the end of May, then his Fear of Flying course was going to be a complete disaster.

JALIL

'You are on an aeroplane that is accelerating down a runway at 3.20 m/s^2 for 32.8 seconds until it finally lifts off the ground. How far would you have travelled before take-off?' Mr Yashir offered the whiteboard pen around his A-level physics class. 'Anyone like to have a go? Anyone? Ok, someone at least make a start. Jalil?'

As Jalil reluctantly accepted the whiteboard pen, his friend Zain joked, 'Jalil wouldn't have a clue—he'd be too busy changing his undies.'

The class laughed. Jalil forced a smile and flicked his middle finger to Zain under the wooden science bench. He wished he had never mentioned his fear of flying to his friends. Since then they had relentlessly taken the piss out of him for it at every available opportunity. He felt foolish for being surprised about this, after all, that's what he would have done to them. The only means of defence was to show apathy, or to laugh along with them.

He made his way to the whiteboard, and managed to

work out the first part of the equation before handing the pen back to Mr Yashir to finish it off. Zain and Robbo were grinning as he sat back down. Moments later a paper missile flew into the side of his head. His mates laughed and congratulated each other with a complicated handshake. He picked up the paper aeroplane, screwed it into a ball, threw it in the air and headed it back in their direction.

A free period before Computer Science meant they had time to walk to the fried chicken takeaway on St Edmund's Way. There was a similar outlet closer to school, but it was rank! Jalil's cousin swore he once got food poisoning from eating an undercooked batch of chicken wings, but everyone knew that he'd been hammered from drinking a bottle of Strongbow, which was the real reason he had vomited all over his bedroom floor. Still, none of them risked it anymore, especially since Robbo told them that one of his Dad's mates had said the environmental health people once tested the coleslaw and that it contained five different samples of jizz.

'Hey, look who's over there.' Robbo was already cramming the last pieces of his chicken surprise bucket into his mouth.

Further up the high street, Jalil saw the unmistakable profile of Holly Richards, whose ability to pull on his hormones was almost magnetic. The sight of her laughing with her mates outside Boots made his stomach flip. In a bid to conceal any giveaway reactions from his mates, he lifted his can of Red Bull to his mouth and took a long swig.

'Come on, let's catch up with them.' Zain had just been

dumped by a fifth former and was desperate to get any sort of girlfriend as quickly as possible to bolster his pride.

The girls didn't notice them until they were practically alongside. They were still giggling about something or other.

'Alright, ladies?' Zain nodded vaguely at all five girls.

They all managed to say hello before collapsing into giggles again.

'Something we said?'

It was Holly who spoke. 'Sorry, no, we were just examining our holiday supplies.' This was obviously amusing to the girls who doubled up laughing again. 'Hey, when are you lot going to Kavos? We might be there at the same time.'

Jalil caught his breath. His stomach turned several times, the greasy chicken he'd devoured minutes earlier now felt like a rotting carcass in his gut. 'I thought you were all going to Magaluf?'

'Yeah, we were, until we realised we could get to Kavos for nearly two hundred quid cheaper.'

Becka smiled. 'That's two hundred quid to spend on part-ay-ing,' Zain replied. 'We're going the second week of the holidays. The third of August. What about you lot?'

'Tenth. We might see you out there. You can tip us off on the best places to go.'

Zain tried to regain some cool, but his bright eyes could not disguise his thrill at this news. 'We will, yeah. Well, me and Robbo will. Jalil's not coming.'

Jalil willed Zain to shut the fuck up.

Holly turned her attention to Jalil for the first time. Her

blue eyes, caked in heavy mascara, pierced his soul. He had a momentary panic that her stare had penetrated his thoughts, that she might somehow glean the truth about his nocturnal activities, and the starring role she played. Jalil was fucked off with Zain for starting this conversation.

'How come?' Her tone gave nothing away.

Before Jalil could answer, Zain had beaten him to it. 'Because he's too chicken to fly. Can you believe he's passing up a holiday in Kavos cos he's too scared to get on the aeroplane?'

At least two of the girls raised their pencilled-on eyebrows in exaggerated shock. The others just laughed.

An urge to beat Zain to a pulp engulfed Jalil. He had a split second to control his reaction. Again, past experience told him that to make any sort of big deal of the matter just encouraged them. It took all the will-power he had to force a small laugh, before saying, 'Yeah, of course that's what it is, man.' He forced himself to look into Holly's blue eyes, shrugged his shoulders and simply said, 'Finances.'

'But you're always working whenever I go to town.'

Jalil worked in the men's department of a fashion retailer. He didn't realise that she even knew where he worked. He had never seen her in the shop. Before he had a chance to ride the small wave of flattering hope, he was crushed again, by Robbo this time.

'Bollocks, Jalil, you're loaded.' Then, turning to Holly, he sniggered and continued to back up Zain's version of events. 'He's scared he'll crap his pants when we take-off and he'll have to sit in shitty skids all the way to Kavos.'

Holly wrinkled her nose in disgust.

Jalil felt like dying, right there on the spot. 'I'm just broke, man,' he uttered. He had wanted to tell them that his wages were being saved for a mixing desk, but the lump in his throat had caused his voice to wobble, so he shut up.

He needed the Fear of Flying course to fix him. It was more important than ever before. There was no way he was letting Robbo and Zain go on holiday with Holly without him. No fucking way.

FRANNIE

The accounts department of Manchester Aerospace Engineering comprised three banks of desks situated on the ground floor of a two-storey, 1960's concrete commercial building, adjacent to the small factory which produced the aircraft valves. The interior of the building had been revamped a few years earlier—the oppressive labyrinth of rooms with their flimsy yellowing vertical blinds had been removed, creating a more modern, open-plan working environment.

Frannie averted his gaze from his screen and the spreadsheet he was working on, distracted by the bottom that was perched on the corner of his desk. Looking up, Frannie realised that the arse belonged to one of the accounts assistants, Nathan who was nodding towards the boss's office.

'I've just heard he's definitely retiring this year,' said Nathan.

Frannie nodded. 'Aye, I've heard that too.'

'That'll be you in there in a couple of month
there' referred to the conspicuous glass and chrc
which provided an office, albeit not a particularl\
one, for the company's Finance Director.

Not wanting to give anything away, Frannie shrugged.
'Who knows Nath, who knows?'

'Come on mate—it's got to be you! You've practically
been doing the job for him for the last few months. If they
don't give it to you there's something wrong.'

Frannie gave Nathan a grateful wink. 'Cheers, lad.' The
vote of confidence was nice, but he wasn't about to reveal
that he might not even apply for the job. He had hoped
the Fear of Flying course would encourage him to at least
put his name forward for consideration, however, after the
inaugural meeting, he felt even less confident about his
promotion than ever before. Far from calming his nerves,
Frannie had left the first lesson feeling even more shit-
scared than before he had entered the classroom.

When Nathan left, Frannie tentatively opened the
email that had arrived several weeks earlier. The one he'd
been trying to forget about. It was from Head Office—
they were practically offering him the job on a plate. All
he had to do was submit a formal application. But aside
from a cursory reply, thanking them for the email, Frannie
had done nothing with this information. He hadn't started
the dreaded task of updating his CV with the occasional
pointless training courses he'd been forced to attend. He
hadn't printed off the job description in preparation for
the inevitable interview. He hadn't mentioned the email
to anyone. Not even to his wife, Kim. Especially not

Kim—not after the way she reacted last time a promotion opportunity came up that he hadn't applied for. Frannie knew that as soon as he told anyone, the promotion would become real, and reality meant a constant sickness in his stomach at the thought of the visits to the head office.

Nothing that Hugh had said at the last Fear of Flying lesson had made any difference to the physical sense of dread that sat like a stone in his gut. The only practical advice had come from Will, the PhD student, who had asked them to record any moments of anxiety between the lessons. He logged out of his email account and pulled his wallet out of his inside jacket pocket. He searched through the collection of receipts until he found the scrap of paper on which he had written the details of Will's website. He signed in and found the anxiety log. He thought carefully for a moment and clicked number four on the scale. In the box underneath the numbers he typed the following description.

At work thinking about the flights to Spain I'll have to endure if I take this promotion. Have butterflies in stomach and sick feeling rising to throat.

Pushing open the front door to his home later that evening, Frannie's sense of smell was assaulted by an artificial scent. As he scoured the area in between the pristine magnolia walls and ivory-coloured carpet for the offending item, his eyes fell upon a small collection of shopping bags. John Lewis, Next, Marks and Spencer. He sighed, loosened his tie with one hand and placed his briefcase down next to the hall table. He hadn't even tossed his keys into the shiny purple bowl which sat atop the table and whose only purpose seemed to be to receive keys, when his son Simon appeared lethargically in the hallway, his mother chivvying him along from behind.

'What's that bloody smell?' Frannie asked, half-irritably.

'Summer Passion, Summer Breeze and Summer Ocean. Mum was getting tired of the last one, weren't you Mum?'

'Hello Hannah, love—didn't see you there. Alright, Simon, lad?' After greeting his children Frannie finally addressed his wife Kim. 'Honestly, I don't why you bother with those awful air fresheners. You spend your whole day cleaning the house for real—why do you have to go and cover the smell of actual clean house with that bloody filth?'

Kim ignored her husband and continued with what she had been doing when he arrived—organising their two children. It was obvious from Hannah's attire that she was heading out to a ballet lesson. Simon however, was being urged to find a jacket quickly, despite his protests that it was the middle of summer and that at the age of sixteen he should be allowed to decide whether he needed a jacket or not.

Frannie smiled at his daughter. 'So, how was school?'

'Fine.'

'Lessons ok?'

'Yeah.'

This exchange was typical of late. 'Very informative,' he muttered sarcastically.

Sometimes, purely for selfish reasons, to make him feel like a better parent, he would attempt to prolong the agonising conversation. On other occasions, like today, the effort seemed too great. He had just decided to save them both from their misery when Hannah animatedly offered some information.

'Ooh, guess what?' She didn't wait for anyone to respond. 'Jason Pressly got suspended today.'

Frannie knew a couple of Hannah's friends, but this name wasn't on his radar. 'Who?'

Hannah seemed annoyed. 'Dad!' she moaned. 'Jason *Pressley*. He joined our class in year *five*.'

The system of numbering school years had changed since Frannie was at school and he had no idea what age year five related to.

'Mad hair? Sometimes used to get dropped off to school in a camper van?'

Frannie knew she was getting annoyed with him, but he still had no clue who she was talking about. Kim had always taken care of school matters, including the school run. There was no reason why he should possibly be expected to know who she was talking about.

'Remember when we did *Oliver* in year six for the end of term show? He was the orphan with the henna tattoos of Man United all over his arms.'

Frannie had a vague recollection of Kim being disgruntled about the situation at the time. 'Maybe?'

'Mum thought it was some sort of hate crime against that writer guy.'

Kim had bustled back into the hallway halfway through the conversation. 'Charles Dickens,' she tutted. 'And I'll have you know, I spent weeks organising props and making costumes for that show. He completely ruined the effect!

Hurry up—we're going to be late.'

'Hang on a minute,' said Frannie. 'Hannah was just telling me something about school. So this Jason kid, got suspended?'

'Yeah. We were in P.S.H.E., learning about reproduction, *again*,' she said rolling her eyes for dramatic effect. 'Jason waited 'til Miss Evans was pointing to the diagram of the male reproductive organ, then he took a snapchat and sent it to, like, *all* of his contacts. I think he put a rude caption on it too, but I didn't see it because I'm not one of his followers.

Frannie was lost. Snapchat? Followers? Peeshee? He had read an article in *The Daily Mail* a while back about a device ladies could use to go to the toilet whilst standing up. Something about protecting their modesty. 'What the hell is Peeshee?'

Kim shook her head. 'Honestly, Frannie. She's been doing that subject since she started high school. Do you ever listen?'

To avoid an argument, Frannie said nothing in return. He turned to his son. 'Where are you off to?'

'Violin lesson,' replied Simon flatly.

'Another one? Didn't you have one yesterday?'

Simon wasn't given the opportunity to reply.

'He has an exam coming up, Frannie. His Grade Eight! I discussed this with you ages ago. He's having an extra weekly lesson leading up to the exam to prepare him. If he passes this one he'll be eligible for the National Youth Orchestra.' She sang these last three words in a rather manic fashion whilst simultaneously fluttering her hands about, jazz style.

Frannie shook his head and took a deep breath. 'That violin teacher will be able to retire soon, the amount of brass we've put his way.'

Kim shot him a glare that said they would talk about this later. As she ushered the kids through the hall past their father she shouted over her shoulder, almost as an afterthought, 'Your tea is in the oven—I turned it off about five minutes ago. It might need a quick blast in the microwave.' Then they were gone.

Frannie pulled at the plastic shopping bags as he walked past them. Curtains and cushions. They didn't need any more soft furnishings. The house was like a show home as it was. He stepped heavy-heartedly over the shopping bags and walked through the lounge and into the kitchen. He opened the oven door, took out the foil wrapped plate and uncovered it. A bland looking meal of white fish, boiled potatoes and green beans awaited him. He let the plate fall carelessly onto the round pine dining table and sank onto the chair. He wasn't sure whether it was the unappetising low calorie food or the thought of his next credit card bill after seeing Kim's shopping bags, but something had made Frannie's appetite disappear. As he sat down to eat his dinner alone in a scenario that was becoming more and more usual these days, Frannie wondered whether he could afford to let this promotion slip past for a second time.

RACHEL

It had not been a good day for Rachel. Comparatively speaking, Rachel's 'good days' probably involved more stress than your average person could deal with. It all came down to levels of expectation. Rachel had her own gauge of what constituted a good or bad day. She measured each day as it came, against a series of events which had preceded it. Rock bottom was Emergency Admission, which thankfully, was becoming less and less frequent now that they finally seemed to be finding the right balance of drugs for Poppy. Next came Home Seizure, which didn't necessarily mean that Poppy's fit had occurred at home, just that Rachel had been able to deal with it herself. The next measure on the scale was Brook Farm Disaster—even the very thought of that day out still made Rachel's heart sink. General Crap related to a generally good day which was spoilt by any number of small things such as other parents staring at Poppy in the park, casting judgements on her behaviour without knowing why she didn't always 'conform'. Other children asking Poppy to join in with their games was tough, only because it pulled at her heartstrings when she had to watch her daughter fail to keep up with the game and often be abandoned after a short time. And sympathy—that had to be the worst.

Rachel couldn't abide people's sympathy over their situation. She was not, nor ever would be some sort of charity case, so when the hospital suggested that Poppy should be nominated for a 'Wish Come True' all expenses paid trip to Disneyland, Rachel told them exactly where to stick it, adding that if Poppy wanted to go to Disneyland she would damn well take her there herself! Not one of her finer moments, and one that she was now bitterly regretting given her acute fear of flying, especially since the first Fear of Flying lesson had only magnified her fears.

There were good days too. Milestone days, which were as vivid in Rachel's memory as in that of any other parent—things like the walking, the talking, being able to count to ten. Only, Rachel felt that these days were much more special for her, because unlike most parents, she never once took for granted that she would get to see them when it came to her youngest child.

Top of the scale was Grandma Silky's Birthday. Rachel's mother-in-law wasn't really called Silky (her name was Kathy) but she had a cat of that name, and Poppy used it to distinguish between her two grandmothers. They had gone to the party through a sense of duty, fully expecting to spend a stressful couple of hours following Poppy around the busy function room, making sure she didn't abscond or get herself into any situations with the other guests, only to find that Poppy had been brilliant—she had managed to eat her food without choking or making too much mess, she had sat quietly through the speeches, completely mesmerized by a coloured glass necklace that one of the party guests had been wearing and who had graciously allowed Poppy to sit on her lap and turn it over and over in her hands. At one point Poppy's head was inches away from the woman's chest as she pulled the glass beads close to her eyes. In spite of all their reservations they had had fun, and when they finally tumbled into bed she remembered them actually having the energy to make love.

Today though, had been a bad day. Almost a Brook Farm Disaster. Only marginally better.

'I should have cancelled.' Rachel's jaw was tense, and the kitchen surface was in danger of being worn down with the strength of her scrubbing. 'I should have bloody known better.'

Charlie sat staring into his tea for a few more moments. 'Come on, Rachel,' he said gently. 'It's not the first time, and it certainly won't be the last. It's happened and there's nothing we can do about it.'

'It's not the fact that it happened that's upset me Charlie, it's more *where* it happened.'

'She had an episode in the swimming pool—so what?'

Rachel wanted to cry, scream and lash out at her husband all at once. 'You really don't get it, do you? The swimming pool is my,' she struggled to find the right words, 'my safe place. It's the one place I can take her where I know that everything will be okay. Poppy and Jasmine both love it. Poppy can play about in the little pool and for a couple of hours she is just the same as everyone else. I've never had any problems with her in the pool. It is the only place I can take her without a feeling of dread building up inside me hours in advance. And now it's gone.' She paused. 'If you hadn't been called into work…'

'Come on now Rach—I had to go. It was an emergency. Their shower was leaking through the kitchen ceiling and the water was running right into the electric sockets. I could hardly refuse to go could I? The whole house could have caught fire! And anyway, the Hardmans are good customers—they put a lot of business my way and they always pay up.'

Rachel scrubbed harder at the pristine worktop. Bloody Jessica Hardman with her detached house and her fancy car and her perfect kids! She was blaming that stuck-up cow for this disaster. If Charlie had been with her at the pool instead of her mum it would not have happened. He would have smoothed it over with the other child's parents. Charlie had a way of dealing with other people that she simply didn't have.

Charlie sighed. 'So, what *did* happen?'

Rachel stopped scrubbing and wrung the dishcloth weakly in her hands. 'Oh Charlie, it was awful.'

He rose from the kitchen table, wrapped his arms around her shoulders and kissed the top of her head. 'Come and sit down. It can't be as bad as the Brook Farm Disaster?' His eyes smiled.

Rachel took a deep breath and began to tell Charlie about the trip to the swimming pool. 'It was all going so well until Poppy spotted the new toys.'

'Toys?'

Rachel looked at Charlie pointedly. 'Dolphins,' she nodded.

The look on Charlie's face said it all. 'Oh,' he said slowly.

Dolphins were one of Poppy's obsessions. She had a few others—water, jigsaws, a couple of TV shows and cats. The dolphin obsession started when her Aunty Clare bought her a 200-piece dolphin jigsaw for her fourth birthday which Poppy completed in less than half an hour. When anything to do with the creatures came on television, Poppy would move her face right up to the screen, as if she was trying to get into the television with them. Rachel had managed to find some old clips of 'Flipper' on YouTube which Poppy asked to watch several times a day.

'I had spotted them straight away, but we'd been there nearly an hour before Poppy saw them. She got hold of one, and was happy playing with it on her own—filling it up through the hole in the back then squeezing the rubber to make the water squirt out of its mouth.'

Charlie raised an eyebrow. 'So how long was it before she spotted the others?' He gave a tight smile in a way which showed he knew exactly what had happened next.

'About five minutes. I foiled a couple of her attempts to take the toys off the other kids, but then Jasmine swallowed a load of water and was crying for me, so I asked Mum to watch Poppy whilst I sorted Jas out and, well, let's just say Mum wasn't quick enough.'

'So what? She snatched a toy off a kid? She's done it before?'

'Oh, Charlie it was really awful. I saw what she did from

the edge of the pool. There was a little girl, she was only about two years old, standing on the steps of the island in the middle of the pool. Poppy noticed she had a dolphin and went to take it off her, but as she grabbed it, the force of Poppy's hands knocked the girl off balance and she fell backwards into the water. The girl's father started shouting at Poppy, calling her a horrible little brat and shouting at her to come and apologise.' Rachel swallowed down a painful lump in her throat. 'Mum didn't help matters. She just got all upset and marched Poppy away from the horrible man. By this time everyone was staring at us. Mum was crying, the man was still shouting. I went over to try to talk to him. I started to say that Poppy had some problems, but he just cut me off and started ranting about her bad behaviour. He didn't even give me a chance to explain, so I just thought, sod you! If you can't be bothered to give me a chance to explain and to apologise then I'll just walk away. Which is what we did.'

Charlie's face looked strained. He was generally the more laid-back out of the two of them. Rachel knew that if Charlie had been there he would have spoken to the family and smoothed things over. It had happened before. Rachel sometimes felt worse afterwards because the other parents were often so nice about the situation—full of apologies for shouting at Poppy.

'Do you want me to find out who it was and go and speak to them?'

'No, Charlie. I just want to try to forget all about it.'

'You mustn't let yourself get too stressed by this, Rach. She's not the only kid in the world who behaves badly in public. And you know it's not her fault!'

'I sometimes feel like I'm the only parent who has to deal with this crap.'

'Nah—there must be loads.'

'Yeah? Like who?'

Charlie thought for a few moments before snapping his fingers together and smiling. 'Davy Hertz!'

Rachel raised an eyebrow. 'Davy Hertz? The kid who was in the year above us at school—the one who had Tourette's?'

'Yeah, imagine being his parents! God, the end-of-term carol service at St Stephen's was brilliant when Davy was allowed to go. We used to fight to get a seat near him.'

'That's not funny in the slightest,' said Rachel stifling a grin. 'It's a condition—just like Poppy's.'

'It is a *bit* funny,' cajoled Charlie, nudging her arm. 'O, Come All Ye SHIT FUCK BOLLOCKS!' he yelled.

'Charlie!' warned Rachel, laughing now, but feeling guilty at the same time.

'Hey—we're allowed. It's one of the few perks of having a child with a disability. We can make fun of disabilities because we really do understand how fucking nightmarish they are.'

Rachel shook her head. 'So the one person you can think of who is worse than Poppy in public is a Touretter?'

He took a step closer to her, cupped the back of her head with his hand and said softly, 'Yes, but she's my Poppy, and I love her to bits. Just like I love Jasmine, and just like I love you.'

Rachel was touched. Charlie was not always romantic,

so when he said things like that she knew he meant it.

He leaned in to kiss his wife. He waited until their lips were almost touching before shouting 'TITS FUCK WANKER!'

Rachel blew a raspberry, and hit him playfully on the arm. He had managed to do what she had thought was impossible. When there was nothing to smile about, she could rely on Charlie to find something.

Charlie looked relieved. 'It's not always going to be like this Rach. We've got the appointment with the neurologist next week. If the scan shows up a lesion this time then they can operate and this will all be over. We've been through enough crap, but our luck is going to change. I can feel it.'

PETAL

The journey from the church hall to Petal's flat on the fifteenth floor of her block took eighteen minutes. It often felt like hours, but to hurry it up any more would only serve to draw attention to the fact that she was afraid, and that would be a catastrophic error. As someone who practised and taught meditation and yoga, and more recently had been employed to impart these techniques to assist a group of aerophobes, she sometimes felt a shame in her fear. Other times though, she would berate herself for feeling ashamed, after all, *her* fear was not irrational. According to statistics, there was more chance of winning the lottery than being killed in a plane crash. She was fairly sure that the odds of being attacked by some hooded twelve year olds in the courtyard between the two tenement blocks where she lived were a lot lower.

The unusual heat of the previous week had subsided to leave a pleasant warmth, some of which still remained in the early evening sun. She automatically took a right turn on reaching Jubilee House, the lifts were often out of order and she preferred to take the stairs for fear of being trapped in a lift with the local teenagers who regularly mocked her for her alternative lifestyle. Although she was fit from her yoga classes, by the time she reached the fifteenth floor Petal could feel the muscles burning in her legs and a film of sweat clinging to her body. Home safely, she could now look forward to a long hot bath before working herself up to the talk she planned to have with her life partner, Moon.

On entering the flat it took a few moments for her eyes to adjust to the darkness. At first, the coolness was welcome, but the pleasant sensation evaporated after only a couple of steps. She pushed open the living room door and wafted away a choking concoction of incense and marijuana fumes. The light from the sun glowed gently through the flimsy yellow curtains.

'Petal, my lovely.' The greeting was enthusiastic enough to warrant a broad grin but not enough for her visitor to rise from where he was sitting on the floor.

'Ash,' she nodded as politely as she could. 'I didn't know you were coming round?' She directed her gaze towards Moon at the end of the sentence to convey a subtle question. It was pointless—he had clearly smoked too much dope to pick up on such nuances.

'I have some exciting news. Thought I'd come to deliver it in person.'

The jealousy Petal felt in that instant was physical. Her heart-rate increased and without knowing it she had held her breath. Could Dawn be pregnant? She couldn't possibly have the conversation with Moon tonight if that was the case. He wouldn't think she was being serious.

'Go on?' She forced a smile.

'I've persuaded JJ to take his van down to Stonehenge for the Summer Solstice Festival. Me and Dawnee are going, and,' he paused for dramatic effect, 'there's room for you two as well.'

Petal exhaled. Was that it? 'Oh, right.'

Ash looked slightly crestfallen. When Moon spoke it was clear to Petal that he was completely stoned. 'What's up babes? Quiet class again?'

Yes the class had been quiet. Numbers had been declining on a steady basis over the last twelve months or so. New state of the art gyms with mirrored walls and smooth flooring were springing up around the neighbourhood. Petal's customers were discovering that they could pay a fraction more and exercise in relative comfort rather than in the freezing cold church hall that Petal rented, with its splintered floor and cobwebbed ceilings.

'Eight for the first class and five for the second,' she answered.

'Oh well,' Moon shrugged, 'at least you covered your costs and made a few quid.'

A few quid was precisely what she had come home with. She sighed. 'I'm going for a bath.'

She poured a generous amount of one of her favourite bath products into the running water. She knew that she shouldn't be using it—there was nothing remotely organic or natural about it. It had been a gift from one of her yoga students last Christmas, and she hadn't had the heart to refuse it. Anyway, it was amazing! The smell was delicious, and it produced a quantity of bubbles unlike anything she bought herself at the organic market. It was her guilty pleasure. She undressed and swished her hand in the water to whip up the bubbles. The water was freezing! She draped a towel round her, stuck her head out of the bathroom door and shouted.

'Moon, there's no hot water. Has it been ok today?'

Moments later Moon appeared at the bathroom door, a puzzled expression exaggerated on his face. A thought occurred to Petal. 'Moon? You *did* pay the gas bill last week didn't you? It was overdue.'

Moon's mouth hung open as he trawled his ever-depleting memory cells for the information. 'Er, the gas bill?'

'Yes Moon, the gas bill.'

'It said we had until the twenty-sixth or something to pay.'

Petal moaned, 'It's the twenty-seventh today, Moon. We've been cut off? For goodness sake—why didn't you just pay it when I asked you? You know our finances are tight. It's a tricky balancing act to get everything right. I have the file next to the fridge and everything is worked out to the penny and to the day.' Petal struggled to contain her temper. 'You said you'd pay it on your way to the skip on Tuesday!'

'Chill out Pet, it's cool, I'll do it tomorrow.'

'I need a bath now, Moon. In case you hadn't noticed, I've been out working this evening. I'm cold, sweaty and I don't want to wait until tomorrow.'

'I don't mind you being sweaty babe—it's all natural.

There is such a thing as being too clean you know. It kills off your natural aura.'

Petal didn't acknowledge this. Instead she marched down the short corridor into their bedroom and slammed the door behind her. She was cold, hungry and pissed off. She threw herself into bed with nothing to do but wish for tomorrow to arrive.

McKENZIE

McKenzie jabbed the *end call* button on his mobile phone several times before hurling the handset onto the small blue futon in his attic studio. It hit with such force that the phone rebounded onto the floor at the feet of his bandmate, causing the battery to fly out.

'Fucking wanker!' he growled.

Little Gee replied with a mixture of amusement and irritation. 'Don't let him wind you up—he's a tool!'

'Whose band does he think this is? Just because he's offered us a record deal he thinks he's the Big Daddy. Tried to tell me about the importance of my own fucking band!'

'Our band!' corrected Little Gee.

'Yeah, you know what I mean.' McKenzie unplugged a set of headphones from the synthesiser and coiled the lead violently around the headband. 'Six years we've been fighting to get this band off the ground to where we are now, then he turns up acting like he's the fucking Godfather.'

Little Gee shrugged. 'Never seen it.'

McKenzie frowned. 'Think Robert De Niro from *Meet The Fockers* but without the funny bits. And don't tell me you haven't seen that, cos I know it's one of your top ten films ever, you simpleton!'

'It's a great film,' he laughed. He placed the last of the kit into the hard case ready for the following day's trip, then spun round to face McKenzie. He held up his index fingers and thumbs together to form a circle. 'So you're not in his 'circle of trust' anymore?'

'Obviously not. He was checking to make sure I don't miss the flight again. Got a ten minute lecture on the importance of publicity tours. Talking to me like I'm a bloody three year old.'

'Look, I don't like the slimy twat any more than you do, but if we want to stay sweet with Dark Star Records then we've just gotta suck it up. And whatever you think of him, we wouldn't be able to do all of this publicity crap without him. Dark Star are big, man. They've got more money than, I dunno, the whole of…Wales!'

This was all it took to break McKenzie's bad mood, his default setting generally being effervescent bordering on manically cheerful. He folded over at the waist and emitted a high pitched laugh. 'Fucking Wales? I thought you were gonna say some third world country or something! That's well Walesist!'

'Whatever, man. *We're* the Urban Phantoms. Me, you, Kitty and The Prof. Alfie—he's just the manager. The man who makes things happen. We all know he'd drop us the minute things started to go a bit Pete Tong, but we'll *always* be The Urban Phantoms.' He banged his fist against his chest. 'It's in here, man.'

The Urban Phantoms were the result of years and years of hard graft. McKenzie (aka Big Mac), Kitty, Little Gee and more recently, The Prof, had all played a significant part in getting the Urban Phantoms to where they now found themselves. From their infancy in the music room of their local comprehensive, where McKenzie and Little Gee (or George as he was known then) used a basic synthesiser to piece together some simple 2-step garage tunes, through to their house party days, then to the small club circuit where they had noticed the trend towards more of an R&B vocal vibe, right through to the present. The addition of Kitty with her grungy chic beauty and crystal voice, and The Prof who was a technical genius and came with his own equipment, added the missing dimension to the band.

The present was a pretty fucking exciting place for the Urban Phantoms. A rave review in *NME* had propelled them from a small time East London band to one of the hottest up and coming acts in the UK. Their website received more hits in the week of the *NME* review than it had in the whole two years since it had been launched, and they had sold a few thousand downloads of their track *Under the Radar* as a result of it. It was at that point that they had started to attract the interest of a couple of record companies. Both McKenzie and Little Gee had been pissed off about the timing of this interest. Both of the companies who were sniffing around them had been sent their demos on several occasions prior to the review, and both record companies had replied each time with a standard 'Thanks, but no thanks' email. Only after they had managed to break into the market themselves did the companies decide to show some interest. Little Gee had wanted to tell them to shove it. McKenzie would have liked to as well. After all, their interest would have been much more helpful to them two years earlier. However, McKenzie did have some business acumen, and knew exactly where the balance of power lay when it came to record companies. Which was how they found themselves signed up with Dark Star Records, and how McKenzie now found himself taking a bollocking from his manager.

The most irksome thing about the whole situation was that McKenzie couldn't complain. Alfie, in spite of being a mouthy Essex boy in a suit, with, in McKenzie's opinion, no idea about either the mechanics or the heart of music, had managed to negotiate some pretty unbelievable deals for them in the six months he had been 'in charge'. The *piece-de-résistance* was a series of arena gigs supporting an A-List American band who were touring the UK in November. The result of that was that they had several months of publicity to do. Radio and cable TV interviews had been lined up on a series of low-budget music programmes in the UK as well as the Netherlands and Scandinavia. Which was where the bollocking came in.

A week ago to the day, McKenzie had been scheduled to take part in a student music programme in Glasgow. It was fairly low rent stuff—broadcasting via a podcast to the local student community. He had packed all his gear, rehearsed some of the PR shit that Alfie had told them they had to include (even though he would usually never say anything so wanky) and had told the rest of the band he would meet them at Stansted airport the following morning for the flight. He had fully intended to be there. He had told himself that he could do the short flight no problem. Reassured himself that it was only an hour. He had set off in his nine year old Citroen Saxo and had arrived at the short stay car park in plenty of time, but instead of getting straight out of the vehicle he had made the mistake of sitting in his car for a fraction too long. It was long enough for him to hear the roar of the engines preparing for take-off. Long enough to witness a huge airliner wobbling then straightening as it came in to land. Long enough for the sickness to take hold in his belly and the sweat to seep through his carefully chosen T-shirt. Long enough for him to decide to fuck the whole, stupid idea off and drive home.

He had made the excuse that his car had broken down in the Blackwall tunnel. That by the time the RAC had sent someone out to fix it he had been too late for the flight. The rest of the band seemed okay with that, but Alfie had been unimpressed. He had lectured him on exactly what he should have done in order to make sure he made the flight. Which is why he felt the need to phone McKenzie the night before the Amsterdam trip. To make it clear that another no-show would be completely unacceptable. He had told McKenzie that letting the rest of the band down would not be an option this time. Especially as they had a live performance on the back of this interview. The fact was, McKenzie knew he'd let the rest of them down, and no one felt more shit about that than he did. He didn't need Alfie to point this out. It was *his* band, not Alfie's, and having that mouthy tosser lecturing him about his responsibilities made him furious. He knew he had to get on that flight. He was doing something about it. The first step was booking himself on to the Fear of Flying course (in Manchester, where he hoped he would be anonymous) and had already been to one lesson. It hadn't helped of course. He had come out of the lesson about a hundred times more terrified than when he went in, leaving him with a problem. What possible excuse could he come up with for missing the flight to Amsterdam?

FLIGHT DAY MINUS 3 WEEKS

Hugh was amazed. Thankful but amazed. Four of his students had turned up for the second Fear of Flying lesson in spite of the dismal first session. He had been tempted to throw in the towel after week one, when, if truth be told, even *he* would have been reluctant to board an airliner after hearing all of the tales of doom and disaster. Only a midweek visit to Marguerite's den of temptation (a neat little bungalow in Pendlebury) had motivated him to continue with the course. Having recently quit her voluntary job as deputy manager of the Help the Aged charity shop due to an argument over the moral correctness of selling a DIY vajazzle kit, Hugh's wife's increasing presence at home meant his once regular visits to his mistress had been curtailed. He was lucky if he got to see Marguerite once a month, and the 'boys' trip to Marbella was pulling at his groin area with gusto. If the trip was to become an annual affair, so to speak, he would need to solicit some half-decent testimonials from his students at the end of the course to vastly increase his numbers for next year.

He gave a final glance at the standard-issue school clock on the wall before deciding to press on with the lesson. It was just his sodding luck that one of the people who had not returned for week two was the pretty blonde lady, and not one of the more mouthy or hysterical ones. Still, he felt slightly more prepared than he had been the week before. He realised he had made a novice mistake allowing his students too much of a say in the lesson. This week he was going to try to keep audience participation to a minimum.

As Hugh fiddled about with the wire connecting the laptop to the projector, Will reminded the class of the importance of using their phobia logs. 'It's extremely important that you make a note in your logs each time you feel any sort of anxiety.'

Frannie raised his hand. 'I feel anxious every time my wife tells me she's been to town. That woman can spend money like you wouldn't believe.'

Will laughed along with the rest of the group, simultaneously holding up his index finger.

'In all seriousness though, yes, I'd like you to include any moments of anxiety you might be experiencing. It doesn't necessarily have to be related to flying, although I imagine many of you will already be feeling anxious at the thought of the end-of-course flight in three weeks' time.'

Will was interrupted by a low rumble of discontentment and a shuffling of bottoms at the very mention of the graduation flight.

'Part of my thesis is to establish whether phobias are a completely stand-alone reaction to an external stimulus, or, whether they stem from other, seemingly unrelated sources. Please feel free to mark down any moments of anxiety in your logs, remembering to score each incident from one to ten, one being the lowest, ten being…'

'…a change of underwear moment?'

'Thank you, Frannie. I wasn't going to word it like that myself, but yes, ten being a moment of severe anxiety and stress. Also remember that you can use the chat facility on the website if you are feeling anxious. It sometimes helps to have someone to talk it over with who understands how you are feeling. Unless you have experienced a severe phobia yourself, it can be difficult to comprehend someone else's reaction.'

Hugh concurred privately with Will. He had never experienced this type of fear before. Moments of anxiety, yes—catching a nasty bout of VD from an air-stewardess after a stop-over in Moscow he remembered as being a pretty stressful time. That wasn't irrational though—his wife Pat would have done a lot more damage to his nether regions had she found out. Being scared of travelling in a perfectly well engineered mode of transport though, was something he truthfully found bizarre.

After a good deal of wire-swapping and switch-flicking, Hugh managed to set up the projector. 'I'm going to play two short video clips of aeroplanes in various stages of flight. This will include preparation for take-off, the take-off itself, cruising, preparation for landing and, finally, landing.

McKenzie frowned and raised his hand. He was wearing thick-framed spectacles this week in an attempt to remain incognito. His no-show for the flight to Amsterdam had created a furore at Dark Star records (he had told them that his Gran had died, knowing that even a shrewd bastard like Alfie couldn't argue with that one) and some apologies were published on the Urban Phantoms website, as well as in the Dutch music press. McKenzie was fairly sure none of his fellow students were subscribers to the Dutch music publication *FRET*, but still, he didn't want to take any chances. 'Why two videos? Is it, like, a good example and a bad one? Cos I'm not sure I wanna see the bad one, man. You're supposed to be making us feel better, not worse!'

'No, no, nothing like that at all,' said Hugh, trying hard to disguise his irritation with this early disruption. 'The first one is the video for a propeller plane. The second one is a jet engine. They make different noises, which is why we will be examining both types.'

Jalil had been momentarily distracted by McKenzie. The voice was familiar...or was it the face? He trawled through his mental database to try to work out if McKenzie had been a pupil at his school—albeit a few years older. Nah, the accent just didn't fit. McKenzie was a proper Southerner. Hugh's response to McKenzie's question re-captured his full attention. 'A propeller plane? Aren't they from, like, about a hundred years ago?'

'Not at all!' replied a bemused Hugh. 'Many domestic or short haul flights still use prop planes.'

'Which one are you using for them,' Frannie caught himself 'er, I mean *us* for the end-of-course flight?'

Jalil shook his head. 'There's no way you're getting me on one of those Wright Brothers efforts!'

Rachel disagreed. 'No, love. Don't you remember what that lady said last week about the birds flying into the jet engines. I think I'd prefer a propeller. What's better Hugh—a bird flying into a jet engine or a bird flying into a propeller?'

'Well neither is exactly ideal,' he snapped. 'Can we just get on with it?' Hugh instructed Will to dim the lights. 'Now the first sequence is for a jet plane.'

The gentle hum of an aircraft's engine filled the room, becoming gradually louder and louder as four faces blanched whiter and whiter.

Hugh raised his voice to a gentle shout to make himself heard over the audio. 'This is the sound of the engines spooling-up for take-off.'

Frannie raised his hand. 'Can I make a note in my anxiety log, please?'

The others sniggered. Hugh pressed on. 'You may feel some vibration as you travel down the runway. This is simply the wheels passing over the centreline lights. A bit like when you drive over cat's eyes.'

Jalil smirked at the word 'vibration.' At eighteen years old, there were some words that just triggered an infantile reaction. Organism was another one. Jalil and Robbo had once spent an entire lunchtime in detention after pissing themselves laughing every time the biology teacher said the word. In fairness, they probably wouldn't have done had Zain not mispronounced it the previous week whilst reading from the overhead projector.

'The journey down the runway usually lasts around twenty seconds, after which, the nose of the aeroplane will tilt upwards and you will lift off.'

Rachel shuddered. 'What happens if it climbs at too steep an angle, Hugh? I'm terrified it'll tip over.'

Hugh tried to dismiss this one bluntly. 'It won't. It can't.'

Rachel countered, 'It can, Hugh, I've seen it before.'

Hugh strained to hear over the noise of the video. 'When have you seen this impossible feat happen, Rachel?' His eyes challenged her to come up with something to back up her claim.

'Last year, we went to visit Charlie's sister in Farnborough. This plane did a somersault—like you'd see on a roller coaster! There was all this smoke—red and blue and…'

Hugh looked at Rachel incredulously. 'Are you talking about the Red Arrows, Rachel?'

'Well, yes, but…'

Hugh cut her off immediately, and once again wondered why the nice quiet blonde lady couldn't have come back this week instead of this imbecile. 'Moving on, now the noise you might have just heard if you hadn't been too distracted by Rachel's eloquent recreation of the Farnborough air show, was the clunking shock absorption of the landing gear on take-off.'

Hugh was distracted by another raised hand.

'Can the tail of the aircraft bang against the runway if the pilot takes off too steeply?'

Hugh couldn't understand why they couldn't just watch the bloody thing and ask questions later instead of constantly interrupting his video presentation. Anyone would think they didn't want to be cured. 'Nooo,' he said, his tone now sounding slightly bored. It *could* happen—he knew of incidents where this had *indeed* happened, but they were very rare indeed and there was no way that this lot would know about them. He knew that if he was too honest with them, none of them would come back for the third session. He took a slow, deep breath and visualised his golfing trip to Spain. 'Any aircraft you would be travelling on would have a device called a tailskid to prevent this.'

Jalil smirked again at the word skid.

Twelve minutes later, Hugh was fairly confident that his class were feeling much calmer about the graduation flight in three weeks' time.

As Will flicked the lights on, Frannie finished off the mental balance sheet he had been compiling in his head for the last few minutes. If he cancelled his Sky TV subscription, vetoed all the unnecessary present-buying his wife felt the need to partake in *and* forfeited his lunch a couple of times a week, he reckoned he might be able to afford to let the promotion go by after all.

McKenzie silently cursed Hugh for showing the video. The noises had brought back the all too real memory of sitting in his car at Stansted airport. The fear had caused him to perspire, and he would now have to endure the three hour train journey back to London in a sweat soaked shirt.

Rachel had felt sick at the thought of the plane flipping over mid-air. She compared it to the sensation of being on a roller coaster which, incidentally, she hated too. At that moment she questioned the whole notion of taking a trip to Disneyland. It had never been her decision in the first place—it was that bloody hospital and their interfering that caused all this. Well they could bloody well sod off! She would just take Poppy and Jasmine to Alton Towers and get Charlie to stick a Mickey Mouse costume on.

Jalil had popped his ear bud in and pressed play on his iPod as soon as the landing gear started to make that archaic clunking noise. It was okay for him—he had already decided he was not taking Hugh's terror flight. He was not a stupid boy—nine GCSEs if you don't mind. Still, he couldn't help feeling a bit sorry for the other poor bastards who were going to be subjected to it.

PETAL

Petal tipped out the contents of the hessian sack onto the small Formica breakfast bar and wondered *when* exactly it was that her life had become a light-entertainment parody. Whilst the contestants on the TV show *Ready Steady Cook* battled it out to create a meal out of a mishmash of surprise ingredients for the benefit of momentarily amusing the general public, Petal lived like this out of necessity.

She sighed. Two loaves of sliced white bread, a box of croissants, a packet of chocolate covered doughnuts, half a dozen browning bananas, a punnet of soft strawberries, a bruised aubergine, a dented tin of cream of mushroom soup and three mystery tins whose labels had disappeared.

'Not bad today, Pet.' Contrary to Petal's feelings on the matter, Moon seemed fairly pleased with today's haul.

Petal raised an eyebrow. 'Did they not have any wholemeal bread?'

'Nah, not today. I think those travellers from the other side of the embankment have been down again. They need to stick to their own territory! It's bang out of order stealing from someone else's skip. No bloody respect, that lot!'

As her thirty-ninth birthday approached, Petal couldn't help assessing the state of her life. Ten years ago, free-cycling food from supermarket skips had been an exciting and eco-friendly way to live. Moon's radical lifestyle and boundless optimism had spread effortlessly into her soul, igniting a fire in her spirit that she believed could drive a change in the world. They had been an unstoppable force, living the good life for themselves and for everyone else on the planet. Nowadays her fire no longer raged, and her charred spirit merely smouldered. She had hoped to make a special meal tonight. She had even bought some elderflower wine from the farmers' market for the occasion. Unless the mystery tins held anything amazing, it looked like it was going to be aubergine stir-fry for the second time that week.

'They aren't exactly stealing, Moon. It's not like we're paying for the food either.'

'It's a matter of honour, Petal. Everyone has their own patch and you don't stray into anyone else's. You just don't do it! Everyone knows the Sainsbury's on Trafford Lane and the Aldi on Church Street are mine and Ash's territory...*and* Old George from the park—but he's not been round much lately. I think his chest is bad again. Ash was dropping a bag of stuff off for him on his way home. Anyway, the point is, you don't steal from your own. The amount of good food that gets chucked away in this city is horrifying. There is enough for everyone who wants to live like this without getting into turf wars. It's like with window cleaners—you don't go near someone else's patch. Anyway, we did well today. It's not every day you get strawberries!'

Petal picked up the punnet of soggy fruit. A pool of bright pink juice ran in small rivulets as she tilted the plastic container to inspect the berries. A small amount of white, candyfloss-like mould had begun to form around some of the stalks. She banged the punnet back down on the counter in frustration, then immediately felt guilty. It wasn't Moon's fault. It was she who had changed, not him. His enthusiasm for the cause had been the trait that had most attracted her to him when they first met. The fact that she now found it plain irritating was not his fault.

'And chocolate doughnuts!'

Petal resisted the urge to point out that covering stale doughnuts in chocolate and sprinkles was just a way of extending their tired life by another day, therefore the doughnuts on the table were likely even worse than the plain ones they had found the day before. She rubbed her tummy. If the conversation went well tonight she would have to start eating a more balanced diet. Cheap, sweet carbohydrates would be a thing of the past. She took a deep breath and tried to remain positive. She surveyed the three labelless tins and tried to gauge which looked the most promising. A nice tin of stewed steak, or even a tin of mixed beans could save the stir fry. After a moment's indecision she went for the middle tin and pulled on the ring pull before she could change her mind.

Petal slammed the two plates of food down on the table and sloshed out two glasses of elderflower wine. She told herself that she would need to improve her mood after the disappointing discovery of the contents of the mystery tin. She needed to be warm, charming and convincing.

'This looks lovely, Petal,' said Moon genuinely as he examined the *Thomas the Tank Engine* pasta shape on the end of his fork.

Petal sliced into her aubergine frittata and covered the forkful with the cheap tomato sauce from the tinned pasta meal. 'Hmm,' was all she could manage. Her creative culinary skills had enabled her to save them from a second aubergine stir fry that week, but she was unsure as to whether her negotiating skills were quite as polished. She took a large swig of her wine which tasted disappointingly low in alcohol. She didn't know how to bring the subject up. Should she mention someone in her yoga class who'd just had a baby? Should she tell Moon that the thought of nearing the end of her thirties had suddenly set her biological clock ticking? Should she drop some subtle hints? She looked at Moon who was hungrily wolfing down the frittata and *Thomas the Tank Engine* shapes and decided that she should just come out with it.

'Moon, I think we should have a baby.' She held her breath at the end of the sentence and watched silently for his reaction.

Moon had stopped mid-forkful. His brow crumpled in confusion; half of an engine—it looked like it could have been Gordon—spilled out of his lips as he muttered the reply. 'Eh?'

She swallowed. 'A baby.'

Moon looked genuinely perplexed by the statement. 'Why?'

Petal had anticipated a number of responses Moon could have given. *Why* was not one of them. She stalled. 'What do you mean, *why*? Why does anyone want a baby? Because it's one of the most natural, primeval instincts known to mankind. The need to reproduce. Create life. Can you think of anything more amazing than creating a new life?'

Moon put his knife and fork on his plate and pondered this. 'Err…'

Petal helped him out. 'There isn't anything more amazing, Moon.'

'The thing is, Petal, we're free spirits, me and you. If we had a baby it'd tie us down.'

'To what, Moon? This flat? The only time you ever leave it now is to go and do the skip run and to score some weed from Ash.'

'That's only because we can't afford to fix the camper van. If I could get that up and running again we could be back on the road, like we used to. And anyway, that's a good point. How could we have a kid when we're this broke? We couldn't afford it. It wouldn't be fair.'

'I've got my regular yoga class, and if this Fear of Flying course goes okay then I'm sure Hugh will ask me back again. And there must be loads of other anxiety courses I could get myself on.'

'But if you're doing that who would look after the baby? *I* don't know what to do!'

'I don't bloody know either, but we'd learn. *You* would learn. Or failing that, you could get a job!' Petal knew this was a touchy subject, but she didn't care. It was all or nothing now.

'I've got a job!'

'A paid job, Moon! Freecycling stuff from skips is all well and good but it doesn't pay cash. You mentioned window cleaners earlier, you could do something like that. Low overheads —all you'd need to get started would be a bucket, a cloth and a ladder.'

Moon looked horrified. 'I'm not stealing anyone's patch.'

'Grr, it doesn't have to be window cleaning. You could just get a job! Anything!'

Moon shook his head. 'I can't believe you're asking me to sell my soul.'

Petal slammed her hands down on the table. 'For fuck's sake, Moon, I'm suggesting you get a job, like everyone else, not sell your soul.' She glared at him. 'And there's no need to look like that.'

'Like what?' he whined.

'Like somebody's shat in your teapot!'

'I can't believe after all these years you're turning into one of them, Petal. A sheep! A follower! You want me to go and slave my guts out for a few quid that the government will then steal off me in taxes and spend on new runways so we can clog our planet up a bit more; on schmoozing up to the fat cats of the big banks; on H_2O.'

Petal was thrown off track for a second. 'What the fuck has water got to do with it?'

'Eh?'

'Water—H_2O.'

Moon replied. 'H_2O—the new train line thingy.'

'Do you mean HS2?'

'Whatever!'

Petal took one, deep inhalation, then breathed out seven short breaths. It was a technique she had learnt on a course at a commune years earlier. She found it really did have a calming effect, and she planned to use it on her flying students during the next lesson. She simultaneously mentally blocked out any fears that were already seeping in regarding the paternal intelligence genes that might be passed on to any future child of theirs.

'All I was trying to say was this: wouldn't it be nice to get out of here?' She swept her hand in the semi-circle in the air above her head. 'To have some more space? To be able to choose what type of bread we eat, rather than wait to see what nobody else wants at the end of the day? I'm not turning into a capitalistic ogre, Moon, but sometimes, *just sometimes* it would be nice to have some of the nice things that other people have. A new scarf, some perfume. Just occasionally. Not all the time! And yes, a child. There are millions of people who are far worse off than we are, but they still manage to bring up their children, because they have love! That's far more important than money.'

Moon groaned. 'It's not just the money thing though. I mean, don't you think that our world is overcrowded enough as it is? I don't believe we should put an extra burden on the planet by adding another human being that it then has to sustain.'

Petal felt tears prick her eyes. She looked at him pleadingly.

'I'm not saying that it's wrong to want to share your love. I totally get that, Petal.' Moon thought for a second.

'How about getting a dog?'

Petal scraped her chair back, picked up the plates and chucked them into the sink. She marched down the short corridor to the bedroom, holding in the tears until she had thrown herself onto the bed. She buried her head into her pillow and howled.

RACHEL

Rachel was always one of the last mothers to enter the school playground at home time. This was partly because she always had far too many things to do in a day than there were hours to do them in, but also partly intentional. She had discovered from Poppy's early days in reception class that the school playground brought out the worst in her. She couldn't bear to listen to the constant bragging of other parents at the (if you believed them as much as they seemed to believe themselves) super-human achievements of their offspring. If she had to listen to Stephanie James telling people one more time that her six year-old daughter Francesca had the reading levels of a ten year-old then she couldn't trust herself not to bash the stupid cow over the head with a copy of *War and Peace*. Rachel was certain that even if Poppy ever did master her letters, she wouldn't be boring other parents to death by banging on about it to anyone who would listen. Whilst the bragging was bad enough, Rachel paradoxically found the moaning just as infuriating. All of the other parents in Poppy's class had healthy children. They had no idea what it was like to have to deal with the constant trips to the hospital, the sleep deprivation, the permanent ball of anxiety that never left her stomach. Yet they still complained. They complained about not securing Take That tickets, about a smashed iPhone screen, about a dose of chicken pox. When Rachel heard them complaining, complaining, complaining, for the sake of bloody complaining, she wanted to shake every last one of them by the hair and tell them how goddamn lucky they all were.

This afternoon, it was Aliya's mum who was the source of Rachel's increasing rage. She was whining on about Aliya's older sister having a throat infection and having to miss the ballet exam that she'd practised for. A ballet exam! Rachel wondered what it would be like to have a life where the biggest worry was missing a sodding ballet exam! She tapped her foot on the concrete, imagining what she would really like to say to Aliya's mum. It would go something along the lines of being grateful for having a child who had the co-ordination to be able to dance. Poppy could walk, and, in her own fashion, run, but her movements were clumsy and uncoordinated. She struggled to gauge depth, so navigating steps was a problem for her.

Rachel was relieved when the schoolchildren came running out, just in time to stop this particular train of thought getting her any more wound up. About half of the kids from reception class had spilled out when Rachel spotted Poppy's teacher, Miss Myers, striding across the playground. This was never a good sign. In fairness, Miss

Myers could have been coming out to speak to any one of the parents of the twenty eight children in Poppy's class, but Rachel knew the odds were she was the favourite, followed marginally by Kai's mum and then Lewis' gran.

Miss Myers gave nothing away as she walked through the yard. 'Please be Kai, please, please make it that little shit today and not Poppy', Rachel pleaded silently. She glanced at Kai's mum, who had also clocked Miss Myers' walk of doom. Kai's mum gave Rachel a conspiratory eye roll before glancing in the direction of Lewis' oblivious grandmother. With just a few feet to go, Miss Myers looked up and smiled at her victim.

'Hi Rachel, is it okay if I just have a quick word?' Her voice was sweet and friendly, as if to convey to the other parents they should move along—nothing to see here!

Rachel gave a tight smile, and replied 'Of course.' She made the mistake of glancing over in time to see Kai's mum breathing a deep sigh of relief, and to take in the pitying glances the other parents were casting in her direction. 'Just give me two minutes. I need to find Jasmine and tell her to play for a bit until we've finished.'

She used the time it took her to march round to the junior playground to send a quick text to Charlie.

Been called in again! God knows what she's done. I swear I'm not doing school run any more, you can!

By the time she reached Jasmine, Charlie had replied.

Oh shit. Nice try, but I thought I was banned from going into Poppy's class after parents evening ;-)

Rachel smiled at the private joke.

Well you did spend the entire appointment staring at Miss Myers' tits!

Charlie replied immediately

They were massive! I couldn't help it! Anyway, you admitted you were staring too!

She glanced at her watch, unable to delay it any longer before quickly typing.

I'm allowed, I'm a girl. Gotta go.

Her phone beeped again just as she was winding her way through the clusters of tables in Poppy's classroom.

Good luck babe. Tell her we only want what's breast for Poppy. Haha x

There was something vaguely chastising about the simple act of having to sit on the miniature seats in Miss Myers' classroom. Rachel shifted in her seat, her knees awkwardly jutting at chest level. Rachel knew the drill well. She had already settled Poppy down at another table with the iPad before bracing herself for what Miss Myers wanted to discuss today.

'There are a couple of things I wanted to talk to you about, Rachel.' Miss Myers smiled sympathetically before continuing. 'I'm afraid we've had another water incident today.'

Rachel immediately felt her muscles tense up. 'Go on.'

'We had the water and sand table set up in the outdoor area, and when Poppy noticed that it had been set up she only wanted to play in the water. I couldn't get her to do anything else.'

Rachel tried to play devil's advocate. 'You *know* that playing in water is one of her 'things'.'

'Yes, yes, I understand that. But it became a problem

when the other children wanted to play too. There's only enough room for two children on each side of the table. Poppy wasn't keen on sharing the table space, and I'm afraid Leah and Kai ended up getting soaked.'

'She splashed them?'

'I'd be more inclined to say 'drenched'. I've had to send them home in their PE kits.'

Rachel felt deflated. 'Okay, I'll speak to her about it, but I'm afraid that unless you take the water table away for a while, this might keep happening.'

'I'm not sure that's fair on the other children.'

Fair? thought Rachel. Was it fair that Poppy suffered from epileptic fits every time she went to sleep? Was it fair that her brain activity didn't power down at night time like the other kids, meaning she would wake up exhausted, pale and sickly? Was it fair that she had to be sedated every night just to give her body a rest from the physical movements that the brain activity caused? Rachel began to feel the anger stir in her belly again.

'Where was her support worker?'

'Sorry?'

'Her support worker—the one the school gets paid to provide her with? Couldn't she have intervened before Poppy splashed the other kids?'

'I'm afraid Miss Koslowska was assisting another child at the time.'

Rachel bent down to pick up her bag. 'I'll speak to Poppy about it when we get home.'

'That's not quite everything,' said Miss Myers quickly.

Rachel felt her heart sink. She dropped the bag back on the floor.

'After snack time, Poppy went to the toilet. It appears that whilst she was in there she put the plug in the sink and turned on the tap. There were paper towels stuffed into the overflow. Luckily the caretaker was alerted within minutes, but, I don't have to tell you that it could have been a lot worse.'

Rachel put her head in her hands. 'I'll speak to her.' She didn't believe this would make any difference whatsoever. Poppy didn't do these things because she was naughty. Her behaviour was compulsive and she simply hadn't yet developed the social skills to control it. 'Anything else?'

Miss Myers grimaced. 'We're also having a few issues with hugging.'

'Hugging?'

'Yes, now don't get me wrong, I think it's adorable to see how affectionate Poppy can be, but some of the other children are finding it difficult to deal with being cuddled quite so, er, enthusiastically.'

Rachel knew better than anyone that Poppy's hugs could sometimes be mistaken for attempted strangulation, but she simultaneously felt the primeval urge to protect her daughter. 'So, let me get this right, one minute she is being too mean to the other children, the next she's being too kind to them.'

Miss Myers flushed. 'Well, I just thought I'd mention…'

'I'm sorry Miss Myers, but I can't help feeling that the school should be doing a lot more to help a child like Poppy.'

Miss Myers gave a little cough. 'I have to say I completely agree with you.'

Rachel was taken aback. 'What?'

'I said I agree, completely, Rachel. The thing is, we simply don't have the resources to give Poppy the education she needs. The education she deserves. Yes, we have some support staff here who can make a difference, but as you know Poppy's support worker is shared with five other children in the school. I completely understand how frustrating it must be for you to come here and recognise that Poppy isn't having her needs met, which is why I was wondering…' She paused, seemingly unsure as to whether to go on. '…I was wondering whether you had considered the special needs unit at St Thomas'?'

Rachel felt as if she had taken a blow to the stomach. Her throat constricted, a salty sting assaulted her eyes. She shook her head.

Miss Myers held up two calming palms. 'Before you say anything Rachel, this is just a thought, and in no way am I going to pressure you into anything. I'm only mentioning this to you because I have a friend who works there. The resources they have available to them are fantastic! They have one-to-one support for each child there, and educationally, they are outstanding in terms of progress.'

Rachel looked over at Poppy. Her beautiful Poppy, who was sitting calmly, watching an episode of *Flipper* on the iPad. She already had so much to deal with. How would it help to take her away from her friends, remove her from her community? No—Poppy was going to stay in a mainstream school. There was no question about it. She struggled to keep her composure. 'Thank you Miss Myers, I understand what you are suggesting, but it won't be necessary. We're seeing the neurologist next week, and we're hoping for some good news. I'm hopeful they can find the lesion that's causing this. If they can, they'll operate and she'll be well. This'll all be over. Come on Pops, let's go.'

Working completely on auto-pilot, Rachel managed to put some sort of tea on the table for the kids. Hovering behind them as they ate, she tapped in her password to gain entry to the phobia chat room. It was the first time she had looked at the site, but as Will had asked them to use it when they felt any form of stress, she felt compelled to record her feelings. She typed with two fingers.

Very stressful day.

Feel physically sick. I feel pressure to do this flight more than ever for my family, but I don't know if I can take any more stress. Love, Rachel.

FRANNIE

Whilst the rest of the extended family were busy catching up with the birthday boy and each other, Frannie stole frequent glances at the messages on his Blackberry. First there had been a notification from one of the other members of the Fear of Flying Club on Will's dedicated website. The poor woman seemed to be having a bad day. He knew how that felt! He typed a quick reply

Chin-up, love. See you on Wednesday.

The second message was from the head office. They were reminding him about the job opening. Whilst it wasn't abrupt in its tone, it clearly demanded attention sooner rather than later. He considered sending a quick reply out of politeness, but then the fear gripped him once again and he was paralysed. When Kim appeared in front of him with a mug of tea he was taken by surprise. Panicking, he fumbled with the buttons on his phone in an attempt to blank the screen from her view.

'Who was that?' she asked.

'No one—just work.' Sometimes it was a blessing that his wife wasn't remotely interested in pursuing a conversation with him. He distracted himself by making a third trip to the buffet table, which was largely depleted apart from a slightly wilting bowl of salad. He wondered what percentage of the world's salad crop actually got eaten rather than being purchased, placed on a plate for show then dumped in the bin. As he chewed on a thin strip of Chinese-seasoned beef which he really didn't need to eat, he contemplated that being a lettuce leaf must be a bit like being a reserve goalkeeper. You had to have one, but ninety-nine per cent of the time it would never be used.

'Lovely spread, Sharon,' he said, nodding at his brother's wife.

'Get it eaten,' she encouraged. 'It'll only go in the bin otherwise,' she laughed as she ferried steaming mugs of tea to those who weren't drinking their way through the table full of beers and spirits bought especially for the occasion.

The family had gathered to celebrate Frannie's nephew's twenty-first birthday. Frannie was close to his brother Gary and Gary's three sons, however, he was especially fond of the birthday-boy Joe. Partly because he saw him at work on a daily basis. Joe worked as a packer and forklift driver in the factory at Manchester Aerospace Engineering, although he was hoping to move onto one of the machines when a job became available. The celebration was the first (and Frannie imagined the tamest) in a series of celebrations that Joe had planned.

'I've got a surprise for *you,* too!' shouted Gary, looking at Frannie.

'Me? It's not my birthday,' laughed Frannie, trying to put the promotion out of his mind.

'Wait there, I'll be back in a second.'

Frannie sipped his scalding tea and waited for his brother to return. Within a minute, Gary was striding across the lounge, his crooked teeth exposed beneath the beaming smile. He tossed a small plastic booklet onto Frannie's lap.

Frannie put his tea down. 'Is this what I think it is?' he finally managed after a few seconds of speechlessness.

'If you're thinking it's a Man City season ticket, then, yes,' laughed Gary, clearly delighted with the response. 'Not the whole season ticket, obviously, but there's a spare ticket in there for the derby on Saturday. There's one for Simon too.'

Frannie shouted to his son Simon, who was sitting on a wooden dining chair, head engrossed in something on his iPad. 'Look what uncle Gary's just given me. Only tickets for the bloody derby on Saturday!'

Simon's eyes lit up. 'Wow—how did you get your hands on them?'

It had been a long time since Frannie had seen his son excited about *anything*. He often wondered whether the blanket apathy was a genuine reflection of Simon's personality or if it was simply reserved for his dad.

Gary smiled. 'It's my mate's season ticket. He's going away for two weeks on Saturday morning. Lanzarote. His missus booked it without checking the football fixtures. Gutted is not the word! He's been waiting all season for this. It was going to be his son's first derby match too, but now they can't make it.'

'I've never been to a derby match,' said Simon.

'Ahh, you can't beat them, son,' said Frannie, in high spirits. 'If we're lucky we'll get a classic, like the '72 match. Denis Law. He'd always been a red in my eyes but that day he was our bloody hero. Back-heeled it into the net and sent United down to the second division.'

'Really? Bet he was popular!' laughed Simon.

'He was actually devastated he'd scored. Had to be subbed-off.'

Just then, Kim appeared from the kitchen, coat on, seemingly ready to leave. 'What's going on in here?' she smiled.

Simon took the ticket off his dad and waved it in the direction of his mum. 'Look what Uncle Gary got us! Tickets for the match on Saturday.'

Kim had a quick look at the booklet being thrust under her nose. 'For you? You can't go to that I'm afraid, Simon, you've got orchestra practice.'

'Ahh, can't I miss it this week?'

Kim looked horrified. 'No! You've got your exam in less than a week, and you're already pushing it to learn those new pieces for the National Youth Orchestra audition.'

'But it's the derby, Kim,' said Frannie, not knowing whether she appreciated the magnitude of the match.

'Come on Kimmy, you can't let the lad miss out on his first derby match,' said Gary, nudging her playfully.

Kim sighed. 'And what if he misses out on the National Youth Orchestra after all those years of practice—all because of one silly game of football that he's not even particularly interested in?'

Simon looked crestfallen. 'But Mum…'

'No buts, and talking of orchestra, we'd better get a move on, otherwise you'll be late for your violin lesson.'

Simon slunk back to his dad with the tickets, flopped the season ticket back into his hand and then dutifully went off to get his coat.

Frannie followed him, embarrassed about being so carelessly undermined in front of his family. 'I'll speak to her,' he whispered.

Kim busied herself with her goodbyes. 'Where's the birthday boy? Ahh, Joe, we've got to go now darling. Happy twenty-first. I still can't believe it was twenty-one years ago that you were born!'

Joe gave his aunty a hug. 'Cheers, Aunty Kim, and thanks again for the pressie. You didn't have to do that. It was way too much.'

Frannie's ears pricked up. He had no idea what Kim had bought for Joe, but by the sounds of it, it was far too generous, as usual.

'Not at all, dear.'

'I'll spend it well,' he laughed.

'Sounds like I'll be putting in some more bloody overtime,' said Frannie, attempting to sound like he was joking.

Joe laughed. 'Shut up, you'll be loaded when you get your promotion. Nate was telling me it's pretty much yours if you want it.'

Frannie felt a surge of panic rise in his stomach and wondered whether there was any possibility Kim hadn't heard that. He tried to change the subject quickly. 'So, what are you going to spend your birthday money on?'

As Joe replied, he caught a glimpse of Kim's icy stare and he knew that she had heard. She knew about the promotion and she knew that he had kept the information from her. As Kim swept out of the house with Simon trailing in her wake, he knew he'd be going home to a row.

Frannie pushed open the door and braced himself for the assault. He tossed his car keys into the key bowl and walked gingerly into the living room.

As soon as he spotted the ironing board, he knew he was in for a hard time. Years of experience had taught him that if Kim was ironing in the evening it usually meant she was in a foul mood. A large glass of red wine was balanced on the mantelpiece to her right. The TV was playing on mute.

'Alright, love?'

Kim planted the iron down heavily on the white shirt and pressed a button making an angry cloud of steam hiss into the air. She responded with a grunt and a raise of her eyebrows.

'Where're the kids?'

'Simon's at violin, Hannah's at ballet. Lois' mum is bringing her home. She'll be back soon.' She slammed the iron into its stand and shoved the shirt onto a hanger before hooking it abruptly onto the top of the door.

'Listen…' Frannie tried to formulate some sort of apology in his head, but Kim interrupted him before he could articulate anything.

'When were you going to tell me?' she demanded, one

hand on her hip, the other taking a large slug of wine.

Frannie covered his face with his hand and sighed. 'It's not definite.'

'Well it sounds pretty bloody definite to me.' Her eyes challenged him with an adversary stare. 'How stupid do you think I feel right now, Francis? I mean, your nephew knows, which probably means the rest of your family know, but me, your own sodding wife—I'm completely in the dark!'

'I just didn't want you getting your hopes up. Not after last time.'

'What sort of ridiculous reason is that for not telling your own wife you might be getting a promotion?'

Frannie tossed an imaginary coin in his head, before deciding to go with the lie. 'They haven't even offered it to me yet, Kim, it's just hearsay.' He felt bad about telling an out-and-out lie, but to tell the truth would be to pile on a massive weight of pressure that he simply couldn't deal with.

'Hearsay that I've heard nothing about!' she shouted.

'Come on, if I'd mentioned to you that I might be getting a promotion you'd have had the money spent before I'd even started the job!'

Kim looked wounded by this comment. 'What? How can you possibly say that? Of course I spend money—I have to. No bugger else ever offers to do the shopping, pay the bills, buy birthday presents. I do everything round here, Frannie, everything! It's not like I'm living the life of luxury, going on loads of exotic holidays like lots of people do.'

Frannie knew that this last comment was a barbed dig at his fear of flying. He chose to ignore it and pick up on something else she said instead. 'Exactly! Birthday presents—you always go mad. Christmas is the same. How much did you give our Joe for his birthday today?'

'He's your bloody nephew, Frannie,' she replied, avoiding the question.

'How much?'

'A hundred.'

'A hundred quid! Jesus Christ, this is what I mean! If I'd have told you that I might be getting a promotion you'd have chucked in an extra fifty!'

'It was his twenty-first birthday, Frannie! A hundred pounds doesn't go far nowadays. Sometimes I think you're still living in the 1970s!'

Just then there was a noise at the front door, followed by a shout of hello from their daughter, Hannah.

'Hello, love,' Kim shouted before lowering her voice to a harsh whisper. 'I am so angry with you right now I can't even look at you. We're supposed to be a team. I cannot believe you kept this from me.' She unplugged the iron and twisted the cord around the bottom. 'It makes me wonder what else you're not telling me!'

JALIL

The children who attended Jalil's comprehensive school were fortunate in that they had one of the largest playing fields in the area. Formerly a well-resourced grammar school, St Mary's had two large grassy areas to the east of the sprawling building, where football, hockey, rugby and cricket were played. Its northern boundary was a smaller grassy area which funnelled into a pathway eventually leading to the canal towpath. For most of the children in the school, being led to the northern field in PE portended to an agonising cross country run, out of the school and down to the third bridge and back.

It was a gloriously hot early May afternoon. Jalil, Zain and Robbo had decided to spend their lunch-hour playing football instead of venturing to the shopping parade. They were walking towards the marked out football pitches, Zain bouncing the football against his knee as he walked, when Robbo spotted the girls.

'Whoa, check out Holly and Becka! Dirty slappers!' he

laughed gleefully, flicking his hand in a gesture of disbelief.

Jalil searched for a moment until his eyes fell upon Holly and Becka who were lying on their backs, school shirts tied just below breast level, skirts hitched up. An iPod was playing on loud speaker in between them.

'Let's go and get a better look,' Robbo laughed. The others trailed behind him.

Robbo was practically standing on top of the girls before they noticed he was there—their eyes being closed to protect them from the bright sunlight.

'Thought we were in Kavos for a minute there, ladies.'

Both girls immediately shielded their eyes and lifted their necks off the ground to see who was there.

'Oh, hi,' said Becka.

'Yeah, we're just trying to get a bit of a base tan before the big holiday,' said Holly.

Zain continued talking to the girls, whilst Jalil subconsciously nodded his head in time to the familiar music, wondering how long he could look at the scantily-dressed Holly before he became visibly aroused.

'Have you had a look at any of the webcams? There are some *well sick* clubs out there.'

Jalil felt embarrassed. In the last few months, Zain had picked up several expressions from TV shows and was using them repeatedly. He hoped that Holly didn't think they were all dicks!

Becka nodded. 'We've already made a list of about ten clubs that we're definitely gonna go to!'

Holly laughed. 'We've rated them on the price of the shots, the fanciability of the bar staff and the music, of course!'

Jalil took his chance to change the subject away from the holiday that he was fed up of hearing about. He pointed at the iPod. 'You got the whole album?'

Holly took a moment to gather what Jalil was talking about. 'What? The Urban Phantoms? Yeah, I'm really into them at the minute.'

Jalil was surprised. He was pretty well into his music and prided himself on being the first to discover new bands. He had imagined Holly was more of a mainstream girl when it came to music.

'Cool!' Jalil had downloaded a couple of their tracks after reading a review in *NME*, but he was going to make a point of downloading the whole album as soon as he got home. 'I love *Under the Radar*, it reminds me a bit of…'

The rest of the sentence remained unfinished. First came the shout of 'look out!', now familiar to Jalil. He realised immediately what was going on, but didn't have time to react. The girls were looking up at the sky where Jalil assumed Zain or Robbo had been pointing. In a split second, Jalil had been rugby-tackled to the ground by both of his friends, who were laughing and shouting 'Plane— save yourself!'

They had taken to doing this to Jalil during PE lessons whenever one of them spotted an aeroplane flying above them. Jalil had tried laughing along with them in the hope that they would become bored and stop, and when that hadn't worked he'd tried to be deadpan, telling them that they were fucking lame. That hadn't worked either.

This time, Jalil had banged his wrist at an awkward angle when he hit the ground. He tried to push away Zain and

Robbo, who were nearly pissing themselves laughing. He couldn't appear to be hurt in front of Holly. His face was hot and his wrist was burning. When he looked over at the girls, they were wide-eyed, emitting small embarrassed giggles. He got up, brushed the grass off his trousers and made a hasty excuse to leave the mortifying situation as quickly as he could.

Jalil had not been able to face walking home from school with Zain and Robbo. He told them he was going to see his dad, who lived in a flat about fifteen minutes' walk from his own house. He didn't get on especially well with his dad, and didn't visit him that often, but decided that since he had made up the excuse and was currently walking in that direction, he might as well call in to see the old man and kill two birds with one stone.

A perpetual jobseeker, Jalil knew the odds of his dad being at home at quarter past four on a weekday were relatively high. Sure enough, when he got to the second floor flat, he could hear the television before he even pushed open the door.

'Bloody hell, to what do I owe this pleasure?' asked his dad from the sofa, waving his hand in front of him in a completely ineffective effort to clear the cigarette smoke from the small room.

Jalil shrugged. 'Just thought I'd call in.'

'Kettle's just boiled if you want a brew.'

'Nah, you're alright.'

'How's school?' Jalil's dad smiled. He was genuinely proud that any son of his had the intelligence to stay on for A-levels.

'S'alright.'

'What about that computer project you were telling me about last time? Did you get good marks for it?'

Jalil couldn't remember which project he had mentioned to his dad. They were given regular assessments to complete, and he struggled to think of the one in question. It didn't help that the television was blaring out some World War Two documentary at about a hundred decibels, complete with wailing air raid sirens. 'Er yeah, I think so.'

As his dad continued to press him about his school work, Jalil's attention was distracted by the television, which was now showing grainy shots of fighter pilots in action. He tried to keep the conversation on track, but when one of the planes spiralled out of control, with a trail of black smoke in its wake, Jalil grabbed the remote control off the arm of the sofa and switched the television off.

'Hey, I was watching that,' complained his dad. 'It's history, that is.'

If Jalil didn't see another aeroplane in his entire life he would be happy. 'I just couldn't hear what you were saying, that's all.'

'Jesus, someone's got a right cob on today. What's up? Girl trouble?'

Jalil scowled. 'No!'

'Well, what then? I thought you'd be happy. You've got six weeks holiday coming up soon.'

Jalil shrugged. 'So! It's going to be boring.'

'What do you mean boring? You lot don't know you're born, I tell you!'

'It is though! All my mates are going on holiday. I'm

going to be left here like Billy-No-Mates.'

'Why don't you ask your mum's boyfriend to give you some money? He's bloody loaded isn't he? I bet that flash bastard can afford a cheap package holiday.'

Jalil felt uncomfortable when his dad slagged off his mum's boyfriend, Harvey. Yes, Harvey could be a bit annoying when he tried to be the big man, but it was Harvey who was paying for his Fear of Flying course. His dad hadn't stumped up a single penny for anything for years. Jalil hadn't even bothered to tell him about the course, even though he blamed his dad for creating his fear in the first place by making him watch that stupid disaster film.

Jalil took his phone out of his pocket and pretended to check the time. 'I've gotta go. I'll see you later.'

'You've just got here!'

Jalil wasn't in the mood to talk to anyone. He felt utterly shit. He probably wouldn't even bother going on Facebook later. He would go home, download the Urban Phantoms album and avoid speaking to anyone until the morning.

'Got homework to do. See ya.'

McKENZIE

McKenzie felt like crap. He hadn't slept well the previous night, his slumber having being continuously disturbed with nightmares of plane crashes. He generally suffered from two recurring dreams on this matter. In one, he would be sitting in a regular airliner when suddenly the plane would nose-dive at a sharp angle. The engine noise would suddenly increase to a deafening level, as though the acceleration lever was stuck on maximum. This was always accompanied by an eerie whistling noise as the plane rocketed to the ground. McKenzie would habitually wake up moments before impact, drenched in sweat, his heart hammering in his chest. The second dream was more surreal. The plane would be a jumbo jet which could only take off by accelerating up a series of hills, like a roller coaster. Every time they reached the top of a hill, McKenzie would hold his breath to see whether the plane would take off and stay in the air or whether it would go racing down the other side of the hill.

It was the morning of another promotional visit—this time to Sweden. He had arrived at Stansted airport using public transport. It had meant a horrendously early start, but as he had spent most of the night awake, he had been grateful for an excuse not to fall back into his twisted dreams. He knew that if he was going to make it on board the flight to Gothenburg he would need a little pharmaceutical help, which meant that he would be unfit to drive. Luckily, he had a list of contacts on his mobile phone who could score him some diazepam without asking any questions. He had swallowed one of the little white pills with a mug of vodka and orange before leaving the house. He wasn't usually a vodka drinker, but to be able to stomach any alcohol at six am he had opted for the most flavourless.

He asked the check-in assistant for a seat next to the emergency exit. If that thing was going down he wanted to be in control of getting himself out as quickly as possible. On clearing security, he headed straight for one of the small bars, where he downed another three large vodkas and a second Valium. He was so anxious about the flight that he knew he couldn't speak to anyone. Not until they landed safely on the other side. Provided that they *did* land safely. In the hope of avoiding Alfie and the rest of the band, he waited until the last call for the flight before walking to the gate.

Kitty gave him a little wave as he fumbled his way into his over-wing seat. She was sitting a little further back, next to Alfie, clearly relieved that he had made it onto the flight.

Within moments, a stewardess was crouching next to him, telling him how to open the exit in the event of an emergency. McKenzie concentrated harder than he had ever concentrated in his life. His brain felt a bit foggy due to the mixture of alcohol and diazepam, and he confirmed every instruction she gave him with a serious 'um hmm'. When the general safety demonstration started, he also gave that his full attention, but he panicked when he realised that he couldn't remember the exact instructions she had given him to open the emergency exit. Was it pull in, then twist and kick it out, or was it twist then pull down and kick out? When the stewardess walked up the cabin checking passengers' seatbelts, he stopped her to go over it with him again.

With take-off approaching, he was glad he had managed to secure a seat away from the others. Obviously he didn't want them to see that he was petrified of flying, but also, he was keen to avoid questions about the death of his grandmother. He had told Alfie that this was why he had been unable to fly to Amsterdam the previous week and was hoping Little Gee hadn't remembered that one of his grandmothers had died when they were in year ten and that the other one was alive and well and living in the Isle of Dogs.

As the engines roared in preparation for take-off, McKenzie screwed his eyes tight and sang a song in his head. He was gutted that headphones were not permitted during take-off as he would have liked something to drown out the terrifying sound. Hurtling down the runway, McKenzie felt his guts turn to liquid. He gripped onto the armrest urgently as the plane tilted backwards and made its ascent. On reaching cruising altitude he opened his eyes, but kept his hands firmly on the armrest, only removing them when the cabin crew arrived with the alcohol trolley.

The television studio was a cramped, partitioned-off area in a former factory building on an industrial estate on the outskirts of Gothenburg. McKenzie had slept for most of the hour-long car journey. Squeezed in between Little Gee and Kitty on a stylish but uncomfortable lime-coloured sofa, and with the bright studio lights burning down overhead, McKenzie still felt drowsy. As the teenage host of the satellite music show *Euro Download* asked them question after question, McKenzie failed to stifle a large yawn.

'Some of our viewers might have downloaded your latest track *Under the Radar*. Is this typical of your style of music?' asked Ana, in immaculate English but with an accent that was slightly west of the Atlantic.

Little Gee took this question. As McKenzie's bandmate explained the band's evolution from a 2-step garage vibe to the garage/R&B cross-over style they were currently producing, McKenzie felt his stomach cramp violently. He had been experiencing terrible gut spasms since he got off the plane. He rocked forwards slightly and folded his arms across his stomach. In leaning forward he let out an audible fart. It took a few seconds for the toxic smell to reach the band. Kitty's professional gaze didn't leave the host, however, a small involuntary wrinkle of her nose upon sensing the noxious smell was unavoidable.

'Fuck, sorry about that,' muttered McKenzie, wafting his hand on top of his lap.

The host, Ana, continued with her questioning. 'That sounds great—well we're going to be hearing some of your music shortly. Given your evolution from one style to another over the past few years, you must have had some pretty strong influences. Was there any artist or band in particular that you were trying to emulate?'

Kitty nodded to indicate that she would like to answer this one. 'I think that my joining the band was one of the catalysts for the R&B sound. I was brought up on R&B—my parents used to listen to Stevie Wonder and Mariah Carey. I think Beyoncé is probably my all-time idol. She has the most beautiful voice, and she's a fantastic role model for women of all ages.' As Kitty continued, McKenzie's body began to slump slowly to his left until it came to rest against the singer's right arm. The presenter's eyes flicked towards McKenzie, who was sandwiched between Kitty and Little Gee.

McKenzie felt a sharp nudge in his left rib. He sat up abruptly. He wished the presenter would hurry up and finish. He was struggling to keep his eyes open and he needed to find a toilet fairly quickly too.

'The big news for the Urban Phantoms is that you're going to be supporting The Black Eyed Peas on their next UK arena tour. I guess when you get a deal like that you know you've made it. What advice would you give any young bands out there who haven't made it yet?'

McKenzie opened his mouth for the first time in the interview to directly answer one of Ana's questions. 'All record companies are tossers,' he slurred. 'They'll suck at your soul like slimy leeches, then they'll...'

'Ha, ha,' laughed Little Gee nervously. 'Every band needs a joker. McKenzie's ours. Isn't that right, Prof?'

The Prof, who had scanned the wings of the tiny studio for their manager's reaction, laughed uncomfortably along with Little Gee.

'Okay, so whilst the band get ready to perform their latest track, *Under the Radar*, I'll give you a preview of what's coming up after the break.'

The cameras stopped rolling. The video would be edited in at a later date. McKenzie stumbled over electric leads and other bits of equipment. He reached the keyboard that he had set up himself about an hour earlier. 'Hey, this is just like mine!' he exclaimed, his memory of the day's preceding events utterly obliterated by the drugs and alcohol.

The Prof and Little Gee fiddled with some of their own equipment before counting down to the beginning of the track. McKenzie started to add his own magic to the familiar tune, but he found that his hands weren't working properly. His fingers fell clumsily on the wrong keys and the sound jarred sharply in contrast to the rest of the track. He turned his head away from camera to complain to the Prof. 'This synth is shit—I can't play it. I need mine!'

The Prof glared back at him and continued mixing the track to the best of his ability.

When he woke up, hours later, the hotel room was dark. The heavy curtains had been drawn and the only sound came from the bathroom. Water was gushing. The sound of the tap made his thirst even more urgent. He sat up but immediately regretted moving too quickly as his head and eyes were pounding. Little Gee walked back into the twin room and glared at McKenzie.

'What time is it?' asked McKenzie, still groggy.

'Eight o'clock.'

'What time's the interview? I must have fallen asleep in the car—I can't remember getting into bed!'

'No shit!' Little Gee grabbed his wallet off the desk, shoved it into his back pocket and strapped his watch around his wrist.

'Sorry, man. Do you want me to do anything?' he asked, scratching his head.

'I think you've probably done enough,' laughed Little Gee bitterly.

'Eh?' McKenzie was picking up bad vibes. He'd done what they asked hadn't he? Got on the flight. He was in Sweden at eight o'clock in the morning (or evening— although he was getting the impression that now was not a good time to ask for confirmation of this). 'What's going on mate? Is Alfie pissed off with me again?'

Little Gee swung round to face McKenzie directly for the first time. 'Alfie, and the rest of the band!' Little Gee thumped his fist down on the flimsy desk. 'What the fuck did you think you were doing? This was our big fucking break, man. You of all people should know how much this means to all of us.'

'Look, I'm sorry, I just can't remember…'

'You can't remember because you were too off your face! Why the fuck did you bother turning up to an interview in that state? Jesus Christ—I wouldn't mind but you're not a piss-head or a druggie, but you've managed to convince the whole of fucking Sweden that you are, which means they probably think the rest of us are too!'

McKenzie was stunned. He felt an urgent need to be sick. He jumped off the bed and ran into the bathroom, where he choked up a stomach full of vomit. Hands shaking, he wiped his mouth. He looked at the ghostly grey reflection in the bathroom mirror and splashed cold water onto his ashen face. He walked slowly back to the bedroom and flopped down onto the bed. A couple of memories started to trickle back into his consciousness. He groaned, then willed the rest of the memories to remain obscured. This wasn't good. Fuck, what had he done?

He lifted his head out of his hands and looked tentatively at Little Gee. 'How bad is it?'

Little Gee looked gutted. 'As bad as it gets. Alfie says you're out!'

FLIGHT DAY MINUS 2 WEEKS

Hugh's class had almost suffered another casualty. McKenzie had seriously considered jacking the course in, having no further reason to attend after being kicked out of his own band. He had spent the last two days in bed, leaving the sanctuary of his duvet only to use the toilet and to fetch fresh water. The drug and alcohol hangover had been horrendous, and the downer he was experiencing was one of the worst he'd ever had. He'd ignored the calls and texts from his bandmates and from Alfie, who had summoned him to a meeting at Dark Star records at the end of the week. His decision to leave his bedroom and catch the train to Manchester had been a spur of the moment one. He suspected that the ringing on the intercom was probably Kitty or Little Gee wanting some sort of face-to-face explanation for his spectacular fuck-up. Unable to face anyone yet, he decided that one way to delay the inevitable would be to jump on a train where he could forget about being the front man for the Urban Phantoms. Here, he was just another aerophobe, with people who understood how it felt to be so terrified that you could act in a way that was unrecognisable to even yourself. Well, they would have understood if he had told them. He was still far too ashamed of his behaviour to share his recollections of the last few days with anybody. However, listening to the others in the group made McKenzie feel better than he had in days.

'I still don't understand,' puzzled Rachel. 'If the engine fails, how does it stay in the air?'

Hugh felt like banging his head on the table, wondering which part of his reasonably detailed thirty minute explanation she hadn't understood.

'It's like I just said. I mean—I could go into the physics of it if you want.' He picked a green marker off the desk and began scribbling a complicated formula on the whiteboard. 'If you want the science of it, it's a balance of minimum control speed in the air, sizing the vertical tail and the effect of bank and angle weight.'

Rachel turned to Jalil who was sitting next to her and pulled a face which suggested that she was sorry she spoke.

Hugh continued. 'But you don't really need to understand all of that, Rachel. All you need to know is that pilots have options after an engine failure.'

Rachel shuddered. 'The thought of being up in the sky and an engine cutting out, well, it's the stuff of nightmares.'

Hugh tapped his marker in the air and gave a half smile. 'Ironically, the higher up you are when an engine fails, the better!'

Jalil screwed his face up, thinking that Hugh was a

proper div for suggesting this. 'Eh?'

'Think about it. The more altitude a pilot has, the more time he has to get things under control.'

Frannie laughed sarcastically. 'If I was 5,000 feet in the air and the engine cut out, the last thing I'd be thinking would be *I'm glad I'm so high up.*'

'How long would the pilot have, Hugh?' asked McKenzie. 'Before it, you know, hit the ground?'

'Well the whole point of the presentation I've just given you is to let you know that it's very unlikely such a situation would develop. The pilot would fly the plane using the single engine he had at his disposal and would control the plane until he could land it safely.'

'Yeah, but say he couldn't control it…how long before it would crash?'

They've done it again, thought Hugh. Every week they manage to bring the conversation round to disasters. For a bunch of people who claimed to be completely terrified about plane crashes, they spent an unfortunate amount of their time discussing them. Why couldn't they just listen to what he was saying and believe that air travel was perfectly safe?

'I really don't want to dwell on…'

Rachel's palms covered her cheeks as she imagined the unthinkable. 'Can you imagine? Can you just *imagine* being up there,' she nodded her head and raised her eyes skyward 'and knowing that the plane was going down? *Knowing* you only had one more minute to live. What on earth would be going through your mind for that minute?'

Jalil shook his head. 'I don't know, man? It would be,

like, the last minute of your life. Ever! What would *you* do?'

'I'd scribble a goodbye note to all my family and friends in the hope that someone would find it,' said Rachel, solemnly.

Jalil thought of his mates and their relentless piss taking. 'I'd write a note to my friends saying *I fucking told you so!*'

The rest of the group laughed. Frannie said, 'If I knew I only had one minute left to live I'd text my wife my PIN number for my credit card. At least one of us would be happy! Then if I had any time left after that, I'd eat the biggest amount of non-Weight-Watchers crap I could get my hands on.'

Petal listened to the conversation with interest. It was a fascinating concept…what would you do with your last minute on Earth? If she was in that situation she wouldn't be able to achieve her main goal of becoming a mother— not in just one minute. There were other things she had never experienced though: swimming with dolphins; staying in a hotel; eating McDonald's. Her anti-capitalist principles had prevented her from ever entering any of the major fast food franchises, but, she had to admit that when she walked past the McDonald's on the high street after a double yoga session it did smell delicious! Yes—she imagined ordering a Big Mac—with cheese—and ketchup. And a large fries!

McKenzie laughed. 'I'd be looking carefully out of the window, calculating the exact time to jump. Honestly, man, why don't people do that? Wait 'til the plane is about to hit the ground then jump up in the air at the last minute?'

'Oh yes,' agreed Rachel. 'I'd try that as well. I'll tell you another thing I don't understand too. You know if you're standing at the front of the plane, and you jump in the air?'

The rest of the group nodded to show they were listening.

'Why don't you end up at the back of the plane?'

'Exactly!' laughed McKenzie. 'I don't get that either. I mean, you're jumping straight up in the air, and the plane is whizzing forwards at like, 500 miles an hour. You should end up at the back, yeah.'

Hugh pinched the bridge of his nose and sighed. These people were for real? He had seen programmes on television before where really stupid people were exploited in the name of entertainment but he had been cynical about how much of their idiocy was real and how much was stage-managed for effect. He had often wondered where they dredged these foolish people up from, but now he had his answer. He picked up the board rubber and wiped away the physics equation he had written only moments earlier. Thank God he had finished his part of the lesson. Petal could deal with them now.

Petal stood up looking pleased with herself. 'Could I ask you all to move the tables and chairs to the side of the room, then come and sit in a circle on the floor?'

No-one budged an inch, except to swap stealthy cringes. Petal clapped her hands. 'Come, come. I did say that this week we'd be practising some anti-anxiety techniques. This week we're concentrating on breathing.'

Frannie laughed. 'Yeah, I think we might have that one covered, love. I know *I've* managed to do it for forty-six years without any help.'

'You might be surprised to find out that you're not doing

it properly! Now let's get these chairs and tables moved.'

Reluctantly, the group moved the furniture to the back of the classroom. As Petal poised herself in a cross-legged yoga position on the floor, the others stood gingerly around the edge of the room. In a bid to delay the inevitable cringe-fest, Jalil found a sudden interest in studying the poster on the wall that illustrated the life-cycle of a newt. Frannie had his hands in his pockets.

'Well, come and sit down then!' urged Petal.

Rachel was the first to sit down. 'This is how you get piles, you know, sitting on a cold hard floor!'

'Get what?' asked Jalil.

'Piles—it's like having a bunch of grapes hanging out of your backside,' explained Rachel.

Jalil's eyes widened as he wondered whether he would ever be able to eat grapes again.

Frannie groaned as he squatted down onto his knees before sliding onto his bottom. 'Jesus Christ! I've pulled muscles I didn't even know I had. I've no idea how I'm going to get back up again.' He looked at Petal and laughed. 'And don't even think about asking me to cross my legs like that!'

Petal addressed the whole class. 'If you can cross your legs then that's great—if not, just stretch your legs out straight in front of you with your hands either side of your bottom, or straddle your legs and place your hands on the floor in front of you like this.' Petal uncrossed her legs and then flung them apart until they were almost in side splits.

Jalil and McKenzie sniggered.

'Whoa there, Petal, we don't need to be seeing that now,'

joked Frannie, who was genuinely uncomfortable with Petal's immodest pose.

Rachel was astonished. 'I don't think I've ever met anyone that bendy! That's amazing. How do you get like that? Were you born like that?'

'Lots of yoga,' admitted Petal. 'I could get you into splits if you came along to my yoga classes.'

'After two children, love? I don't think my pelvic floor would cope. Even with a Tena Lady I reckon you'd be mopping the floor afterwards.'

'Bloody hell,' complained Frannie, trying but failing miserably to get back up off the floor in protest against the turn of the conversation. 'It's bad enough having to sit on the floor doing breathing exercises without you two talking about women's parts.'

Petal laughed. 'Sorry Frannie, sit back down. We'll get on with the breathing.'

'Oh goodie,' he mumbled sarcastically.

'So, you need to sit up straight, shoulders back, head up from your shoulders. Really raise that head towards the ceiling. We are aiming for one big, deep breath in, hold it, then seven short breaths out.'

'Hey?' said McKenzie. 'How can you breathe out more than you breathe in?'

'Watch.' Petal took a deep inhalation of breath through her nose, then puffed out seven shorter breaths through her mouth.

Jalil turned his face away from the circle and whispered to McKenzie. 'I'm not doing that, man. It looks *well* gay!'

'The idea is that you regulate your breathing. If your

breathing is too shallow or too fast, which often happens when you are nervous, your body will not receive the oxygen it requires. This can increase anxiety levels and can even induce panic attacks. It's kind of self-perpetuating. Most of us don't breathe properly on a day-to-day basis, never mind when we are in a state of heightened anxiety. Here—put your hands like this for a moment.' Petal placed one of her palms across her chest and the other across her abdomen. 'Everyone take a couple of breaths in and out for me.' The class duly followed her instruction, albeit self-consciously. 'Tell me where you can feel the rise and fall of your breathing. In your chest or your belly?'

'Chest,' muttered Rachel.

'Yeah,' agreed the others in a rather muted fashion.

'That's what I expected. You are all breathing into your chest area. What I want to see from all of you is some really deep breathing. The breath should go all the way down into your belly. Put your hands across your stomach and try again. Really try to see some movement in those hands.'

Frannie took a deep breath and tried to make his hands move. 'I reckon I'm at a disadvantage because my gut is bigger than everyone else's. More weight to shift. Tell me again, why is this better than a large vodka?'

The very mention of the word vodka made McKenzie's stomach contract. His face blanched and a cold sweat broke out between his shoulder blades. The hangover was still physical, even after two days. He wondered whether he had induced some sort of alcohol poisoning. He turned his attention towards Petal. If he was going to ever fly again (which seemed even more unlikely now than ever) then he was going to have to rely on something other than drugs and alcohol to get him through it. He was going to give this deep breathing thing a try—even if he did look like a total twat in the process.

Seeing that everyone else was giving it a go, Jalil reluctantly joined in. He was with Frannie though—surely a can of cider would be far more effective than this bollocks.

'Alcohol is a false friend. It often exaggerates the emotion you are experiencing at the time, making you more anxious than you were initially. It can also cause dehydration which may make you feel sick and dizzy. This breathing technique *really* works. Once you've mastered it, it can be used in any situation, at any time. It's free, it won't get you sacked for using it at work. Midwives use it to get pregnant women through childbirth.'

Rachel interjected. 'Have you actually *had* a baby, Petal?'

'Well, no, but…'

'Well if you ever do, I bet it'll be pethidine and an epidural that will get you through—not deep breathing. Honestly when that baby's coming out of your…'

'Right, that's enough of this talk.' Frannie was flailing about on the floor trying to get back up on his feet. 'I thought I'd signed up for a Fear of Flying course, not some bloody feminist class on women's private parts.'

As the rest of the class took immediate advantage of the opportunity to leave their first controlled breathing session, Petal remained momentarily on the floor with her hands on her tummy. One day, she thought. One day she would know.

RACHEL

Rachel's kitchen table was littered with leaflets. She had tried to read them several times over, but her whole body had gone into some sort of frozen shock, and instead of penetrating her brain, the words swam together on the page. Severe Myoclonic Epilepsy of Infancy; SCN1A; abnormal functioning of sodium ion channels; levetiracetam; carbamazepine; GEFS+; PCDH19[4]; phenotype correlations; valproic acid monotherapy… Only one paragraph had stuck clearly in her mind. The one which said, in black and white, that Poppy only stood an eighty-five per cent chance of reaching adulthood.

Whilst Rachel sat motionless and shell-shocked, Charlie paced the kitchen, flinging open cupboard doors before banging them shut again, looking for the bottle of whisky they had bought several Christmases earlier.

Rachel's mum, Jean, had brought the spectacles with her that the optician had prescribed, but which she rarely used, preferring to hold the newspaper at arms-length. The dainty gold chain rested on her shoulders as she studied one of the leaflets on Dravet Syndrome.

'I don't understand,' said Jean, genuinely confused. 'I thought they were going to do a scan to see if they could find a lesion. What happened to that? Can't they keep looking?'

'The test results show that she has Dravet Syndrome, Mum. There's no point looking for a lesion now.'

'But why not? There might be one, and if they operate on it surely it would make her better? The sodding NHS isn't what it used to be. It's all about saving money these days. Well if they won't do the scan, we'll pay for her to go privately. I'll sell my house. I don't need it! We'll take her to America. They must have specialists there who can find what's wrong with her…'

Rachel interrupted her mum with a calmness that belied the turmoil that was churning her insides to pieces. 'They *know* what's wrong with her, mum. It's Dravet Syndrome. It's genetic. You can't fix a syndrome. It's completely unfixable.'

Jean took her glasses off. Her hands were shaking a little and there were tears in her eyes. 'It can't be. Remember when she was a baby—the doctors said she might grow out of this. Are you saying they've changed their mind?'

Charlie found the dusty whisky bottle in the cupboard above the cooker. It had been stashed at the back along with some paper cups and plates, cocktail sticks and serviettes. He slammed a glass on the worktop, poured in a generous amount of the amber liquid and took two large mouthfuls. He rarely drank. Neither of them did. They had to be alert twenty-four hours a day and ready to drive to the hospital at any time.

'She's not going to grow out of this, Jean,' he said with an anger that was directed towards no one in particular. 'That's it! That's her lot! How do you think *I* feel? I'm her dad and I can't fix this. I can't tuck her into bed and tell her that everything's going to be okay, because it isn't. I'm her dad, Jean! I should be able to make things right for her.'

'You're not a doctor, Charlie.'

'No, but I *am* an electrician! If you're renovating an old house, I can re-wire it. If you're shower's fucked, I can fix it. Cooker's not working, I can find the problem and sort it out. But my own child has a brain that's not wired up right. There's a short circuit somewhere that's causing her all sorts of damage, and I can't do a bloody thing about it! I can't help her, Jean!'

Then, without warning, he let out a long and painful whimper before breaking down in tears.

Rachel remained motionless at the table. She was unaccustomed to seeing Charlie break down over Poppy's illness. Usually, she was the one who took everything to heart, the one who saw doom and gloom everywhere and who would cry on his shoulder when the injustice of Poppy's condition got too much for her. Charlie was the one who looked on the positive side. Made her smile. The joker. The one who made everything okay again. Yet despite his need for comfort, she remained in her trance-like state, concentrating on breathing in, then out again, just like Petal had taught them. She had spent the past couple of hours crying. Her eyes were red raw and her stomach felt like it had been kicked at full force. Her body didn't feel like her own anymore, and she was worried that if she didn't concentrate hard enough, she might become detached from it altogether. Which is why all she needed at that moment was to breathe. In for one, out for seven, in for one, out for seven.

Jean wiped away the tears that were running down her cheeks. She crossed the kitchen to embrace her son-in-law who had pressed his hands to his eyes to stop his emotions from pouring out.

Without warning, a sound from the baby monitor startled Rachel out of her inertia. She bolted for the stairs. Poppy had been asleep for about an hour, and it was typical that if she was going to have a fit it would be around this time. Charlie followed behind her.

'Get the box!' she instructed.

Charlie made his way quickly to the cupboard in their bedroom where they kept a supply of Poppy's anti-seizure medication.

Rachel managed to get Poppy into the recovery position. It had taken years of experience for her to go against her maternal instinct which was to cradle her seriously-ill child and instead, leave her convulsing on the bed or the floor, but any saliva in Poppy's lungs could prove catastrophic, so she manoeuvred Poppy's tiny, jerking limbs as best she could. Charlie swept past Jean, who had her hands held to her face in shock, crying.

'Go downstairs, Mum,' ordered Rachel firmly, knowing from the early days when she relied on the assistance of the ambulance service how distressing it was to stand watching helplessly from the side-lines.

Rachel snapped open the pre-loaded syringe of midazolam and swiftly but calmly attempted to administer the correct dosage for Poppy, injecting the clear fluid into the lower gum, then massaging Poppy's cheek to aid the process.

'Come on, Pops,' she said brightly, even though she knew it was unlikely that Poppy was aware of what she was saying. 'Let's get this into you.'

Poppy's jaws had clenched firmly shut, and the amount of saliva she was producing made it impossible for Rachel to tell how much of the medication had actually been absorbed. The noises coming from the tiny, golden haired child were primeval. Rachel had hardened herself to this over the years, and in the height of the emergency she was able to block out the distress that the sounds caused her. It would be later on, at a quiet, unexpected moment, or in the dead of night, that the guttural echoes of her helpless child would come back to haunt her.

'How long has it been, Charlie?' she asked urgently. She knew that if the drug was to have any effect it would be evident within about two minutes.

'Hurry up!' urged Jean through shaky sobs. 'She's going blue! Look, Rachel, her lips are blue. So are her fingernails. I'm calling the ambulance.'

'No, Mum! If we can get this into her she should recover. I know what I'm doing.'

'Why don't you pop your head in on Jasmine to make sure she's asleep?' Charlie suggested compassionately.

As they waited for the drug to take effect, Rachel prepared

the second dosage as a precaution. One dose was usually sufficient to bring Poppy round, but on the occasions when it wasn't, a second dose could be administered, meaning an ambulance would then need to be called. They had been in this situation before, however, and there were risks with administering a second dose, so they both waited anxiously for signs that the seizure was passing.

'What if this dose isn't enough?' asked Charlie.

'Then we call the ambulance.'

'What about the second dose?'

The problem with the midazolam was that it was a muscle relaxant. Whilst this was of great assistance in stopping the seizure it could not be isolated to prevent it relaxing all of the muscles in the body, including the breathing muscles. The last time Poppy had been administered a second dose, her lungs practically stopped working and, had the ambulance not arrived when it did, she would probably have died. Neither of them needed reminding of this; however, when Poppy's convulsion hadn't eased after the first dose they found themselves once again caught between a rock and a hard place. Should they do something to help her right then, and administer the drug or should they leave her suffering in case the second dose stopped her breathing?

Rachel reassessed the situation. 'Let's call the ambulance now,' she said.

Charlie waited with Poppy as Rachel ran for the phone and dialled 999. 'Has the child suffered from fever or illness in the last forty eight hours?' the operator began.

'No. Listen—it's not a febrile convulsion, she has Dravet Syndrome. I've told you I've administered the midazolam.

We just need the ambulance!' she explained impatiently.

'Is the child conscious?'

'No—I just need to know if the ambulance is on its way so that we can give her a second dose.'

'I understand,' said the operator slowly. 'I just need to ask you a few more questions before I dispatch the ambulance.'

'Why?' cried Rachel. 'I'm more of an expert in this than you or any of your paramedics. I'm telling you we need the ambulance right now. I know what I'm talking about!'

'Of course you do, madam. Just try to remain calm. Just a couple more questions. Is the child in a safe place where she cannot fall, bang her head or harm herself?'

'Yes!' shouted Rachel.

'And are all pets safely out of the way?'

Rachel felt like exploding. 'For fuck's sake—I'm hanging up now. Just send the goddamn ambulance.'

JALIL

Jalil wondered whether to bother going on the night out. He felt like staying at home and writing the *entire* day off as a disaster. Deciding to go, though, might mean an evening in the company of Holly. He had daydreamed about chatting with her at the nightclub—finding a quiet corner where they would become so engrossed in their conversation that before they knew it closing time would arrive, then, realising their friends had given up on joining their intimate *tête-à-tête* and gone home, Jalil would have to accompany Holly back to her house. On the way they would laugh about how the evening had gone before finding the perfect Hollywood moment to kiss each other senseless.

It *could* happen. It was Becca's eighteenth and Holly would definitely be there. Pretty much the whole of the sixth form had been invited. If he could *just* manage to get a few minutes with her on her own—away from her mates, and definitely away from *his*, he reckoned he might be in with a small chance of getting off with her. After all, they *did* have a lot in common. The Urban Phantoms made for good common ground. If he decided to go out he would definitely try to engage her in a conversation about them.

But then again, the shame of knowing that they witnessed yet another 'friendly' attack on him by Robbo in the common room today made him squirm. There was also the fact that Becca probably wouldn't be keen on admitting Robbo or Zain to the party after they had blatantly taken the piss out of her fake tan earlier that day. Becca and Holly had come into school looking like they had been coated in creosote. Zain had laughed and asked Becca if he'd be seeing her at temple at the weekend. Then Robbo had joined in, telling them that if they were aiming for the colour of Jalil's undies after a trip on a 747 they had got the look spot on. Jalil could have swung for the dickheads on the spot. It was bad enough taking the piss out of *him* in front of the girls, but unlike lads, Jalil knew that girls didn't take kindly to being publicly humiliated. Becca would be quite within her rights to take revenge by refusing them entry into the VIP area of the club she had apparently booked. Jalil didn't know if he could take any more mortification for one day.

He took his three best going-out shirts out of his wardrobe and chucked them on the bed. The club was in town. It was a proper, big night out. They had wangled their way into a few of the local nightclubs before now. Jalil being one of the oldest in the year had no problem, but Zain and Robbo were a few months younger and had often been refused entry. If they were going to be allowed in they would have to look the part. No jeans. No trainers. If he was going to go, he needed to be at the bus stop in ten minutes to meet the lads. He chose the plain black shirt, chucked a decent pair of trousers on and stepped into some patent brogues. Before he left he applied a liberal spray of his most expensive aftershave. He was going to go. Holly was too important to give up on.

They had planned to arrive fairly early, but Deansgate was already buzzing with summer revellers. They stopped short of the club for a quick pep talk.

'Shoulders back. Head up. Look confident, yeah,' said Robbo.

They were just about to make their way towards the intimidating bulk of the black jacketed, ear-piece wearing door staff when Robbo stopped short of his next rousing sentence.

'Even better!' he smiled.

All three of them were now looking in the direction of Bridge Street, where three girls they vaguely recognised from the lower sixth were tottering along in high heels and short dresses.

'I don't get it,' said Zain. 'That Maz is a right minger—what do we want to saddle ourselves with them for?'

Robbo frowned. '*They*, my friend, are going to get us in that club. Everyone knows bouncers let couples in loads easier than lads on their own.'

'*I'm* not asking them,' huffed Zain.

The girls were almost upon them before they spotted the boys.

'Alright ladies,' said Robbo. 'You're all looking fine tonight if I may say so.'

Maz smiled whilst the other two scowled pityingly.

'So, are you heading for Becca's party?'

'Yeah. You?' replied the tallest of the three, whose name none of the boys knew.

'Indeed we are. Listen, you know what the door staff are like in these places. We were wondering if we could go in with you. Pretend we're three couples.'

All three girls wrinkled their noses in disgust. Jalil and Zain were pretty offended by their reaction and went to walk away, but Robbo continued valiantly.

'Come on. There's a drink in it for you when we get inside.'

The girls looked at each other, weighing up the trade-off.

'A double—and that's my final offer.'

The tall one nodded. 'Okay then—but just 'til we get inside, yeah.'

'You'd better believe it,' muttered Zain under his breath.

'Happy Birthday,' said Zain, handing two glasses of vodka and Red Bull over to Becca and Holly.

They were standing in the so-called VIP area—a small, slightly raised section of the club that had been roped off with a flimsy black cord tied between two short chrome posts. It was only half past nine so the club was still fairly empty. There was a small crowd of sixth formers gathered in the area, along with some other people Jalil didn't recognise. Most worrying of these, were two older lads (Jalil guessed they were about twenty-four) whose words Becca and Holly seemed to be hanging on. Holly had really gone to town on getting dressed up. She was wearing a tight monochrome dress which showed off of her newly-bronzed legs. Little was left to the imagination.

'You'd better enjoy it!' Zain added, shouting to be heard over the reverberating bassline of the music. 'That round just cost me thirty-five quid!'

One of the older lads smirked. 'I don't touch that stuff. Waste of money man!'

Jalil perked up. Maybe this bloke was some sort of do-gooder. After all, he didn't know anyone his age who refused to drink alcohol. He couldn't see Holly going for someone like that.

'Yeah?' questioned Zain.

The stranger looked at his mate and smirked. 'There are much cheaper ways to have a good time, aren't there?' He gave Holly an unapologetic squeeze round the waist.

Jalil might have known. Holly was going to be into much cooler, older guys. Bad boys. How could a little nobody from school possibly compare to that?

Jalil could see that Zain looked shocked. 'Ah no, not us, man. We're not into any shit like that,' his friend replied.

The man pulled a *suit-yourself* sort of face. 'Your call, boys. If you want to chuck your cash away that's your own business.' He tapped his nose. 'If you change your mind, come and see me, I'll sort you.'

Then he leaned over and whispered something into Holly's ear, before laughing and stroking her hair.

The guy was a dick. There were no two ways about that. But if that was what Holly wanted, then maybe Jalil could be that person. He was damned if he was going to let the knobhead call them 'boys' in front of Holly.

'Go on then,' said Jalil, before he could change his mind.

The older lad looked surprised but impressed.

'What?' said Zain, horrified. 'Are you kidding?'

Jalil was sick and tired of being treated like a cowardly little kid. He looked at Zain with challenging eyes before returning his gaze to the dealer. 'I said, count me in.'

The dealer nodded. 'Good lad! That's what I like to see. Some common sense. Fifteen quid will get you a buzz that'll last you all night long. You won't regret it. You see my mate over there.' He gestured to the shorter guy whose acne was visible even in the dark of the nightclub. 'He'll meet you in the toilets in five minutes.'

Zain and Robbo turned to walk away. When they were out of earshot they turned on Jalil.

'What the *fuck* do you think you're doing, man? Are you completely insane?'

Jalil eyed them both with a little of the aggression he'd been suppressing over the last few months. 'What—you guys think I'm too chicken to do it?'

'It's not a question of being chicken—it's about being a fucking moron if you do.'

Jalil shrugged. If it took something like this to get Holly to realise he wasn't a pathetic coward, then so be it. If his mates didn't like it, then tough shit. It was them who had made him look like a wanker in the first place. He pushed between the two of them, barging Robbo with his shoulder on the way through.

'Don't fucking do it!' shouted Zain angrily.

Five minutes later, Jalil found himself in the central toilet cubicle of the club, cradling a little green pill in his hand, wondering who was the coward now? The other two might willingly jump on an aeroplane, but they had never scored drugs in a nightclub. Which of those two things took more guts, hey? He looked at the tiny round drug. It was smaller than he'd imagined. Pastel green in colour and with a frog carved onto it. He steeled himself to swallow it, wondering whether the magic pill could really create that perfect euphoria—a moment where he was just the same as Holly and her friends. He took one deep breath followed by seven small exhalations, just as Petal had shown them, before dropping the little round tablet into the toilet.

McKENZIE

The meeting at Dark Star Records was brief. In contrast to the last time he had been to the record company headquarters, McKenzie was not invited past the reception desk on this occasion. The offices were pulsing with activity. The curved reception desk on the fourth floor provided a physical barrier between the visitors and the executives who were busy making record deals in the uber-stylish offices behind it. When Alfie swept out from behind the partition, he was holding a stack of papers and a pen.

Alfie placed the papers on the table, clicked the top of his pen and made a cross next to two paragraphs on the front page. 'I'm sorry it had to come to this, but I'm afraid I had no choice.'

'What's this?' asked McKenzie.

'Your exit contract. I need you to sign and date where I've marked, please.'

'Hang on a minute. Does it really have to come to this? Yes—I made a massive mistake, but I promise it won't happen again.'

'You're right, it won't.' Clearly Alfie was still pissed off about the interview.

'There can't be that many people who saw it, Alfie,' pleaded McKenzie. 'I'll make it right, I promise.'

Alfie raised his voice slightly. '*Anyone* who saw that interview is one person too many for my liking *and* for the liking of the chief executives here at Dark Star Records. You know it's not just *your* neck on the line here. *I* signed you in good faith! My bosses want to know how I didn't spot that we had a prolific drug user on our books when our research usually flags that up before you've even had your first interview.'

'But I'm really not...'

Alfie held his hands up to stop McKenzie's protests. 'It's too late McKenzie. I've already got three more people lined up for auditions to replace you. Now if you'll just sign these please.'

'I'm not signing nothing 'til I've read the whole thing.'

Alfie sighed. 'Fine. I want them back on my desk by next week at the latest.'

He tossed the papers onto the coffee table and stood up to leave. Before heading back to his office he turned to McKenzie one final time. 'I'm fucking gutted that you blew this, kid. I had big plans for you, you know. You let both of us down.'

McKenzie let his head fall into his hands. He took one deep breath in, then blew out seven smaller breaths. He picked up the bundle of papers, and trudged towards the lifts, detecting a glimmer of pity from the receptionist on the way.

The journey from Canary Wharf back to Stepney was made even more depressing by the sight of the bars and restaurants already teeming with Friday evening trade. It was difficult for McKenzie to forget that whilst most people were celebrating the end of their working week, he was mourning the end of his career. He took the DLR to Limehouse station and contemplated going back home to his empty flat. On a whim, he decided to go and see his mum. She had known about the meeting and would doubtless be on the phone to him soon to find out what had happened. And anyway, her house was warm and welcoming. It would be good to sit with someone who was on his side.

The smell of the house hadn't altered since he was little—a mixture of fatty pastry and Dettol. He automatically shoved the door closed behind him, knowing without even thinking about it, that it would stick with around fifteen degrees to spare. When he turned around, a small boy was smiling at him from the end of the hallway, standing barefoot on a heavily-patterned carpet.

'Hey, squirt.' Although he loved his five year old nephew, he couldn't help feeling disappointed. He'd needed to be with his mum. To have her undivided attention. He heard laughter from the back room which he recognised to be his sister's and his gran's. His heart sank. He couldn't do this in front of them. Was it too late to sneak back out again and go home? 'You're in trouble,' smiled his nephew, Kaiden.

'Am I?' McKenzie replied.

'Mummy and Nan said you've been told off.'

Fucking great, thought McKenzie, realising that his life-destroying meeting had been the subject of discussion for the entire family.

'Did they?'

'Did you have to sit on the naughty step?'

McKenzie smiled. If only! 'Grown-ups don't get sent to the naughty step.'

'That's not fair! I always get sent to the naughty step.'

'You're not naughty, are you?'

Kaiden kicked his toe against the carpet, looking sheepish. 'Only sometimes. Ben is really naughty. He's in my class at school. He did a swear at the teacher.'

McKenzie laughed. 'Ben sounds like fun—what did he say?'

Kaiden's eyes widened solemnly. 'Mummy said I'm not allowed to say that word.'

McKenzie crouched down to Kaiden's level. 'You can tell me—I won't tell Mummy,' he whispered.

Kaiden looked unsure. 'Promise?'

'Promise.'

'He said 'fackuf'.'

McKenzie stifled a laugh. 'Yes, Mummy's right, 'fackuf' isn't a good word for little kids to use.'

'Mummy said it's not really his fault—it's because he has older brothers who let him play *Call of Duty* which is a shooting and swearing game. And his favourite programme on telly is *Gogglebox* and that's got loads of swears in it. So is your teacher mad with you?'

McKenzie thought about Alfie. 'Yes, a bit.'

'Was your behaviour unacceptable?'

'What?' laughed McKenzie.

Kaiden shrugged. 'It's from Supernanny.' Then, bored of the conversation, he spun on his bare feet and charged off into the back room.

The house was a 1960's two-up two-down mid-terrace affair. Small and clean, although his mum's collection of ornaments and photo frames cluttered every available surface.

He sighed and followed the voices through to the small back sitting room which was the preferred room of choice—the front room being a dumping ground for paperwork, coats and other things his mum preferred not to have littering the sitting area.

McKenzie's mum stood up on his arrival and kissed him on the cheek. 'Well?'

He slumped onto the sofa next to his mum, choosing to avoid the discussion for as long as he could. Seated in the hard-backed arm chair to his left was his grandmother. She was a naturally slender woman, who, despite moving to London from the Dominican Republic over forty years earlier, had never acclimatised to UK weather. Wrapped up as usual in several layers of cardigans and shawls, her frailty was accentuated. 'Hi, Gran. How are you?'

'Not doing bad for a corpse,' she said reprovingly, then laughed to show that she was joking.

McKenzie groaned. This was far worse than anything that tosser Alfie could throw at him. Shame burned through him to the core. 'Gran—I am *so* sorry. Really, I am…'

She patted her dark, wrinkled hands to stop his apology.

'It's fine, boy. It was actually nice to feel useful for a change. Although when Tash told me I had passed, I was shocked. I thought, dear Lord, if this is heaven then you've been having a proper fine joke with us children on earth. No angels, no gates, no harps. Just my own little street with the litter blowing from the takeaway. I was more relieved when I realised it was all your invention.'

McKenzie glared at his younger sister. Bloody Tash. What possessed her to tell their gran about his cover story?

'Come on, son, don't keep us hanging. What did they say?'

He threw his head back and inhaled deeply. 'I'm out, Mum. They don't want me back.'

'What?' she screeched indignantly. 'But that's crazy? All because of one stupid interview?'

Tash laughed. 'I heard about that! Getting trashed on TV—what the hell is that about Big Mac? I mean, it's fine by me and all. You're making me look like the number one child for a change. But seriously?'

McKenzie didn't like it when his family used his stage name. It didn't feel right in these four walls. Especially not now. But Tash was right—he had always been the golden child of the family (Tash getting pregnant at sixteen had sealed that one for good).

'Shut up, Tash. It wasn't like that. I'd just had too much to drink to see me through that flight.'

Tash raised her eyebrows as if she knew it wasn't just alcohol that had been self-medicated that day. He glared at her, warning her to keep her mouth shut in front of his mum and gran.

'It can happen to anyone,' said his mum. 'And they know you don't like flying. You told them about your Fear of Flying course didn't you?'

McKenzie pursed his lips and stared at the ceiling.

'McKenzie?' his mum pressed.

'No! It's none of their damn business.'

McKenzie's mum sank back into her chair in dismay. 'But that explains everything,' she said angrily. 'If you tell them about that they'll understand why it happened and they'll let you back in.'

'They won't let me back in, Mum.'

'But it's worth a try.'

'It's not worth a try!' he snapped back. 'It'll just make me look like more of an idiot in front of the entire nation.'

'But there are lots of famous people who don't like flying,' pleaded his mum. 'There was that footballer —you know, that thingy-me-bobby one.'

'Dennis Bergkamp, Mum. He's the only person people can ever think of, and do you know why he is scared of flying? It's because he was on a plane, travelling to the World Cup when the engine cut out!'

'Well, whatever—he still did well for himself. And anyway, how can they have the band without you? You write all the songs.'

'With Little Gee, yeah.'

'And what has he got to say about all this? George has been your best friend since school,' her hands were on her hips now, demanding an answer.

McKenzie shrugged.

'Well I think he should quit too if they are not going to

let you back in. One-for-all and all-for-one. I've seen it on *The X Factor!*' she exclaimed as if that were the benchmark for all musical matters. 'A band comes on and Simon takes a liking to one of them but not the others. There are tears and all sorts of crying shenanigans, then the other one says he won't do it without the rest of the band. Simon pretends to think about it then tells them he admires their team spirit and lets them all go on. It's how they work, these record bosses. This Alfie boss man will be just waiting for George and the others to vouch for you.'

'Mum, this is not *The X Factor*. This is real life—not television. Little Gee is not going to chuck his entire career away to save me. It was me who messed up, *not* him.'

McKenzie's mum huffed. 'Just you wait until I see him!' she muttered. 'And we're boycotting his uncle's grocery shop from now on.' She raised her voice and repeated slowly for the benefit of her mother. 'We're-not-shopping-at-Fruitopia-any-more-Mum!'

McKenzie's gran nodded along in the corner, not having kept up with the conversation whatsoever. 'So when are you going to be on the television?' she asked him, genuinely.

FRANNIE

Frannie had come home early from the night out. It was the second in a series of celebrations to mark his nephew's twenty-first birthday. He had been flattered to have been invited out with all of Joe's friends, and, although he wasn't interested in going clubbing with them, he had gone along for a quick pint in the pub before the youngsters headed into Deansgate to go clubbing.

Man City's game was on Match of The Day, so when the phone rang at quarter past eleven, Frannie was distracted and frustrated with the interruption. He answered the phone, his eyes still fixed on the screen. The referee had just called over Kolarov to issue a yellow card which, in Frannie's opinion was unmerited.

'Hello,' he mumbled through a mouthful of contraband crisps, still frowning in protest at the replay.

'Uncle Frannie, it's Joe,' came the distressed voice from the other end.

'Joe, what's up? You know City are getting shafted here by the ref.'

'I'm at the hospital. Simon…he…he collapsed.'

Frannie felt the handset shake against the side of his face. 'What? What's happened?' he said urgently.

At that moment Kim appeared in the lounge, pulling the fleecy cord of her dressing gown belt around her waist. She was blinking against the light. 'What's going on?' she frowned. Frannie ignored her.

'I don't know. Honest, I don't know. One minute he was standing having a drink and the next he was slumped with his back against the pillar.'

'Which hospital?' asked Frannie urgently.

'Manchester Royal Infirmary.'

'We're on our way. Kim—get our Gary over here right now to stay with Hannah.'

Joe was waiting in the reception area of A&E when Frannie and Kim arrived.

'Where is he?'

Joe's face was pale, making the red rims of his eyes even more noticeable. The shock of what had happened had sobered him up abruptly. 'They've taken him straight through.'

Frannie marched to the reception desk, tapping his feet impatiently as he stood in a short queue. A&E was Saturday night busy. Girls with mascara tracks smudged down their faces clutched their high heels in their hands; others bore the signs of a nasty fall with their laddered tights and bleeding wounds. A man with vomit down his shirt slouched comatose on a plastic chair, whilst a young mother held a fevered screaming infant close to her chest.

The place smelled of cleaning products and putrid bodily fluids.

When he reached the desk, he spoke quickly. 'Our son, Simon Bentham, has been admitted via ambulance in the last half hour. We don't know what's happened, or what's going on but we would like to see him.'

'That's fine,' the receptionist replied calmly. 'Can I just take a few details?'

As Kim confirmed all of Simon's details with the receptionist, Frannie quizzed his nephew on what exactly had happened.

'I swear, Uncle Frannie, we were taking care of him. When we got to the club, he only had *one* bottle of beer, then he asked for Coke. I know because I bought him one, then it was Maya's round and she said that she got him a Coke as well. She's on her way here in a taxi—she'll tell you the same.'

'Frannie, we're going,' said Kim.

'I'll wait here for Maya. Can you let me know as soon as you know anything?' pleaded Joe.

'Of course,' said Frannie over his shoulder.

They followed the nurse through a set of double doors, then along a long corridor off which branched several smaller corridors. The nurse stopped at the ward station to pick up some paperwork, before leading them to a trio of plastic moulded chairs fixed to the wall of one of the smaller corridors.

'Simon is currently being treated by Doctor Ashmal. In order to help him select the best course of action for Simon, I just need to ask you a few questions.'

'Okay,' they nodded, still shell-shocked.

'Is Simon a regular drug user?'

'No!' exclaimed Kim. 'He *certainly* is not. He's only sixteen. He's a good boy. He would never dream of doing anything like that.'

'Thank you, Mrs Bentham, I know this is a distressing time for you, but I really do have to ask as it might help Simon's recovery. Are you aware whether either Simon or any of his friends may have experimented with drugs or other illegal substances in the past?'

Kim began to get angry. 'I understand that you have to ask these questions, but I'm telling you, you're barking up the wrong tree. Simon is not a drug user of any sort. Never has been and never will be. He's never even been on a big night out before. He's only sixteen.'

'Mrs Bentham, from the information our paramedic team passed on to us, it seems likely that Simon has suffered a reaction to some sort of toxin. We're not the police. We are just interested in making him better. At the moment he's hooked up to a saline drip. However, we do have some medication which can reverse the effects of certain drugs, for example, if Simon had taken heroin, we might administer naloxone—'

'He is *not* on heroin or any other drug!' Kim cried angrily. 'I want to see my son...now!'

Frannie urged Kim to calm down and asked the nurse to repeat what she had just said. He was finding it difficult to take in the information. As she calmly went over the facts for a second time, Joe and Maya appeared.

'Is he okay?' asked Joe.

Frannie shook his head. 'They are still sorting him out. We haven't seen him yet.'

'But he's going to be alright, yeah?' asked Joe, his face pleading with the nurse to say *yes*.

'He is still unconscious. If we knew what he had taken we might be able speed up his recovery,' replied the nurse.

Frannie spoke calmly but firmly. 'Listen, if you two know anything—*anything* that might help then please speak up now.'

Joe began to cry. 'It was just a night out! I like a pint, but *you* know I'm not interested in any other shit. Maya doesn't even drink! They were both on Coke! Coca-Cola!' he added.

Maya was shaking. 'I think it was meant for me,' she whispered.

'What do you mean, love?'

'I think my drink was spiked. You're always reading about that date rape drug. I think it was meant for me. Our drinks were on the same table. I bet Simon picked up the wrong can of coke.' She whimpered. 'It should be me in there.'

The nurse interjected. Maya's sobriety seemed to have convinced her that she could be trusted to give the correct information. 'Did Simon consume any alcohol this evening?'

'Just two bottles of beer,' said Joe. 'One with his dad in the local pub, and one more a few hours later at the club. Apart from that he was drinking Coke.'

Maya nodded.

The nurse made notes. 'I'll pass all of this on to Doctor Ashmal, then you can come and see Simon.'

The small side room off the busy corridor was functional and sparse. One flimsy chair stood next to a trolley of sterile, plastic wrapped bandages and cardboard kidney shaped bowls. A large, blue metal pedal bin took up an entire corner. Frannie noticed that the wall mounted hand-sanitiser was situated perfectly at head height for visitors choosing to sit down. Simon lay on the portable hospital bed, his best shirt unbuttoned, with a drip attached to his arm. A large clip on the end of his finger measured his oxygen saturation levels. Kim cried the moment she entered the room.

'I *told* you we shouldn't have let him go,' she cried angrily.

Frannie tried to rationalise with her. 'It was a freak accident, Kim. It could have happened to anyone.'

'He's just a child, Frannie. I told you I didn't think he should go.'

'He's sixteen, love. You can't wrap him up in cotton wool forever. I was *working* when I was his age.'

'Well excuse me for wanting something better for him!'

'Hey, I know you're angry, and you want to lash out, but this isn't my fault. It was an accident, so don't bloody take it out on me. And whether you like to hear it or not, you *do* baby them. Both of them! If you ask me it's *more* independence he needs, *not* less.'

Kim raised her voice. 'If taking an interest in your child and giving them opportunities is babying, then yes, I'm guilty. At lease I *take* an interest—unlike you!'

'What the…are you serious?' Frannie shook his head. 'It'd be nice to get a chance to spend more time with the kids—I couldn't agree more. You've got them into some sort of regimented routine—constantly ferrying them from one activity to another. If it's not violin, it's football or ballet or orchestra or choir. The poor kids don't get a break, Kim! It's ridiculous. If they want to do these things let them do them—they're both old enough to sort themselves out. Simon can walk to his violin lesson. Or get the bus—you don't need to drive them everywhere. And I'm sorry that I have to work, but it's me who has to pay for all of this stuff. I can't be out earning the brass and at home at the same time. You can't have it both ways, Kim.'

'I cannot believe that while our son is lying in a hospital bed, you're moaning about bloody money!'

'And I can't believe that you're blaming me for this.' He gestured towards Simon.

'I just want our kids to do well in life. I want them to work hard, get good jobs and have the lifestyle that we'll never have. What's wrong with that? What's wrong with me wanting the best for them?'

'Because the best for them isn't about how many exams they pass or how much money they'll earn. Not to *me* anyway. It's about them enjoying life, Kim. Having friends, having fun. When was the last time you saw either of them just mucking about having some fun? It's not about how much money you've got in the bank, or how many fancy holidays you have…'

'I wouldn't know about fancy holidays, would I? In case you hadn't noticed your ridiculous fear of flying sees to that nicely! I have to book activities for the kids for their summer holidays so they don't get bored because you won't travel anywhere!'

'They're probably bored silly of being organised. Just give them a break, Kim, for fuck's sake.'

'Muuuum.' There was a small groan and some movement from the bed.

'Go and get the nurse!' Kim ordered.

Frannie's gaze lingered on his wife for a couple of seconds before he paced out of the room towards the nurse's station.

As the nurse took various readings and marked information in Simon's notes, Simon came round slowly.

'Looks like he's over the worst of it,' smiled the nurse. 'The doctor might want to move him onto a ward, just to keep an eye on him, given his age. I'll phone ahead to see if they have any space.'

Both Frannie and Kim insisted on staying the night on the ward with Simon. As he slept off the effects of the drug, they sat in icy silence. Frannie tried to remember when the divide between himself and the rest of the family had developed. It couldn't have been a sudden thing—surely he would have noticed. Gradually though, over the years, the very foundations of his family unit had shifted beneath his feet. If there had been an earthquake in their marriage, he would have felt it, but the gradual seismic shift had taken him completely unawares. He thought about his job and the promotion. Only hours earlier, this had seemed like the answer to all his problems. Now, he wasn't sure.

The doctor signed Simon off shortly after nine a.m. Frannie and Simon waited in the foyer for Kim to return from the loo before heading home.

'Hello, love,' came a voice Frannie half recognised. He looked up to see a dark haired, tired-looking woman balancing a paper cup of coffee, a chocolate muffin, and a packet of crisps in her hands. It took a moment for him to place her as one of his fellow Fear of Flying students.

'Hi, Rachel. What are you doing here?'

Rachel huffed. 'This is our second home, unfortunately. My daughter was admitted last night. She has,' she paused, unaccustomed to the finality of the new diagnosis, 'Dravet Syndrome.'

Frannie looked blank.

'It's a type of severe epilepsy. She's had it since she was a baby. This fit was a bad one. Her lungs were affected. She's on IV antibiotics as a precaution against it turning into full blown pneumonia. We've had that before and believe me, we don't want it again. It was touch-and-go that time.'

'Rachel, I'm sorry, I had no idea.'

'Well, why would you? It's not something I broadcast. Anyway, I'd better get back. I'll see you on Wednesday?'

'Well, yes, assuming you're able to make it.'

'Oh, I'll be there,' she nodded. 'This just makes me even more determined.'

Kim appeared just as Rachel was walking away. She frowned. 'Who was that? What's happening on Wednesday?' She had heard the last part of the conversation.

'Oh, just work stuff. She's new. Her kiddie is in upstairs ... not well at all. Come on, let's get home.'

PETAL

The journey from Manchester to Stonehenge had taken several hours longer than planned. JJ's van had broken down once before they had hit Altrincham, then again on the M6 just north of Birmingham. Petal had spent nearly two hours breathing in exhaust fumes from passing, fully functioning vehicles from her vantage point on the embankment, whilst mentally calculating how long it would take her to walk the 100-odd miles home. Sharing the back compartment of the VW camper with two fully-grown adults (one of whom was clearly a stranger to soap and water), a slobbering whippet, a jumble of camping equipment and the finest post sell-by-date food that Aldi had to offer was not how Petal had envisaged spending her thirty-ninth birthday. She had only agreed to the trip as it had appeared marginally less depressing than spending the day in Jubilee House, tiptoeing around the subject that Moon had been so keen to avoid since Thomas-The-Tank-Engine-Gate.

'You *did* sort out the camping permits didn't you?'

asked Petal. After several hours in the van, the Wiltshire countryside looked inviting out of the grubby back window of the camper and she was keen to get the tent up as quickly as possible to regain a modicum of personal space.

'All under control, Petal,' replied Ash.

'So you have them? In your possession?' asked Petal, rather more firmly this time.

'Don't you worry about it, love. Old Ash has got it sorted.'

'Moon?' Petal's glare demanded further explanation.

'It's fine, Babes,' Moon nodded, eyes slightly unfocussed from his last joint. 'Ash's mate's brother is on the gate. He's sorting us out.'

Petal's lips pursed so tightly that she felt some of the skin crack. Fighting to stay in control she began to breathe deeply—in for one, out for seven. Then again—in for one, out for seven. All the way to Stonehenge.

Petal hadn't been to the Summer Solstice Festival for a number of years. It had been a regular event when they lived on the commune in Devon, and when she was a child her parents had taken her every year until they became discontented by the growing druid influence over the hippies. Even from the back of the camper van, the festival seemed more organised than ever before. Dozens of hi-vis clad volunteers patrolled the entry queue, directing drivers into their lanes. They rumbled along for another twenty minutes until they arrived at their gate.

'Are you Barry the Badger?' asked Ash, leaning over JJ to speak to the car park attendant out of the driver's window.

'Are you taking the piss?' came the surly reply.

'No, man, I'm looking for Chas' brother, Barry. You not him then?'

'Er, no, and in case you hadn't noticed there's a two mile queue behind you. I just need your tickets.'

'Well, you see, Barry the Badger has our tickets. He was supposed to be working on this gate. If you could just phone your boss and find out where Barry is, then we'll be out of your way.'

The man on the gate gave a pitiful laugh. 'Come on guys, you're holding up the queue.'

On cue, a range of beeps of differing tones came from the lane behind them.

'But he has got the tickets. Honestly…'

'Listen, I'm going to have to ask you to turn around and go back, otherwise the only person I'll be calling is security.'

'Are you seriously not going to let us in, man?'

The tabard-wearing man picked up his walkie-talkie and poised his hand over the button.

'Okay, okay, we're going!' Ash held his hands up in surrender and muttered 'for fuck's sake.'

The man allowed them into the field to turn the camper around, before they set off on the drive of shame back down the queue. The lane was narrow and each vehicle they passed had to squeeze into the ditch to allow them their retreat. More beeps and insults were thrown their way as wheels spun to force campers and cars back on track. Petal bent over with her head in her lap to avoid the shame of facing the other drivers. Over an hour later they parked the camper in a general car park about a mile away from the stone circle. The five-pound charge was covered by a whip round, although Petal found herself putting three quid in to cover her own share and Moon's, plus JJ's since it was decided that the driver shouldn't have to pay. Ash covered the remaining two pounds for himself and Dawn.

'We'll just come back here to kip,' said Moon brightly.

'What—all of us?' said Petal, pulling her hand knitted calf length cardigan tightly around herself despite the midsummer heat.

'Yeah, it'll be fine. You know how these things go— we'll probably just stay up near the circle partying anyway. Doubt we'll need it.'

Petal rummaged through the supplies she had packed and filled a small rucksack with essentials before beginning the long walk up towards the majestic stone circle.

Once she reached the hub of the festival, Petal began to relax. People of all denominations had come from far and wide to celebrate the longest day. The mood was celebratory, the vibe of peace and acceptance contagious. It was good to get away from Manchester. Away from Jubilee House with its teenage gangs who laughed at Petal and Moon for their alternative lifestyle. Here, everyone was accepted. It felt like coming home. Here it didn't matter what brand of shoes you wore. In the immediate crowd surrounding her, Petal could see wellies, sandals, jelly shoes, walking boots, trainers and lots of bare feet. Adults with floral headgear mixed with cloaked pagans and trainer wearing indie-kids. Drums sounded and people danced. Children watched in awe as entertainers juggled with fire and performed acrobatics. In the distance, a mass outdoor yoga group was in session.

'Fancy some yoga?' asked Dawn.

Petal nodded. She enjoyed teaching yoga, but found that much of her time was spent going over the basics with her beginners groups. It would be nice to do some advanced classes with people at her own level.

As they waited for the advanced class to assemble, Petal and Dawn surveyed the festival from the periphery.

'You are so lucky, being brought up with all of this,' Dawn gushed. 'Me and Ash were fortunate to find this lifestyle when we were teenagers, but you, your parents were the original hippies. The real deal!'

Petal sighed. She missed them. Her mum had died four years earlier of an aggressive cancer that took her life quickly. Petal and Moon had moved up north so that Petal could care for her mum through her last months. Her mum's refusal to accept any form of chemotherapy had accelerated the end. Her father, unable and unwilling to remain in his wife's void, was last seen heading east in his camper van in search of a kibbutz. Petal didn't know how far east he got as he had never been great at keeping in touch. She hoped that he had made it to Istanbul, which is where he had often talked of going, but for all she knew he could be living his dream in Grimsby. In the meantime their own lack of funds had delayed any move back down to Devon. The flat in Manchester was only supposed to be a temporary measure, but then the cash had run out, their van had died a sad death, and Moon and Petal had got stuck in the rut that they found themselves in to this day.

'Do you ever want more, Dawn?' asked Petal, gazing into the distance and picking tough stems of hay from the dry earth.

Dawn looked genuinely confused. 'More than what? We're free spirits—what more could you want?'

'Hmm,' pondered Petal.

The yoga session was just what Petal needed. Her body felt beautifully fluid after being cramped up in the camper van for hours on end. Her mind, too, was open to possibility. They stopped at a catering van and bought some delicious Thai noodles. There was no point ordering anything for the boys as they might not find them again for hours. Then they wandered around the site, stopping at different tents and enjoying music and entertainment from every corner of the globe. By the time they bumped into the men again, hours later, it was clear that Moon, Ash and JJ were too stoned to hold a conversation.

'I was just telling Ash, we're thinking about getting a dog, aren't we Petal?'

Petal felt her newly relaxed body begin to knit into small gnarly knots again. 'Are we?' she said sharply.

'Yeah, you know,' he drawled. 'The pitter-patter of tiny paws and all that.'

Petal glared at him. She couldn't believe he was bringing the baby conversation up in front of their friends.

'I think that matter is still up for discussion,' she snapped.

'Ahh, you guys should have a *real* baby,' prattled Dawn.

Ash laughed. 'I dunno about you, mate, but I'm always too stoned to get it up.'

Moon took another drag of his spliff and descended into a fit of giggles that lasted almost a full minute.

Petal was furious with him. It was her thirty-ninth birthday and she was fucked if she was going to spend it with people who were sullying her aura.

'I spotted an old friend of my mum and dad's in the weaving tent on the way up here. I'm going to say hello. I'll catch up with you again later.'

She stomped off, away from Moon, away from Ash, and JJ and Dawn. It was her birthday and for one night only she was going to be exactly who she wanted to be. The sun had gone down and lights, music and drumming beckoned her from different directions. She pulled a bottle of elderflower wine out of her rucksack and drank about half of it straight from the bottle. She followed the sound of a swirling rhythm and found herself amongst a group of people who seemed lost in the music. Tentatively at first she joined in, swaying conservatively in time with the music. Soon, others were dancing with her, swaying and swirling, clapping and writhing to the beat. As she danced, faces swam in front of her—people who were feeling the same rush as her. She watched people smiling, kissing, hugging. Some of them may have been fuelled by narcotics, but others, like Petal, were intoxicated by the music. One face caught her eye time and time again as it smiled at her through the dancing. It was a handsome face, older than her own, by a number of years. His eyes were brown and his skin a little weathered by the sun. His hair and beard were greying, but his soul was very much alive. At first, contact was sporadic—there were little touches as the music took them in each other's direction. Then, as one melody swam into another, their dancing became closer. Song by song, the other dancers faded from her vision, until it was just him. The first kiss was a gentle, experimental gauge of what was to come; the second, slower and deeper.

'You're beautiful,' he told her. It was a long time since Moon had said anything like that, let alone meant it. This stranger made her feel truly beautiful. 'Do you want to come for a walk?' he asked.

She nodded and took his hand as he led her out of the crowd.

His tent was sparsely furnished. He had arrived earlier that day and had headed straight for the festival after pitching up. The foam camping mat was warm to sit on. She pulled the remaining wine from her rucksack and they shared it out in plastic mugs.

'Cheers,' he smiled. 'To my exquisite flower of summer. The beautiful Petal.'

She blushed and took a demure sip of her wine. Before she could put it down he leant over to kiss her again. This time, the kiss was hard and urgent. Petal dropped her mug and threw herself headlong into the kiss. Within seconds he was on top of her. She pulled his smock over his head and helped him to unbutton the fastening on her best tie-dyed skirt.

'Do I need anything?' he panted.

Petal paused only for a fraction of a second. 'No,' she whispered.

Minutes later, after he had collapsed on top of her, Petal

felt an exhilaration unlike anything she had felt before. Without trying to draw attention to what she was doing, she surreptitiously tilted her pelvis upwards to assist the process. She crossed her fingers and prayed for the best birthday present anyone could give her.

FLIGHT DAY MINUS 1 WEEK

'One week until the big test,' smiled Hugh. If anyone had asked him after week one whether he believed that he would have any students left at this stage of the course, he would have replied with a categorical 'no'. Granted, the course hadn't been the resounding success he had anticipated, but then again, how was he to possibly predict the ludicrous obstacles that his students conjured up for themselves? The four people who sat in front of him might not provide sufficient funds to facilitate his holiday with Marguerite, but at least they had been loyal enough to stick it out until the end. And anyway, in his view, the course had taken a turn for the better in recent weeks. He was fairly confident that they would all board that flight next week without causing him too much embarrassment.

'I think we can all say that we have learnt a lot over the past few weeks. So today, we're going to do a quick revision session, just to reinforce the fact that we now all know. That is, that air travel is by far the safest form of transport.'

The students smiled nervously at each other. Jalil had been studying McKenzie since they arrived for the session. He'd had the nagging feeling for weeks that he recognised him from somewhere but had been unable to place him. Today was different though. In a bid to impress Holly, he had gone onto the Urban Phantoms website to try to be as knowledgeable as possible about the band in case they got the chance to chat about music, and that's when he had seen the picture of McKenzie. Well, it looked like McKenzie, but he wasn't sure. On the website the singer was called Big Mac. He wore baggy black jeans, gathered at the ankle, with bright white t-shirts, fraternity jackets and lots of gold chains. McKenzie, meanwhile, looked like an office boy in his Marksies' jumper over a check shirt. He looked away as McKenzie caught his eye for a second time. He didn't want McKenzie to think he fancied him, or anything, with his staring, so he turned his attention back to Hugh who was prattling on about the flight next week. The flight— yeah right! He had already decided to text Hugh with some phoney illness to avoid it.

'We know that the statistics speak for themselves. Not wanting to dwell on fatal accidents,' he began. He could see that all four students perked up in their seats when they heard their favourite topic, and he was sure that Rachel was about to open her mouth and add some gem of wonder on the matter. He continued quickly to avoid any interruption. 'There is more chance of you being struck by lightning, becoming a premiership footballer or giving birth to natural quadruplets than there is of you being killed in a plane crash.'

Petal automatically put her hand on her stomach. She hadn't even considered the possibility of multiple births. She immediately pictured herself walking through the park with a double papoose strapped round her chest, stroking the two perfect downy little heads sticking out of the top.

Rachel gave an exaggerated, audible shiver. 'Sod that! I'd take the plane crash any day. Could you *imagine*, four tiny humans inside one woman, then four scrikin' babies, four sets of shitty nappies, four…'

Petal recoiled, wondering how anyone could say such a thing about the wonder of nature.

'So you get the idea,' shouted Hugh, wondering why he hadn't come up with a better analogy. 'We've also learnt that there are mechanisms that have been designed and built into modern aeroplanes to avoid situations such as tailskid and wind-shears. That pilots have gained years of flying experience before they are even considered to be allowed to fly commercial passenger planes. That these same pilots have been trained to control a plane whose engine has failed. And that these same pilots are supported by an army of highly qualified ground staff in air traffic control who are watching every movement of your plane from the moment it takes off, to the moment it lands safely on the other side.'

The class nodded sceptically along to what Hugh felt was a rousing speech.

'Despite this, as we have heard from Will, the very nature of a phobia is that it is irrational.' He coughed in a bid to cover his discomfort in dealing with something that he did not, and probably never would, fully understand. 'So, it is important that when we board that plane next Saturday, you all remember to use the, er, coping techniques that Petal has shown you. In fact, that's what we will be moving on to now.' He looked over at the hippy lady who, he noticed, looked a lot more smiley than usual. 'Petal?'

'Oh, yes, calming techniques,' she said, snapping back to the classroom from her baby-filled reverie. 'If you could all push the tables and chairs back a bit before finding a space on the floor, that would be great.' There was no way she was shifting furniture around in her possible condition.

Frannie went to assist Rachel who was struggling to manoeuvre a double desk on her own.

'How's the little 'un?' he asked tentatively.

Rachel gave a tight smile. 'She's still completely floored. The IV meds seem to have prevented full blown pneumonia this time,' she tapped the desk with her hand several times 'touch wood—but she's very weak. She has no appetite. If she doesn't get anything down her by tomorrow then they're going to have to tube feed her, which is just awful. She's had it done before and she hates it. I'm going straight back to the hospital as soon as we finish here.'

'Right,' Frannie nodded, unsure of what to say next.

'What about your lad?' she asked.

Frannie gave a large sigh. 'He's fine now, no thanks to those bastards peddling their dodgy drugs. It was his first ever night out. He wasn't even drinking—well, two beers he'd had but then he was on Coke. Some knob-head spiked his drink. We're pretty sure it was one of the girls being targeted but Simon picked up her drink by mistake. It's bloody frightening. You think your kids are sensible so they'll be safe but it doesn't always work like that.' He shook his head.

'I know, it's everywhere. Did you see the front page of tonight's *Manchester Evening News*?'

'No, not yet.'

'Hang on, I've got it here.' She rummaged in her handbag. 'Something about some dodgy drugs. Here it is.' She flattened out the newspaper on the desk. The front page showed a picture of a policeman holding a plastic bag containing some tablets. The inset photo was a close up of the confiscated tablets. They were small green tablets with a picture of a frog on them. She read the headline and sub-heading out loud. 'Contaminated Ecstasy Hits Manchester—Several Hospitalised. Police have warned people over the risk of taking ecstasy after three teens were admitted to hospital on Friday night after taking what appears to be a contaminated version of the popular club drug. The tablets in question are easily identified by their pastel-green colouring and an inscription of a frog.'

Frannie shook his head. 'I don't understand why kids can't just go out and have a few beers, have a dance and enjoy themselves.'

Rachel shrugged and was about to shove the paper back into her handbag when Jalil asked her if he could have a look. He had heard the conversation and when Rachel had produced the newspaper his stomach dropped.

'Can I see that?' he asked.

'Keep it, love—I've read it.'

'Cheers,' he muttered, already distracted by the headlines. As the others joined Petal in the small circle on the floor, Jalil was devouring the article, hands shaking slightly, mouth dry.

'Come on, mate—if I'm doing this then you are too!' shouted McKenzie.

Jalil looked up from the paper. 'What? Oh, right.' As he found a space on the floor, he noticed a foul smell. It had the sharpness of ammonia. He wrinkled his nose. 'What's that smell? It stinks like cat piss down here.'

Rachel glared at him pointedly. She'd taken the spot next to Petal and realised that Petal had been sporting a new perfume this week.

Jalil's comments didn't go unnoticed by Petal. The perfume had been her birthday present from Moon. Apparently, during Thomas-The-Tank-Engine-Gate she had complained about her lack of perfume (amongst other things) so he had decided to buy her some for her birthday. Unfortunately, it wasn't the fragrant bottle of Chanel that she longed for. There was no ornate glass bottle, or shiny box to caress its delicate wares. No tissue paper or ribbon to adorn the luxury within. Instead, Moon had asked Dawn for a bottle of her organic rose and patchouli cologne, which she made in batches in the kitchen of her flat before flogging them for £7.99 at the farmers market. Dawn had obliged, and this evening in a moment of guilt she had doused herself in the stuff in front of him before leaving for the class.

Petal began by demonstrating the breathing technique that she had shown the group the previous week. 'Big breath in,' she instructed slowly, using her arms to indicate direction of airflow, in case anyone had been confused by the term 'in'. 'Then out for seven.' She made a small O shape with her lips, then blew out seven exaggerated audible blows.

The group reluctantly copied her.

'It's extremely important that when you blow out, you blow every last bit of air out. Right from the bottom of your belly.' She put a protective hand over her tummy. 'Then breathe in again, ensuring you take a big, deep breath. Inhale from your diaphragm. Remember, the key to this is to control your breathing. Take your time. Breathe slowly. The idea is to get as much oxygen into your system as possible. If you breathe too quickly you will hyperventilate and make matters worse. Nice big, deep breaths in, then out for seven.'

'I feel like I'm back in ante-natal classes,' said Rachel. 'We only went to one. Me and Charlie got the giggles when the midwife put on the birth video. The woman giving birth clearly hadn't been introduced to the concept of waxing! My Charlie whispered something about her having a minge like that fella who plays for United—Fellaini is it? The couple next to us heard, cos he's got a right gob on him has Charlie. Well then that fella started laughing, but his wife didn't see the funny side of it, so she started giving us these dirty looks. That just made me laugh even more. I nearly peed myself to be honest. We left after the break— didn't bother going back.'

'Okay,' interrupted Petal. 'I think we've all got the hang of that now. Well done! Now, breathing techniques are one way of coping with extreme stress, but there are other things that you can do to stay calm in situations of anxiety. Which brings me onto our next technique—nursery rhymes.

'What?' said McKenzie, spitting out the *t* sound at the end of the word in disbelief.

'Nursery rhymes,' smiled Petal. 'Who remembers singing nursery rhymes as a child?'

'Well, yes, as a child. But in case you hadn't noticed, we're all adults here, love,' frowned Frannie.

'It's not as absurd as you might think. Lots of people find that singing nursery rhymes helps them through very stressful situations. The rhythm helps to control breathing. The idea is that the rhyme itself is so familiar it requires little concentration. Even if you're distracted by other things going on around you, you can continue to say the rhyme without thinking about it and that will help to keep your breathing in a nice steady pattern. Also, the familiarity of the nursery rhyme provides an element of comfort in times of severe stress and anxiety. Let's try one. Who knows *Row, Row, Row Your Boat*?'

Despite this proposal being met by a circle of frowns and raised eyebrows, Petal pressed on with the song.

'Row, row, row your boat, gently down the stream,' she chanted, nodding her head up and down in time to the rhythm.

'Is she serious?' Jalil whispered to McKenzie, who accidently let out a loud snort of laughter.

'Merrily, merrily, merrily, merrily, life is but a dream. Come on, join in. You must know this one?' she urged.

The four students looked at each other in disbelief— each waiting for the others to join in.

'And you, Hugh!' she urged.

Hugh, horrified, immediately found some urgent photocopying which needed doing as far away from the classroom as possible.

'Okay, if you don't know that one then let's each try our own. I can see you're all a bit shy about this so let's close our eyes and each do our own.'

Rachel muttered. 'For fuck's sake,' before mumbling the words 'Twinkle, twinkle little star…'

Surprisingly to Jalil, the next voice to begin singing was McKenzie, who chose *Mary had a Little Lamb*. Reluctantly, Jalil racked his brains for a nursery rhyme to humiliate himself with as the others began their task.

'Up above the world so high…'

`Mary had a little lamb…'

'Merrily, merrily, merrily, merrily'

'Like a diamond in the sky…'

'She tied it to a pylon…'

'Life is but a dream'

'Twinkle, twinkle little star…'

'Ten thousand volts went up its arse…'

Jalil suddenly creased up laughing. 'Yeah, that's more like it.'

'Georgie Porgie pudding and pie…'

'How I wonder what you are.'

'And turned its wool to nylon.'

'Kissed the girls and made them cry'

'When the boys came out to play, he kissed them too cos he was gay.'

Petal was pleased that McKenzie and Jalil were joining in with the exercise. She had worried that they would refuse to, but she could see that they were laughing and joking, and chanting rhymes to each other.

On the spur of the moment, Jalil decided to ask McKenzie the question that had been niggling at him for weeks. 'I've been trying to think where I recognise you from. Now this is gonna sound a bit mad, but there's this band—the Urban Phantoms—and you look *well* like their main man.'

Stomach lurching and heart racing, McKenzie forced a smile and shook his head. 'Who? Never heard of them?'

Jalil looked crestfallen. 'Oh. They're just this really cool band I'm into at the moment. Honest to God man, you're the double of the singer. He's called Big Mac. I just thought that with you being called McKenzie...'

McKenzie interrupted. 'Nah, man. I mean, do I look like a pop star?' He gestured to his conservative outfit. 'And you've just heard my singing!'

'Yeah, suppose,' shrugged Jalil. 'You should check them out some time though. They're mint.'

A moment later, Hugh tentatively poked his head round the classroom door. He still had some information to impart about the flight, but was buggered if he was going to get dragged into Petal's nursery rhyme nonsense. 'Are you almost done, Petal?' he asked.

Petal addressed the group. 'How are we all feeling about next week? Relaxed? Anyone need more practise?'

'No we're grand, absolutely grand,' nodded Frannie a little too enthusiastically.

'Fine.'

'Brilliant,' came the chorus of the group who had

already scrambled to their feet before she could change her mind and humiliate them any further.

'So,' Hugh clapped his hands together. 'The next time I see you all will be at the airport.' He had to raise his voice slightly over the shuffling noises. 'Just a few practical reminders. We will be taking off from City Airport—not the main Manchester Airport. Now even though it's not a big commercial airport, you will *still* need to bring some photographic ID with you as we will be entering UK air space, and we can't be too careful after 9/11.' Hugh realised immediately that he shouldn't have added that last bit. He continued hastily. 'City airport is not too far away from us. It is situated on Liverpool Road, over Eccles way. You need to get on the A57 until you get to the M602. Get onto the M602, but leave at the first junction to get back onto the A57 towards Irlam. Turn right onto Liverpool Road, then carry on until...'

Hugh stopped short as Will, who had been observing the entire lesson, as usual, interrupted him. Will held up a piece of A4 paper in front of his mouth to shield his comments from the group and whispered something in Hugh's ear.

'Oh,' frowned Hugh. 'Oh, yes. Er, Will has just drawn my attention to something.' He looked at Will for assistance. 'Will?'

'Sorry guys,' Will smiled, 'I can't help but notice that none of you are writing this information down.' He laughed. 'Now, it *may* be that you all have super-duper memories, and that you can absorb vast wads of information in a split second. *Or*,' he hesitated. 'Or, it *could* be, and I'm just hazarding a guess—could be completely and totally wrong—it *could* be that you're not taking notes because none of you intend to actually take the flight next week.'

Nobody spoke. Rachel hung her head and scraped at a sticky patch on the desk with her thumbnail. Frannie coughed and rocked back and forth on his heels, staring intently at the light fitting. McKenzie and Jalil both gazed at their shuffling feet.

Hugh's face crumpled. He looked devastated. For a moment, Rachel almost felt sorry for him.

'Hugh, mate,' stuttered Frannie. 'It's not that we don't appreciate what you've done for us. I know that I'm much happier about getting on a plane than I was three weeks ago.' He looked round at the others for help. They nodded.

'Yeah, yeah, me too,' they lied.

'It's just that, well, I'm not sure we really *need* to take the flight to prove that we've got over our fear. Do we? I mean, we've done all of the *important* stuff in the classroom haven't we?'

'Yeah, I totally agree, man,' said McKenzie. He danced his thumbs back and forth in the air in a show of respect. 'Big up for Hugh here everyone! You've been wicked. I know that next time I get on a plane I'll be chillin' out big time. We don't need to drag everyone out to that airport next week to prove it, do we? I mean, Hugh, mate—I bet you've got a *million* and one better things you could be doing, right?' He joined his hands together and swung them over his right shoulder. 'I know you love your golf—I'd feel terrible if you missed out on your golf next week. The weather is probably gonna turn to shit again soon, man, and then you'd be all, like, "man, I shoulda gone golfing last week."'

'Yeah, I agree with McKenzie,' said Jalil. 'I bet you're like, top of your golfing league. What if some crappy division-two-style golf dude comes along cos you're not there and, you know, kicks your ass off the golfing leaderboard or something. I mean, we'd feel terrible.'

Hugh put his head in his hands.

Rachel thought for a moment. She was terrified that if she went on that plane, something would happen. She was the only person who could look after Poppy properly. Poppy—little Poppy, who was at this very moment lying in a hospital bed. Little Poppy, who would love nothing more than to see Mickey Mouse and all of her beloved Disney princesses. Before she built up the hopes of Poppy and Jasmine, she *had* to know that she could do this. She *had* to know that she wasn't going to back out at the last minute and destroy their dreams.

She took a deep breath. 'I'll do it, Hugh,' she said solemnly.

Hugh took his hands away from his head and looked at her, in grateful surprise.

'On one condition,' she continued.

His face immediately fell again.

'That *this* lot,' she gestured to McKenzie, Jalil and Frannie, 'come too.'

The others did a double take. McKenzie looked like he was in physical pain.

'I mean it,' she said. 'Truth be told, I don't want to go up in that bloody plane either, but I know that if I don't

155

do it, I'll never get over my fear. And it's the same for the rest of you. None of us want to take this frigging flight, but we have all come here for the last three weeks, we've sat, we've listened to Hugh's terror tales, we've meditated, we've breathed like we're about to give birth, we've sung bloody nursery rhymes for God's sake. If we give up now then as far as I'm concerned it's all been a complete waste of time. Now I'm going to go to the airport next week and get on that plane, much as it will go against every instinct in my body. But I'm not going alone. What was that famous saying—from the three Musketeers?'

Jalil, who had studied the novel for GCSE English replied 'You are very amiable, no doubt, but you would be charming if you would only depart.'

The subtlety of his response went over Rachel's head completely.

'No, not that one. "All for one and one for all," or something like that.'

The three men, none of whom wanted to tell an out and out lie, stalled for time.

'Well if you won't do it for me, do it for my little girl. She's lying in a hospital bed, braver than any of us will ever be. I can't change her condition. I can't promise her that she'll get better and never have to go back to hospital again. What I *can* do, is promise her that I'll take her to Disneyland so she can have some joy in her life. Some *pleasure*, instead of the endless rounds of medication and specialist appointments and seizures.' Suddenly she burst into tears. 'But I can't do it by myself. I can't get in that plane next week on my own. I need you lot with me.'

Frannie was the first to break. 'Alright, love, alright. We'll come. Won't we lads?'

McKenzie and Jalil nodded, shamed into submission. 'Yeah, don't cry Rach, we're in,' said McKenzie.

Will interjected. '*Not* that I don't trust you all to back out again, but I was thinking, it might be a better idea if you all meet here and travel there together. From what I've seen today, it's not drugs or alcohol or deep breathing that's going to get you all through this flight—it's camaraderie. Does anyone have a people carrier or a minibus?'

There were various mutters of 'no' and 'sorry' until Petal interjected. 'My friend has a camper van—I'm sure if I asked him we could borrow it for a few hours.'

'Great,' clapped Hugh. 'That's sorted then. So we'll meet here next week, say,' Hugh looked at his watch, 'nine o'clock?'

'Nine o'clock,' they mumbled in agreement.

FRANNIE

Frannie navigated the twenty minute journey from Salford Community College to his home with his mind elsewhere. He had never really had any intention of taking the graduation flight. He had been fairly certain that he would only ever board a plane again if it was a question of life or death. He hadn't bargained for Rachel's emotional plea. Fingers gripping the steering wheel of his Ford Mondeo, he cruised past the park, with its marked-out football pitches filled with brightly-coloured teams. He didn't even glance across to see if Simon was amongst them. The parade of shops on Lee Terrace usually evoked a pavlovian reaction from Frannie on his drive home, even before he sensed the smell from the chippy. Instead, the terror of having agreed to take the flight had replaced his hunger pangs with a sickening weight. The crimson sky would have, on other evenings, given Frannie a small amount of pleasure on his routine drive home. On that particular Wednesday evening, the sky could have been lime green and raining pork pies, and Frannie would not have noticed. His thoughts were on one thing: the graduation flight that he had promised Rachel he would be on the following weekend.

He pulled up on his drive way and trudged through the front door, into his artificially scented home. His mind still elsewhere, he noticed the absence of any radio or TV noise a fraction too late. Kim was in the lounge—standing rigid in front of the ornate hearth.

'You're back early,' she commented.

'What?' Frannie cleared his mind of aeroplanes for a moment and tried to recall what he was supposed to have been doing.

'The football—it's still on isn't it?'

Again, a more clear-headed Frannie would have realised that this didn't portend well. Kim had never taken an interest in Frannie's beloved Manchester City in the entire twenty five years of their marriage (apart from a couple of years just after the birth of Simon where she tried to convince all of their friends and family to call him by his full name, Francis, instead of Frannie. Frannie—who was proud to have been named after the City legend Frannie Lee refused, and, although she still persisted from time to time, it was one battle that Frannie had been determined not to surrender). Frannie remembered that he had told her he was watching the football with his brother.

'Oh, yes.' He screwed his entire face up for a moment. 'It was a rubbish match. I thought I'd make a move early before the end. You know what the traffic is like on the A6 after a home match.' Frannie gave a nervous cough. 'I could murder a brew. Do you want one?'

Kim nodded stonily.

Entering the kitchen, Frannie literally stumbled across a large suitcase and a hold-all. 'What's going on?' he asked.

He turned to find Kim standing in the doorway between the lounge and the kitchen, arms folded.

'You're leaving,' she said in a high-pitched voice.

'What?'

'You're leaving,' she repeated defiantly. 'You're a bloody liar, Francis Bentham. Now I don't know what's going on with you lately—whether it's a mid-life crisis or what, but I will not tolerate being lied to and cheated. I've packed two bags—you can go to your brother's house.'

Frannie felt like he'd taken a blow to the head. 'What are you talking about?'

'Oh, don't come the innocent with me, Mister. I know that you haven't been at Gary's house watching the football—Gary rang about an hour ago to tell me about some article he'd seen in the newspaper about dodgy drugs they'd found in Deansgate last weekend! When I asked him if you were there he didn't know what I was talking about!'

Frannie thought quickly. 'I didn't say I was watching the match at Gary's. I watched it in the pub.'

'On your own?' she sneered. 'When was the last time you went to the pub on your own?'

'I did,' he floundered. 'I stopped off at the Royal Oak, the one by…'

'Just stop it!' she screamed. 'I heard you arranging to meet her!'

'Who?' Frannie was genuinely confused.

'That woman—the one at the hospital,' she spat.

'Rachel?' he questioned.

'I don't know her bloody name. I was coming back from the toilet and I heard you, quite clearly, arrange to meet her on Wednesday.'

'She's just someone from work,' he protested.

'Really—so why didn't you say you'd see her on Monday then?'

'Because her daughter was seriously ill in hospital!'

Kim's eyebrow was doing an angry dance as she debated whether to believe him or not. 'So how come I've never heard you talking about her before?'

Frannie shrugged. 'I don't know. I probably have—you never take any interest in my work unless it's salary-related so I imagine you just forgot.'

Kim went red in the face. 'I'm bloody sick of you going on about me spending money, you tight-arsed bastard!' She paused. 'That's it! That's it!' she exclaimed, as if some sort of penny had just dropped. 'This promotion that you weren't going to tell me about. She knows you're getting the FD job, doesn't she. She knows that you're going to be the big boss and she's trying to charm her way in so she can get a good appraisal and more money.'

Frannie shook his head in disbelief that anyone could put two and two together and get 4000. 'You're bloody mental you are!' he uttered. 'Where the hell have you got that story from? Tell you what—instead of pissing about with housework all day you want to start writing a book with that imagination. J.K. Rowling has got nothing on you!'

'Don't insult me. It all makes sense now. Well this woman, Rachel, is welcome to you!'

'For fuck's sake!' For a moment, Frannie considered telling Kim the truth. Telling her all about the Fear of Flying Club and the truth about Rachel and McKenzie and Jalil. But he just couldn't do it. He needed to do this for himself, not for anyone else. If he told Kim, she would take over, just like she did with everything and pile on the pressure. If he was going to do this it had to be on his own. He shook his head regretfully, picked up his bags and traipsed back to the car.

Frannie sat at his brother's kitchen table, shovelling his dinner greedily into his mouth. A faint wisp of steam rose up out of the newly pierced steak and kidney pudding. He couldn't suppress small moans of pleasure as the saltiness of the pudding and the gravy fused with the sharp, vinegary chips over his flavour-starved taste buds.

'Hungry, love?' joked Sharon, Gary's wife, who was making cups of tea and picking chips out of the white wrapping paper in the process.

'You have no idea how good these taste! If Kim could see me now—well let's just say that'd be another black mark added against my name.'

Sharon rolled her eyes. 'You're a working man. You can't be living off lettuce leaves and bloody couscous! Honestly, I don't know what planet Kim's on sometimes.'

'Well if there was a planet for stubborn, misinformed, angry wives, then she'd be their leader,' he muttered, forking a large piece of pudding into his mouth.

Frannie had spent three nights at Gary and Sharon's house. At first he was in a state of shock. He was stunned that she could even consider the possibility that he would have an affair. It simply wasn't in his nature. However, three days into his stay, Frannie was beginning to relax. Kim's attitude towards him had been frosty of late to say the least, so it was nice to spend some time with people who genuinely enjoyed his company. It was also nice to live in a house where no one was on a diet. Gary and Sharon ate proper food. Their fridge housed cooked meats, cheeses, butter, cheesecake and beer. If you felt like eating a bag of crisps you opened a cupboard and there was a choice of flavours. If he had to find somewhere to stay until Kim cooled off then it might as well be here.

'Have you spoken to her today? Is she still pissed off?' asked Gary who was using his knife to rescue the mushy peas he had just tipped onto his fish and chips without leaving enough space on his plate to accommodate them.

Frannie shook his head. 'She sent me a text with my instructions for the weekend and details of some orchestra concert that Simon's in. That's all.'

Sharon placed three mugs of strong tea on the table then sat down with her chips, eating them straight out of the wrapping. 'She treats you like a bloody slave, that woman.'

Frannie shrugged.

Sharon continued. 'If she's that bothered about this promotion business why doesn't she just get a job herself?'

'She likes to be at home for the kids.'

Sharon laughed. 'They're teenagers, Frannie, not babies! I had to go back to work when Joe was six months old. Most people are lucky to get two years off—what's Kim had? Sixteen years? I'm sorry, I think she's just a lazy cow! You wait, she'll soon realise what she's missing and come running for you.'

'Sharon!' warned Gary, in a tone that suggested his wife may be overstepping the mark.

Sharon opened her eyes wide in defiance. 'Hey, it's better to shit your pants rather than die of constipation!'

'Bloody hell—we're trying to eat here,' moaned Gary. 'And what's shitty kecks got to do with anything?'

'I'm just saying,' she said primly, 'that it's better to say what you think than to keep it all in.'

'Well that's never been a problem for you, Sharon. Bloody verbal diarrhoea you suffer from! That's exactly why you got shifted from women's wear to the food-hall!'

'I was giving honest advice—advice that was asked for! I couldn't have let that poor woman go to her son's wedding in that dress, she would have been mistaken for the bloody marquee!'

'You were lucky that she only complained to Jacqui!'

'If she didn't want the advice then she shouldn't have asked. Anyway, I like the food-hall. You get first dibs on the reduced section and it makes a change from measuring pensioners for bras! It's better for people-spotting too. Closer to the café!'

'You mean nosing!' Gary looked at Frannie and shook his head. 'Honestly, mate, if you want to know anything about anyone—who's been buying what—ask our Sharon. She comes home and tells me that Karen down the road bought two coats in one week! Or that Shagabout Kelly bought four new sets of underwear, which according to

Poirot here, means she's having an affair.' He huffed. 'Like I give a shit!'

'Well I was right wasn't I? Two weeks later Wayne was out on his ear, the kids had been farmed off to Kelly's mum's and the new toyboy was in! And don't pretend you're not interested, just cos your brother's here—you love the Marksies' gossip!' She smiled and gave Gary a playful squeeze on the cheek. 'I could tell you a bit about your Kim, too! There must be more curtains at your place than the Manchester Opera House.'

Frannie's phone beeped to signify a text message. He took it out of his pocket, looked at the message then put the phone back. It was from Hugh, confirming that Petal had secured the use of a minibus to take the group to the airport on Saturday.

Gary and Sharon exchanged pointed looks.

Gary cleared his throat. 'So, she still thinks you're having an affair?' he questioned, adding a small laugh at the end.

'What? Oh, aye,' snorted Frannie.

Gary and Sharon glanced at each other again as Frannie polished off the remains of his dinner.

'But you were just watching the football?'

Frannie's phone beeped again. This time it was Rachel, replying to the group message that Hugh had sent. It simply said, *We've done the hard bit. I'm counting on you. See you on Saturday x.* Once again he looked at it briefly before placing the phone back on the table, wordlessly.

Interestingly, Frannie found lying to his brother more difficult than lying to Kim. 'It was more just a couple of drinks after work. The football was on in the pub.' He got up and placed his plate in the dishwasher, as was the practice at his own house, eager to change the subject.

'Sit down, love, they can wait. You're not at home now,' scoffed Sharon.

Frannie patted his substantial tummy then stretched his elbows out horizontal to his shoulders. 'I think I need to sit on the sofa after that. My stomach is in shock.' He scuttled out of the kitchen before Sharon or Gary could question him any further about his whereabouts the previous Wednesday evening.

When he went back into the kitchen an hour later, in search of a biscuit, he noticed his phone lying on top of the microwave. He picked it up and put it in his pocket before agonising over the chocolate Hob Nobs versus the Double Oreo.

JALIL

The contrast from the cool school hall to the sunny May afternoon outside was stark. Hoards of students exchanged animated comments about the exam they had just sat, comparing notes and trying to establish how well they'd done. Jalil, Zain and Robbo had finished their physics exam, and were talking about the question on circuits and current.

'Lamp B was the brightest,' said Zain, confidently.

'Hang on, was that the one on the outside?' asked Robbo.

'No, it was the one on the left,' said Jalil.

'Oh fuck, I said it was the outside one. I think I've totally screwed this up you know,' moaned Robbo. 'If I don't pass my dad'll kill me. He's only paying for Kavos if I do well. If I fail I'll have to pay him back.'

'Not long 'til Kavos now, mate. Woo hoo hoo!' said Zain.

Jalil suspected that Zain had passed the exam with flying colours. He was a jammy bastard and always scored higher than Jalil, even when he had hardly revised. As for himself, he hoped he'd scraped enough to pass. He usually did okay in exams—they didn't stress him out like they did with some people. Just lately though, Jalil had been finding it hard to concentrate. The graduation flight for the Fear of Flying Club was approaching and, despite his best efforts to blank this from his mind, it kept popping into his head. He had never, ever intended to go on the flight, but Rachel had pulled some serious emotional blackmail. He was sure that Frannie would be going, as he had been the first to agree. That just left McKenzie and himself. If what he suspected about McKenzie was correct (after the last Fear of Flying lesson, Jalil had returned home and googled everything he could find about the Urban Phantoms), he didn't have anywhere else to be, so no doubt he would go on the flight. Which just left him! He was sick to death of being the most cowardly one. The wimp. The chicken. If he was going to be able to live with himself again he was going to have to take the flight.

Then there was the incident at the nightclub. He'd acted like a dick in front of his mates and Holly. He recognised that now. He was just thankful that he'd flushed the tablet away instead of taking it. Seeing the headlines in the *Manchester Evening News* had totally freaked him out. He had told Zain and Robbo that he hadn't gone through with taking it, mainly because they were giving him the cold shoulder, which was the polar opposite effect of what he had intended.

And then there was Holly. Jalil didn't know which smart-arsed academic had been the one to decide that you should take the most important exams of your life at the exact time that your hormones are exploding, but he was guessing that whoever it was had attended a single-sex school. He had been trying so hard to concentrate on his exams, but every time he picked up a text book he thought of Holly on holiday in Kavos. With Zain and Robbo. And it was killing him.

'I'm starving! Subway or Maccy D's?' asked Robbo.

Zain rooted in his pockets, pulled out a handful of coins and did a quick mental calculation. 'Subway, it's cheaper.'

They cut through the school car park and out onto the back field which led to the canal path running parallel to the railway line. Walking a little way ahead of them in the distance, Jalil spotted a group of sixth form girls.

'What other exams were on this morning?' he asked.

'I think it must have been General Studies. That freak, Lyle, had his head in a newspaper in the common room earlier on. Like that was gonna help,' he snorted with laughter. 'I did point out that anything in the newspaper *today* was not going to come up in an exam paper that was printed, like, *weeks* ago!'

'Any others?'

'Er, another piss easy one I think. Oh yeah, psychology!'

Jalil's heart skipped. Holly did psychology, which meant there was a chance that she was in the group of girls up ahead. With the exams in full flow, he knew that there was only a limited amount of time left to see her at school. Then they would probably go their separate ways. He began to pick up the pace. As they narrowed the gap between themselves and the girls, Becca's voice could be heard above all of the others. Jalil found her annoying. She always had to be the centre of attention, even though she was a total dog compared to Holly.

'I chose the essay on Ego,' he heard her say.

'Yeah, me too! It was so lucky that Miss made us revise Freud in class,' said Holly.

'Yeah, I suppose. Although I put that it was all to do with penis size!'

The other girls giggled, wide eyed. 'No way—you didn't!' said Lottie.

'I did—ask Miss when she's looked at them if you don't believe me.'

'So whose theory is that then?' asked Holly. 'I'm sure I'd have remembered that!'

'Tanya Yates!'

'Your mum?' replied Holly.

'Yep, she's always going on about men's attitudes being directly linked to penis size. And she'd know—she's had enough of them!'

'Becca! You can't say that about your mum!' protested Lottie.

'Yeah I can! And anyway, it's original research. They're always telling you to read round a subject and put original stuff in. I reckon I've just bagged myself loads of marks!'

'Hey girls, how was your exam? Hard?' sniggered Zain.

Jalil jabbed him in the ribs with his elbow. They walked along the dusty canal path and compared notes on the morning's exams.

'Have you got any more this afternoon?' asked Jalil.

'No,' answered Becca. 'We're going to have a look at

prom dresses now. There's a little boutique just down from Boots that does the most amazing dresses. They cost a fortune, but we're going to try some on.'

'Are you all going?' asked Jalil, who had not signed up for the prom, mainly because he didn't want to have to go through the mortifying process of asking someone to go with him.

Holly shrugged. 'We haven't decided yet.' She threw a cool look at Becca.

'Oh yeah?' asked Jalil.

'It's my birthday on the fourth of July.'

'Independence Day!' smiled Jalil.

'Yes. And prom night!' replied Holly, raising her eyebrows. 'I wanted to have a party of my own, but now it looks like everyone wants to go to the prom,' she looked at Becca. 'So…' she shrugged.

'Have your party. I'm sure people will come!' he said, genuinely.

Holly twisted her mouth unconfidently. Even when she did that Jalil still thought she was beautiful.

'I dunno,' she whined. 'It'd have to be something pretty special to drag people away from the prom, and I haven't got the money for that.'

'There must be something you could do.'

Holly put on a brave smile. 'Nah, I think I'm going to have to forget it. Anyway, it'll be more money to spend on holiday.'

'Oh yeah, I've heard that you lot are going to Kavos at the same time,' said Lottie.

'Sure are!' said Zain. 'Well me and Robbo are going. And Olly and Whitey. Jalil's not going.'

Don't fucking start this again, thought Jalil.

'Why not?' asked Lottie.

'Funds,' said Jalil at the exact same time Zain said 'Chicken.'

'He won't fly,' said Robbo.

'I fucking *will*—will you quit that story. It's just getting boring now!'

'I don't really like flying,' said Lottie, 'but it wouldn't stop me going on holiday!'

'I'm not fucking *scared*, alright!' snapped Jalil.

'It's alright to be scared,' teased Zain in a baby voice. 'Some girls actually go for the weedy, needy type. Don't you girls.'

The girls giggled.

'Ooh no, I need a man to take charge. One who will fight for me if I need him to,' said Becca. 'Loads of muscles and tattoos! Oh and loads of cash too!'

'No luck there then, mate,' laughed Robbo.

Jalil just scowled. He wouldn't touch Becca if she was the last woman left on earth!

'You know, you can get hypnotherapy for fear of flying,' suggested Lottie helpfully.

Zain laughed and skipped ahead of Jalil, turning to face him before jogging backwards down the path. He held up an imaginary piece of string which he swung in front of Jalil's face like a pendulum. 'Look into my eyes, look into my eyes,' he said in a spooky voice. 'You are feeling very sleeeeepy. When I click my fingers you will not be a scaredy little coward any more. The aeroplane is your friend!'

Jalil tried to bat his hand away but missed. The girls

started to laugh. Once again he felt a rush of anger that started in the pit of his belly and rose in speed and intensity. He clenched his fist and drew it back. His head was now throbbing with a fury he was struggling to control. Jalil was aware of a noise growing louder and louder. For a moment he thought it was the sound of his own rage, building to a crescendo inside his head, but then he noticed the train. In a split second he dropped his arm and bolted over the fence and down the shallow bank. Without stopping to think he launched himself in two long leaps over the train track. The noise of the train thundering along, horn blowing, was deafening, however, Jalil was still able to make out the screams of the girls above the commotion of the train, the rush of wind, and his own heartbeat which was now thumping a resounding rapid pulse directly in his ear.

He lay on the bank on the other side for a few seconds as carriages hurtled past him at express speed. Then, to avoid seeing anyone, he scrambled up the brambley bank and sprinted down the pathway until he reached an alleyway into the adjacent housing estate.

Jalil slammed the apartment door, went straight to his bedroom and threw himself down face-first onto the bed. The curtains were still closed from that morning and he lay motionless in the soothing cool, quiet shade of his bedroom. Within moments his phone rang. He had ignored several calls since the episode at the railway line minutes earlier. Before he'd had time to shut the phone down completely, another text came through. That made eight in total. He let his arm hang down the side of his bed and dropped the phone on the floor. His heart rate had slowed down to a near normal rate and the adrenalin that had surged through his body minutes earlier had all but disappeared. Now, all that he was left with was an overwhelming sense of fatigue and sadness. He closed his eyes and within moments was fast asleep.

He was woken, hours later, by his mum. Taking a moment to come to, his senses were awakened one by one. The smell of smoked fish reached him first as he struggled to open his eyes.

'Tea time!' she shouted into his bedroom.

Minutes later he struggled into the kitchen and slumped into a chair. His body felt heavy, his head fuzzy.

'Brain food,' smiled his mum, placing a large plate of steaming kedgeree in front of him. 'Oh, and Zain called round earlier. I told him you were asleep. He asked if you could ring him later on—something important about exam revision. He said your phone was still off from the exam.'

Jalil felt sick. He wasn't sure he would be able to manage even one mouthful. His mum sat down as her boyfriend, Harvey, came through from the living room and pulled off his tie.

'So,' she enquired tentatively. 'How did this morning's exam go?'

'Oh, that. Yeah, fine,' said Jalil, massaging his temples with his index and middle fingers.

'Do you think you should take a little break from studying?' she asked. 'I don't like seeing you all wiped out like this. It's not worth damaging your health just to get good marks,' she added with concern.

'I'm not working too hard, Mum,' he mumbled. 'I'm fine.'

She glanced at Harvey. 'Is it this Fear of Flying course that's bothering you?' she asked. 'If it's not helping, you know you can quit—any time you like.'

'I'm not quitting,' he whined. 'It's the graduation flight next Saturday and I'm going to do it.'

Jalil's mum looked marginally relieved that she had managed to get to the bottom of the problem.

'You can do it, son,' nodded Harvey. 'I've got faith in you.'

'Thanks,' he muttered. He just wished that he had the same amount of faith in himself. 'Listen, Mum, I've just woken up. Do you mind if I microwave this later?'

'No, no, that's fine. Just make sure you do eat it. You need something decent inside you to keep your strength up.'

He slunk off to his bedroom, feeling even more depressed than ever. He knew that his mum and Harvey would be devastated if they found out what he'd done earlier. He turned on his laptop and logged into the phobia website that Will had set up for the Fear of Flying group. He navigated his way to the profile page. Before he could change his mind he sent a private message to McKenzie.

Big Mac! It is you—I know it is. Listen, I've got a few things going on at the moment and I could really do with your help big time! I know you're at a loose end at the moment, and I was wondering whether you'd be willing to DJ a one-off gig in Manchester. I can't pay you—not straight away—but if you could do this one thing, it might just save my life! I'll see you next Saturday for the flight. Might as well get on the thing—my life is pretty much over here anyway so I've nothing to lose. Cheers mate, Jalil. [thumbs up icon].

McKENZIE

It was two-thirty in the afternoon, and the café was reasonably quiet, having seen off the lunchtime rush for another day. McKenzie nursed his mug of coffee and scanned the local paper which he had spread out across the double table. Little Gee said he would get there as soon as he could. It didn't matter—McKenzie was in no hurry. It wasn't like he had to be anywhere.

He had looked over the adverts on the jobs page several times now, hoping each time he looked that something inspiring would jump out at him. There were loads of adverts for cleaners, chefs and retail staff. Some dodgy 'earn cash from your own home' adverts. But nothing that seemed right for McKenzie. He knew it was unlikely that the perfect job would be staring out from the paper at him, but it didn't stop him from scanning the adverts several times over. Perhaps he had missed it. *Wanted – Musician. Proficiency in the use of synthesiser essential. Composition experience advantageous. Must be able to produce high quality, kick ass R&B*

tracks suitable for mass media. He started from the top again and looked down the list. He needed to get a job, there was no question about that. He had given up his job at a mobile phone shop a couple of months earlier when Alfie had signed them up on a small salary. The thought of asking for his job back so soon was embarrassing—he still had the leaving card dumped on the front seat of his car.

He'd been paid by Dark Star Records a couple of weeks earlier, but he had no idea whether Alfie had stopped his money yet or not. He still hadn't returned his exit contract. His rent would be due in two weeks and he needed to make sure there was something in his bank account.

He turned the page and briefly considered an office job. All the adverts asked for experience. His school had placed him in an office for his work experience when he was sixteen. It was at a massive logistics company in the East End. Little Gee had been placed there too. It was the most boring week of his life. Nobody was interested in training them to do anything. Neither of them even understood what the company did. Their duties involved fetching tea, answering phones, photocopying and filing. Was it surprising that they had decided to make their own fun whilst they were there? Little Gee had started it off by sellotaping the button under McKenzie's telephone receiver down to the base of his phone when he'd gone for his tenth toilet break of the day. Little Gee had waited for McKenzie to return to his desk before ringing his phone and nearly pissing his pants at McKenzie's puzzled face when the phone continued to ring after he'd said hello for the third time. It was only a matter of minutes before they started rolling the experiment out across the whole of the second floor.

On a particularly rainy day, they filled twenty minutes by emptying every hole-puncher they could find into the upturned umbrellas by the main doors. They then spent the lunch hour glued to the second floor window to witness the fruits of their labours.

McKenzie had shared some good times with Little Gee. He was gutted that it was all about to end.

When he saw Little Gee walk past the window he got up immediately, nervous about meeting his friend of many years. Before Little Gee had reached the table, he could see in his face that something had changed. Something in his eyes was guarded. There was a sense of embarrassment in his smile.

'Hey, man. Thanks for coming,' said McKenzie, giving Little Gee an awkward half hug, half pat.

Little Gee just nodded.

'I'll get the drinks,' insisted McKenzie, rushing to the counter before Little Gee could argue, and giving himself time to compose himself for his speech. He had decided to tell Little Gee the truth about his fear of flying. After several days of tossing the idea around in his head he came to the realisation that he owed it to Little Gee to be honest.

His hands shook slightly as he placed the steaming mugs on the table. He caught Little Gee glancing at the jobs page which lay open on the table. He hurriedly folded the newspaper and stuffed it under the table.

'Listen, Gee, I owe you an apology.'

Little Gee blew on his tea. 'I'm listening.'

'About Sweden. I fucked up. I blew it. I could have wrecked it for all of us.'

Little Gee just looked impassive as he sipped at his tea.

McKenzie looked his friend in the eye. 'And I'm sorry. I'm truly sorry, man.'

'Is that it?' asked Little Gee, showing neither anger nor compassion.

'No. I owe you an explanation.' He took a deep breath. He was fairly sure that Little Gee would keep the information to himself, but there was a small part of him that held some doubt. 'It was the aeroplane.' He looked down at the table with its scratched lacquered wood. He scraped his thumbnail into the gummy varnish. 'I'm scared of flying.' He gulped. 'Like, petrified, man.'

He couldn't lift his gaze from the table. He had admitted it. It was out there. He braced himself for the ridicule that he deserved.

'I know.'

McKenzie stopped scraping the table with his thumb and looked up. 'What do you mean, you know?'

'I know!' repeated Little Gee. 'I know all about the self-medication, about the phobia. I know about your fear of flying lessons.'

McKenzie was genuinely confused. 'But, how?'

'Your mum!'

'What? When?'

'A few days ago. She came round and gave me a right mouthful. I haven't been on the receiving end of one of them since she found that johnny in your jeans pocket after you were supposed to be staying at my house to revise for your exams.' Little Gee gave a small laugh.

McKenzie felt a small breakthrough. 'Jesus, I'm sorry! I'll kill her when I see her.'

Little Gee waved his hands in protest. 'It's fine. And anyway, I suppose she had a point. I should have known there was something else going on and not just jumped to conclusions. I've known you long enough.' He laughed. 'Too long!'

McKenzie didn't know what to say so he just nodded, gratefully.

'I'm just fucked off that you didn't tell me, Kenz. I'm supposed to be, like, your best mate. We've known each other since school. If you'd told me I could have helped. Covered for you with Alfie, or even spoken to him.'

'No!' said McKenzie firmly. 'Nobody else is to know about this. Seriously!'

'Well it's too late to do anything now isn't it? You're out! Alfie's replaced you!' He dropped his mug down firmly on the table. 'It's just shit, man. It's not the same band that we created.'

But McKenzie hadn't heard him. He was still reeling from the revelation that he had actually been replaced. He had been holding out some hope that Little Gee could put a good word in with Alfie. It looked like it really was too late. He no longer had any part to play in the Urban Phantoms.

'Who?' was all he could manage to say.

'Some kid called Trey. Technically he's okay but he uses the same effect in all of his loops. It's like, well annoying. Sounds like a wind chime. I think he thinks it's progressive, but to me it just sounds ancient.'

McKenzie nodded.

'The Prof keeps calling him chime-boy.' He laughed. 'The kid was taking it on the chin at first, but now I think he's getting fed up.'

'So, do you think he'll stay?' asked McKenzie, not wanting to hear the answer.

Little Gee shrugged. 'Depends if we can actually get some tracks down together. He insists on using Vocodex, which is fine, but in my opinion he over-oscillates. For filthy dubstep it's fine, but it doesn't suit Kitty, so, you know… you been writing?'

'Bits and pieces. Hard to get back in the zone.' McKenzie had found himself with more time than ever on his hands to write new music, but unfortunately, nothing was working. He wasn't feeling the upbeat, party tunes that usually came naturally to him. Instead his loops were melancholic, whiney and depressing. 'Any news on the tour?'

Little Gee looked embarrassed. 'Yes, we've had the schedule through.'

'And?'

'You don't really want to know all of this, do you?' asked Little Gee, trying to spare his friend the agony of hearing about the success he couldn't share in.

'I do.'

'Well we've got all of the dates through. They've added another seven nights because ticket sales went through the roof. Kitty is jumping up and down because she has her own dressing room at the O2. Oh, and we've got to fill out a rider.'

'No way!' said McKenzie, gutted but unable not to be

impressed at the same time. 'So what are you putting on it?'

'We don't know. You know what it's like. We're used to lugging our own gear, doing our own sound checks. Providing our own drinks. It feels weird to suddenly issue a list of demands.'

McKenzie shook his head, laughing. 'You've got to do that Van Halen thing and demand that the brown *M&Ms* are removed from the bowl.'

'Yeah—we need to put some weird shit in there, just for the hell of it. Dancing kittens or fresh butterfly milk, I dunno.'

'Or,' laughed McKenzie, 'you could make it the most low rent rider ever. That would be hilarious, man. Here we go…Four Gregg's sausage rolls, a bottle of Tesco value vodka, a set of new and unused towels from Primark…'

Little Gee laughed along. Then his face turned serious. 'I miss you, you dick!'

McKenzie put his head in his hands. He felt like crying, but there was no way he was going to let Little Gee see that.

'I'm thinking of quitting,' Little Gee said quietly.

'No, no, that's not happening, man,' McKenzie said urgently. 'You've made it. You're just about to hit the big time. Whatever I did to screw up, *you* deserve this.'

'Your mum was right.'

'Ignore my mum!' said McKenzie angrily. 'She's just looking out for me. She doesn't understand that this is a once in a lifetime offer. She thinks that if we got a record deal before we'll get another one. Or if that fails we just go on *X Factor*. She hasn't got a clue.'

'Maybe she's right. Maybe we *will* pick something else up.'

'Gee—I'm not listening to any of this shit. You've got a band, and a record deal and a rider to go and think about. Don't worry about me. I'll be fine.'

Little Gee scraped back his chair, gave McKenzie a tight smile, and walked dolefully out of the café.

McKenzie sat alone, his hands cradling his chin and mouth, wondering how to start piecing his life back together. He flicked through the pages of *NME* until he found the small ads. Band members wanted. The problem with synth-based R&B was that anyone interested in setting up something like that was likely to be the synth player. They might be advertising for vocalists, but not the main man. Anyone else advertising for keyboards or synthesiser work was unlikely to be his scene.

He put the magazine down and glanced at his phone. That kid, Jalil, from the Fear of Flying Club had messaged him, saying that he knew who he was. He wanted a favour— some gig doing in Manchester. He hadn't replied. It was all very well Jalil knowing about McKenzie's fear of flying, and it was all very well for the public to know that Big Mac was, or had been, a member of the Urban Phantoms, but he did not want anyone to make a connection between these two, very separate, worlds. At that moment, only his family and Little Gee knew that McKenzie, aka Big Mac, had a crippling fear of flying. He was going to do everything he could to keep it that way.

RACHEL

On entering Poppy's classroom, Rachel experienced sensory overload. Yellow and green bunting hung from a sagging string which zig-zagged the length and breadth of the ceiling. A noisy samba rhythm blared from the portable CD player, and a sickly sweet smell emanated from a low table stacked with colourful fruit, sweets and cakes. Poppy was only attending school for half days whilst she got over her latest hospital admission. As Rachel usually savoured the few hours of peace and quiet she got during the day whilst Poppy was at school, the invitation to this parents afternoon was greeted, at best, with mild irritation.

Children were busy pulling their parents (mainly mums) around the classroom, proudly showing off their work whilst the adults smiled enthusiastically before resuming their conversations with fellow parents. Rachel had asked her mum, Jean, to accompany her. She didn't like going into school at the best of times. She couldn't help feeling defensive when faced with any member of staff, so having an ally was preferential. Poppy's one-to-one assistant spotted Rachel and smiled, alerting Poppy to their presence. Poppy made her way clumsily through the assault course of chairs and tables until she reached her mum and grandma.

'Hi Pops. Are you having a nice day?' asked Rachel.

'We're having lots of fun, aren't we?' replied Miss Koslowska when Poppy didn't answer.

Rachel noticed that Poppy had been sitting on her own with Miss Koslowska when they arrived. She glanced around the room. Those children whose parents hadn't arrived yet were busy playing in groups. Rachel's heart ached for her daughter.

'We've been learning all about Brazil, haven't we Poppy?' said Miss Koslowska with a chirpiness that Rachel was certain she could never muster without the help of Class A drugs. 'Can you remember what's happening in Rio this year?'

'Dolphins,' smiled Poppy.

'Yes, they have pink dolphins in Brazil. Clever girl, Poppy. But can you remember what we learnt about the Olympics?'

Poppy nodded, beaming. 'Pink dolphins. Flipper isn't pink. I love Flipper.' She paused for a moment. 'The boy fell into the sea,' Poppy said, before laughing a beautiful, whole hearted laugh.

'It's one of the episodes of Flipper,' Rachel explained to her mum and Miss Koslowska. Rachel was fairly sure that Poppy hadn't digested any of the information regarding the Olympics. Whilst other kids in the class wandered around dressed in football kits, gymnastics leotards and cycling gear, Poppy had wanted to come as a pink dolphin, testing Rachel's creative skills to the absolute limit. A pair of pink pyjamas had been Rachel's best attempt, although now, looking at some of the other costumes, Rachel wished she had made more of an effort.

A small boy in a Real Madrid football kit approached Rachel and Jean. 'Why has Poppy got her jarmas on?'

Rachel smiled. 'She has come as a pink dolphin.'

The boy gave Poppy a suspicious appraisal. 'She doesn't look like a dolphin,' he frowned. He walked a full circle around Poppy whilst she stood still, unaware of the scrutiny she was being subjected to. The little boy stopped and prodded her back. 'She needs to have a triangle right here!'

Rachel forced a smile. 'She doesn't really like having things stuck to her back. Or face paint on her face,' Rachel explained, before finding herself suddenly annoyed that she was justifying herself to a five-year-old.

'Is that because she's different?' he asked. 'My mum said that Poppy has something wrong with her and that's why we have to be nice, even when she's being mean.'

Miss Koslowska took the little boy by the hand. 'Sinha,' she said brightly, 'why don't you come and show me your rainforest animal.'

Rachel blinked back hot tears.

'I'm sure that his mum didn't say it like that, love. She was probably just trying to be nice,' said Jean.

'They think they're all so bloody perfect,' Rachel snarled, ignoring her mum's attempt at pacification. She looked around the room. 'Making judgements on my child!

Who the hell do they think they are? See her over there?'
She jabbed a finger towards a short, slim woman with long
blonde hair who was wearing a coral-coloured boob tube
and oversized sunglasses. 'She's been coming into school
and helping with their topic this term. Right up her street
this Brazil subject is. She used to be one of the biggest
cokeheads going. Surprised she's still got a nose left to hold
up those frigging sunglasses. But here she is, looking like
butter wouldn't melt. Stupid bitch,' she muttered.

Jean gave Rachel a tight smile. 'I know it's hard love,
but, the thing is, unless you've been there yourself you
don't understand what it's like. Maybe you should give them
a chance? Get to know them a bit?'

'Ppffaa! No thanks.'

Miss Myers clapped her hands to get the children's
attention. Dutifully, yet excitedly, they all filed into the step
area to give a performance of some songs they had learnt.
Rachel noticed that whilst not all of the children were able
to sing the whole song, they all knew the chorus. All except
Poppy who was swinging her head from side to side, simply
enjoying the music. When the other children did the actions
for the snake, and the monkey and the parrot, Poppy
continued swaying her head from side to side. For the first
time since the awkward conversation with Miss Myers
several weeks earlier, Rachel considered the possibility of
the special school.

Rachel was exhausted as she pushed open the front door to
her home. It was only four in the afternoon. She had at least
six hours to go until bedtime. Poppy had been restless the

night before, which, although not unusual, combined with the stress of the past week was taking its toll on Rachel. Wasting an afternoon at the school hadn't helped either. She wouldn't have gone back to bed—she never did that— but she could at least have had the kids' tea ready. The thought of having to prepare something now made her want to weep. She bent over slowly to pick the mail up off the porch floor, then went straight through to the kitchen to see if there was a quick fix to be found in the freezer. There was one large pizza in the top tray. That would do for the girls—they both loved pizza. She unwrapped it and put it straight in the oven. Usually she would chop some fresh vegetables to accompany it but she didn't even have the energy to wash and slice a pepper. She looked at the pile of clothes in front of the washing machine. She considered doing something about it, but that would mean taking the clothes out of the dryer, moving them upstairs, then taking the wet clothes from the washing machine and moving them into the dryer, all to make space for the dirty clothes, and that, quite frankly, was just not happening.

She picked the mail up that she had just dumped on the worktop, made her way back into the lounge and flopped down into an armchair. Poppy was lying on her back on the sofa, taking up most of the space. She had her iPad pressed up close to her face watching Flipper. Rachel felt too lethargic even to tell her to move it further away from her eyes. Jasmine was curled up in the corner of the sofa watching some teenage crap on the Disney channel. Rachel ignored the two boring looking letters, which were undoubtedly bills or bank statements, opting to open the heavy cream-coloured, hand-written envelope. Inside was a thick card embossed with violet-coloured hearts. She opened it and a flurry of shiny purple foil hearts fell onto her lap, with some falling down the gap between the armchair frame and the cushion and others onto the floor. She mentally cursed the sender for doing something so bloody annoying. It was a wedding invitation from Charlie's niece and her fiancé. She glanced over at Jasmine who was glued to a programme about a teenage girl trying to get a date with the new kid at school. Then she looked at Poppy.

The diagnosis had changed everything. It was like all form of hope had been sucked out of her body by a powerful vacuum. In that one instant, all of Rachel's aspirations for Poppy's future had been obliterated. Poppy was not going to grow out of her condition. Rachel could no longer hope that her development was merely delayed. It was stunted. Completely. In that moment, Rachel realised that Poppy wouldn't have the usual girly teenage experiences—giggling with her friends about boys, going to discos, proms, to the cinema or out shopping for new outfits. She looked at the pristine wedding invitation in her hand and realised that Poppy would probably never get married. Never have the opportunity to wear a beautiful, ivory gown. She might never have any relationship at all. She looked at the little girl lying on the sofa and felt a physical pain in her chest. Before she was aware of what was happening she heard a sharp sob emit from her throat. She rose quickly from the chair and bolted for the stairs. She locked herself in the bathroom before sliding down the bathroom door and howling into her hands.

Her eyes were still red when Charlie came home, later than she had expected.

'Where have you been?'

'Jessica Hardman's. She had some new wall lights to put up. I told you this morning.' He noticed the red tinge to her eyes. 'Hey, what's up? Are the kids ok?'

'They're fine,' she replied in a husky voice. 'I'll get your tea.'

'Come on, what's the matter? Look, I know you don't like Jessica but she's a good customer.'

'I really don't give a shit about Jessica Hardman and her inflatable chest,' she pattered in a bored tone.

'Really? I've never noticed her, you know…'

Rachel gave him a silencing look.

'You might actually like her if you got to know her. Portia is the same age as Jasmine and…'

'I've officially stopped listening now,' said Rachel as she tossed the ready meal into the microwave and set the timer.

'Well something's wrong. Has it been a Brook Farm Disaster day?'

Rachel shook her head and remembered that dreadful day. The petting farm was only a short drive away. It was relatively small and away from any major traffic, so she could take Poppy there without worrying about her bolting off and getting run over. It was also fairly cheap in comparison to other activities in the area, so they found themselves there a lot when the kids were younger. Poppy had been watching the new piglets feeding from their mother when another family came to join them. Without warning, Poppy held the shoulders of their little girl who had just joined them, and pushed her right over the low barrier and into the pig pen. The mother pig had been startled, leapt up and charged at the bewildered intruder. The child's father unleashed a tirade of abuse towards Poppy and Rachel, threatening legal action and claiming Poppy could have inflicted some pig poo related disease onto their innocent child. Rachel, humiliated and tearful had fled from the barn, turning back only when she realised that Jasmine had not followed. Instead, Poppy's big sister had gone up to the family and calmly apologised for her sister's behaviour, telling them that Poppy had learning difficulties and that she hadn't meant to hurt the little girl. Jasmine had realised that Poppy was trying to let the girl have a closer look, correctly interpreting her sister's behaviour, as she had done ever since Poppy was born. Often, when Rachel and Charlie couldn't understand what Poppy had been saying they would turn to Jasmine to interpret. Rachel had learned several valuable lessons that day. She learnt that children, no matter how young, can often be the strongest in the face of adversity. She also learnt (after she googled it when she got home) that the most likely way of catching a disease from a pig was by actually eating it. Finally, she learnt that hiring a private detective to track down the family in question so she could give them this information in person would be more expensive than she could afford.

'It was nothing like that,' she sighed. 'I just feel floored, Charlie. I can't get past the diagnosis. It's like all the hope we ever clung onto has gone. Vanished. Just like that.' She snapped her fingers.

Charlie sank his face into his hands before placing his

hands firmly on top of hers.

'We can't think like that, love.'

'I can't bloody help it, Charlie. What sort of life is she going to have? She's never going to be independent. Never going to be able to go to the shops on her own. She might not ever be able to read or dress herself. She won't even be able to enjoy nice food anymore if we put her on this ketogenic diet the doctor is suggesting. I mean, let's deny her one of the only pleasures she has in life, shall we!'

'We haven't made any decisions on that yet.'

'I just want to make things nice for her. After your tea I want us to book that holiday to Florida. She's going to see those dolphins, even if the flight kills me!'

'Are you sure? We don't want to make things any more stressful than they already are.'

'I'll be fine—just book it!'

The microwave pinged. Charlie got up and pulled out the anaemic-looking chicken curry, eating it straight from the plastic tray. 'Mmm, this is nice.' He giggled and gave a sarcastic smile.

'Piss off,' she laughed weakly, shaking her head.

'About the future though,' he sighed. 'Maybe we should talk to somebody who has been there? Someone who is going through it too. There must be some support groups for families with Dravet Syndrome. They might be able to give us some hope.'

Rachel nodded. 'Maybe.'

Before going to bed, she searched the internet to see if she could find a forum for parents with Dravet children.

The doctor at the hospital had mentioned a couple of organisations, but with the immensity of everything else she had to digest at the time, she hadn't taken it in. In no time she had found a French site, and a few minutes later a UK-based group. Somehow, even that tiny bit of information—knowing that all over the world there were other families just like hers—made her feel a lot less alone. She logged on and browsed through the site. Mothers and fathers were posting updates on their children's progress. There were reports on the successes and failures of different drugs. Everyone seemed to know each other, messages of support and advice were evident on every page. It was like its own little community. Rachel wondered if she had finally found somewhere she could fit in. She typed her first post tentatively, introducing herself and explaining that Poppy was in the very early stages of diagnosis. Within minutes she had six messages welcoming her to the website and offering advice on anything she needed to know.

She looked eagerly at the pictures that other families had posted. Some were regular family shots of days out, birthday parties, group selfies. Others showed children waving bravely from their hospital beds. Rachel took the most interest in the photographs of the older children. She wanted some reassurances about Poppy's future. She skipped through picture after picture until she came to one which gave her the first hope she had felt in days. A girl of around fourteen years old was smiling into the camera outside the O2 Arena in London, clutching a pair of One Direction tickets. She saw that her name was Daisy. Her long blonde hair hung loose around her pretty face. She was wearing sparkly eyeshadow and mascara which brought out the deep blue of her eyes. Her clothes were boho chic, and she looked about as cool as any teenage girl could be. Immediately, Rachel saw the future she wanted for Poppy. She clicked on the details of the person who had posted the picture and sent them a short message of introduction. Then she turned off the computer and fell into bed happier than she had felt in a long time.

PETAL

Petal had spent the afternoon delivering leaflets advertising her yoga classes. She had hand drawn the flyers herself then had them colour-copied at the library for the extortionate sum of £16.80. She had walked a three mile radius of the church hall that she used for her classes, entering shops, takeaway restaurants, post offices and doctors' surgeries asking if they would mind displaying her advertisements. Some of the proprietors had been quite helpful. Others not-so-much. One middle-aged man (claiming to be the Pizza King) had been blatantly rude, informing her in no uncertain terms that he was not the three-dimensional version of the yellow pages, adding, rather unnecessarily Petal felt, 'And do you think that people who come here to stuff their faces with pizza would be interested in yoga, you stupid hippy woman?'

It had been another hot day, and the sweat from her back had made her dress stick to her body as she climbed the stairs of Jubilee House. Her legs felt tired and she wondered whether her body was telling her that she needed to slow down in preparation for the coming months. Her stomach ached slightly, although she had read that this was quite common and not to be taken as any cause for concern.

She had drained her flask of water before she had delivered even half of her flyers, and had not even contemplated spending a pound on a bottle from any of the shops she had visited, knowing that she could have a free drink when she got home. She barely acknowledged Moon or Ash on her way through the living room to the kitchen, her thirst being her primary focus. She drained a full glass of water, refilled it, then drank half again before she re-emerged into the living room. She had been aware of an almighty racket coming from the small sitting area, and now she was able to fully appraise its source. Moon and Ash were each sat astride a tubular drum, beating out an unfathomable noise with their hands.

'Here she is—the woman who has tamed my mate.'

Petal was in no mood for Ash's snidey, cryptic comments. 'What are you talking about?'

'Zapping his freedom. Making him get a job like all the other sheep.'

Petal was stunned. She looked at her partner, a smile radiating from her eyes. 'Really?'

'Yeah. Thought I'd give it a go, you know, see if I can make a bit of money.'

Petal was now beaming with delight. Perhaps they would now be able to afford a larger flat. Somewhere a bit bigger with room for the baby. Maybe a small garden. 'Where?' she asked, feeling a spontaneous urge to hug Moon.

'Not where—what!' he replied, proudly.

'Okay,' she responded, confused. 'What?'

'Ta-dah,' announced Moon, spreading his hands before him in a visual fanfare of explanation.

Petal's brow crumpled. 'I'm not with you, Moon.'

'The drums, Pet, the drums. I'm going to be a musician. A proper one, like. We're setting up a band.'

'We?'

'Me and Ash. I can't do it by myself—I need some wheels to get around. We're splitting the profits fifty-fifty.'

'After petrol costs,' Ash reminded him.

'That's your new job? Playing bongos!' Petal questioned, her patience withering with every new syllable that came from Moon's mouth.

'They're not bongos actually,' Ash explained knowledgeably. 'They're *djembes*—from Africa.'

Petal flicked her fingers dismissively. 'Whatever! So can you tell me exactly where you plan to perform?'

'Loads of places—festivals, carnivals, gatherings…'

Petal pinched the bridge of her nose in frustration. 'So, let me get this straight. You've got a job as a drummer, and, ignoring for a moment the small fact that you can't actually play the drums, you think you're going to find someone willing to pay you to do it.'

'Uhuh,' nodded Moon. 'Well, maybe not one single person. I mean, if we can get a paid gig from a festival organiser then that's like, a bonus. But we'll probably just start by busking at festivals—until we make a name for ourselves.'

Ash laughed. 'We've got a few names already. Drummer

Dudes; Ash and Moon's Travelling Rhythm Machine—'

'Didn't we decide that one was too long?'

'Oh yeah. Then there was the Off-Beats,' grinned Ash.

'Wasn't it the Beat-Offs?' said Moon, puzzled.

Petal listened in disbelief. 'The Beat-Offs, Moon? Isn't beating-off slang for…actually, never mind, that's perfect for you pair of…' she stopped herself from finishing her sentence by taking a deep breath. 'So, aside from the fact that no-one in their right mind is going to hire you, if you busk at these festivals, you do realise that you'll still have to pay your entry fee? So that's entry fee, petrol money, and I suppose that you'll have to pay Ash back for half of the drums before *you* can even think about making any profit from this.'

'Oh no, babe,' smiled Moon. 'These are mine.' He patted the drums with the tenderness a child would show a new born kitten.

'Yours? Where did you get them?'

'Ash knew someone who was selling them. They were a bargain. Only forty quid—they'd cost about two hundred quid brand new.'

'Hang on. Where have you got forty quid from?'

'We had some savings in the pot,' explained Moon, glancing at the hand painted blue teapot that they kept on top of the kitchen units to store savings.

Petal was momentarily speechless. 'You took the money from the teapot?'

'You were the one telling me I had to invest if I wanted to start my own business.'

'I mean to buy a ladder and a bloody bucket you idiot!

And that money was for a new pump for the washing machine! I've got a plumber coming round next week to install it. What the hell am I supposed to pay him with now?' she screeched.

Ash seemed to sense it was time for him to leave. 'You could always hand wash your clothes, Petal. It's better for the environment. That's what Dawn does.'

'Thank you for your valuable advice, Ash. Any other environmental tips you'd like to share with me whilst you're at it? After all, I've only been into the whole eco scene for, ooh, thirty-nine years?'

'Well, actually, Moon did mention that you're going on a flight next week. Have you any idea how bad that is for the environment, Petal?'

'It's my job!' she screeched at a frequency only audible to dogs. 'In case you hadn't noticed, both of you,' she said, turning her head to each of them in turn to ensure that they both felt the full force of her fury, 'I have a real job. Not a pretend one where I suddenly decide I'm going to have a go at something which I have absolutely no experience at but a real, actual job. A job where I have to turn up at a certain time every week, and deliver a course in something that I'm good at. It's a job that I get paid for. That's right. Not a job that *costs* me money, but one that pays me cash, albeit it a small amount, every week. That cash then gets used to put electricity in the meter, to pay the rent, to buy food to supplement your skip raids. If I don't go on that flight next week, I will not be asked back next time. I will no longer have that job. Which means that you two potheads will have to find somewhere else to prat about with your bloody drums, because we will no longer have a roof over our heads!'

Ash had never seen Petal lose her temper like that. Moon had rarely witnessed similar outbursts himself. Both men looked at her wide eyed, waiting for her to finish her tirade.

As Ash picked up his coat and moved his drum to the side of the room, Petal swore she heard him ask Moon in a low voice 'Is she due on or what?'

Petal sat in the bathroom, using the toilet as a makeshift seat, and waited for her bath to run. She felt embarrassed about losing her temper in front of Ash. The irony that the job she had been spouting off about was to teach calming techniques was not lost on her. She had always prided herself on her laid back, calm attitude to life, and it concerned her that recently she had been feeling angry and anxious on an increasing level. She heard Moon knock on the bathroom door.

'Come in,' she replied wearily.

'I just wanted you to know, that I really thought I was doing what you wanted,' he said in a tone that came across mid-way between apologetic and defensive.

She stared at the black and white lino on the bathroom floor and gave a tight smile.

'I just don't know what's wrong with you lately. You've gone all, you know, stressy.'

Petal lifted her gaze from the floor and challenged him with ice in her glare. 'You do know, Moon! Because we've discussed it.'

'And I've been trying,' he protested. 'I bought you that perfume didn't I?'

Petal felt her temperature rise again. 'It's not about the bloody perfume, Moon! And when you say you bought it, did you really? I mean with actual money?'

'You don't have to buy things with money, Petal. You know I don't work like that. I traded her for some cheese I found. Good stuff it was and all! Mozzarella. Dawn said it wasn't mouldy whatsoever!'

'You should have given me the sodding cheese—it would have smelt nicer!' she snapped, regretting her words instantly.

'What the hell's the matter with you, Petal? Is it still this baby thing?'

Petal gave a hollow laugh. The fact that Moon could even assume that such a primeval longing could disappear overnight—be bought off with some cheap perfume—was astounding. She put her arm protectively across her stomach and wondered whether she really wanted this man to have anything to do with her precious child.

'It's about responsibility, Moon! I know you think I've changed, but in actual fact I haven't. I've just grown. I'm still passionate about our planet. I still believe that we can build a sustainable, peaceful environment for future generations, but not at the expense of a comfortable life for ourselves. The two don't have to be mutually exclusive. And if I can pass on some of my passion—our passion—to a future generation then what can possibly be wrong with that?'

Moon said nothing in reply. He simply turned and walked out of the bathroom, leaving Petal alone with her thoughts.

She turned off the water and felt the temperature of the bath. It was warm but not too hot—just as she liked it. She pulled off her thin layers of clothing, still damp from the heat outside. She peeled off her underwear, letting it fall on the bathroom floor where she stood. The contrast of the crimson stain against the white of her cotton pants was vivid. She remained rooted to the spot for an incalculable period of time—seconds, minutes? It was as if time had vanished, leaving her standing in a void of space, removed from every living thing in the universe. She was aware of her heart racing, and quickly tried to rescue her breathing. In for one, out for seven, in for one, out for seven. She concentrated solely on her breathing—on her very being— worried that if she stopped, the universe might suck her into its predatory black hole.

FLIGHT DAY

Hugh and Will had both arrived at the Community College early. The warmth of the day had yet to develop and a slight breeze rippled through the hydrangea petals bordering the car park. Will scanned his notes in preparation for the most important practical session of his research.

Jalil was the first to arrive. Head down, music playing through his earphones, he appeared from the direction of the bus stop. When he reached the car park and looked up to find only Hugh and Will waiting for him, his face fell. 'Don't tell me I'm the only one here!' he said, horrified. 'I only agreed to do this because the others said they would, if they're not coming then...'

'Good Morning, Jalil,' Will interrupted with a bright smile. 'You're early! The others will be here soon, I'm sure.'

'Well they'd better had be, man, cos I'm not kidding, I'm not going on my own.'

'Look,' said Hugh. 'Here's Rachel.'

A pale-faced Rachel could be seen in the passenger

seat of a well-used people carrier. Will, Hugh and Jalil waved as the car pulled up alongside them. Through the back window, Jalil saw Poppy's tiny face—even paler than her mother's. A long strand of saliva hung from Poppy's bottom lip and trailed down her chin and onto her pretty pink cardigan. Rachel took a deep breath and kissed her husband. She then got out of the car, opened each of the back doors in turn and kissed her two daughters. Her husband opened the passenger side window and shouted over to Hugh. 'Look after her, mate. She's a bit delicate this morning, but I've told her it's all going to be fine.'

'That's alright for you to say,' she muttered. 'I'm bloody shitting myself!'

'Ring me when you want picking up,' he shouted. 'Say bye to Mummy, girls.'

Two little voices shouted 'Bye, Mum.' Rachel turned her head and gulped in four successive throat-fulls of air. Determined not to sob in front of her kids, she reined herself in and gave them a big wave.

'See you later, girls. Be good for Daddy!' She turned to Will, Jalil and Hugh. 'I thought the others would be here by now.'

'Don't worry. They'll be here,' said Hugh, praying that he was right.

To fill time, Hugh went over the itinerary for the day with Jalil and Rachel, even though they had already talked about this in class. He was in the middle of telling them about the qualifications of the captain who would be flying them when Rachel's concentration was interrupted by a loud grinding sound. She looked across the car park to find the source of it.

'Oh my good God! What the hell is that?' she stifled a laugh.

Rattling through the car park was a dirty yellow VW camper van. Rainbows and flowers adorned the outside, juxtaposed by clouds of dark smoke which it belched out. The vehicle came to a stop in front of a parking space before finding reverse gear after three crunching attempts and then parking over two spaces. The four onlookers watched with bemusement as the windscreen wipers suddenly came on, followed by full beam, before the engine was finally switched off. Moments later, Petal climbed out.

'Jesus Christ, I didn't think I'd need those breathing exercises 'til we got to the airport. Now I'm not sure I fancy my chances on the road,' Rachel announced, only half joking.

'Hello,' said Petal.

Rachel noticed straight away that Petal didn't seem as chirpy as usual. She wondered whether she had heard them taking the piss out of her driving (although it would have been pretty amazing considering the noise the van was making). She hoped it wasn't anything more sinister—she had always been slightly suspicious of the dreadlocked-tie-dye types with their meditation and chanting and spiritualism. What if Petal had some super-sensory ability to read people's thoughts? She realised, with some horror, that if that were the case then Petal would be reading her mind right at that moment. She repeated the phrase 'my mind is a blank canvas' to herself five times in a row to throw Petal off the scent.

Next to arrive was McKenzie. He had stayed in a

discount hotel the night before and had wrongly assumed that the rush hour train service in Manchester would operate at a similar level to the London Underground. He had begun to get annoyed when after three whole minutes of waiting, a train hadn't arrived. Asking another person in the queue if they knew what the delay was about, he was told that the next train would be along in fifteen minutes.

'Really sorry I'm late, guys,' he said, jogging the last few paces. 'Trains! Bet you thought I wasn't going to show up,' he grinned. 'Are we ready then? Let's go before I change my mind!'

'Don't worry, you're not the last one. We're still waiting for Frannie,' said Hugh.

'Oh right. Maybe he's waiting for a train too,' said McKenzie. 'I don't know how anyone in Manchester manages to get to work on time!'

Hugh consulted his watch. 'We'll give him another five minutes.'

Will took advantage of the delay to note down some quick thoughts from McKenzie, Jalil and Rachel. All three claimed to be extremely nervous—all eights or nines on a scale of one to ten.

Ten minutes passed and there was still no sign of Frannie.

'He's not coming,' said Jalil.

'He's right,' agreed McKenzie. 'I don't blame him, to be fair.'

'But he promised he'd be here,' said Rachel.

'I'll phone him,' said Hugh. He unzipped his leather document wallet and searched through his papers until he found the course registration documents. He dialled the number and waited.

In the kitchen of his brother's house, Frannie watched his mobile phone vibrating on the kitchen table and waited for the ringing to stop. He'd been waiting for them to call. He knew he should have phoned Hugh and told him that he wasn't going to be joining them, but he knew that Hugh would try to persuade him to come, and he couldn't handle that.

Sharon scraped the leftovers from the previous evening's dinner-plates into the bin and loaded them into the dishwasher. She had a towel wrapped around her hair and was eating a piece of toast. 'Screening your calls?' she joked.

'Aye, something like that.'

Gary appeared through the kitchen door, dressing gown only half fastened, hair still jumbled from sleep. 'Is the kettle on, love?'

'Make it your bloody self,' she quipped. 'I'm trying to get ready for work.'

Gary sank down sleepily onto a kitchen chair. 'You're up early,' he said to Frannie.

'Couldn't sleep,' replied his brother truthfully. Frannie had been awake for most of the night, anxiety sweats drenching his body.

His phone beeped to signal a text. Frannie read it then put it down on the table, wordlessly. Within seconds the phone began to ring again.

'Aren't you gonna get that?' asked his brother, when Frannie made no attempt to answer the phone.

Frannie shook his head. He saw his brother and sister-in-law exchange a pointed look, but decided to ignore that too.

Moments later another text came through. Frannie sighed and picked up his phone.

We're coming to get you, it read.

Frannie felt a surge of panic. He didn't want them turning up at his house and speaking to Kim. He replied immediately.

No!

Seconds later another text came through. *On way!*

He let out a small roar of frustration, picked up his mobile and walked out of the kitchen and into the front lounge. He braced himself for the conversation he was about to have with Hugh, but was thrown completely when Rachel answered the phone. At least he thought it was Rachel—it was very difficult to hear over some almighty noise in the background. 'Rachel, I'm *so* sorry. I really am—I just can't do this.'

'Yes you bloody can,' she replied.

'I know I've let you down—all of you. If it makes you feel any better, you can't hate me any more than I hate myself right now.'

'We don't hate you, you silly sod. We care about you. All of us. Which is why we're on our way to pick you up.'

'Where are you going? You don't know where I live,' he asked, panic in his throat.

'Yes we do. Hugh's got the registration form. Where is it again, Hugh,' she shouted over the noisy engine. 'Derby Road—that's right isn't it?'

'I'm not there,' he said.

'What? I can't hear you!' she protested.

'I said, I'm not there.'

'You'll have to come up with a better excuse than that,' she replied.

'No, really, I'm at my brother's house. It's in Crumpsall. It's out of the way.'

Rachel was not taking no for an answer. 'One of Charlie's sisters used to live over there. It's not out of the way at all. What's the address?'

'Rachel, I really am sorry, but I don't want you to come all this way for me to let you down. I mean it when I say I don't think I can do this.'

'Frannie, we're not going without you. We've all gone through the same thought process as you this morning. Believe me—I wasn't sure I was going to be able to do it. But knowing that the rest of you would be there to get me through is what's got me this far. We're a team, Frannie. We're doing it, and we're not doing it without you. Now where are you?'

Frannie blew out a big puff of air. He paused for a few seconds. 'Okay. Okay. But not here—I'll meet you outside the pub. Do you know the Cleveland? I'll be there in five minutes.'

He hung up and marched back into the kitchen to pick up his wallet and jacket. Both Gary and Sharon were standing wordlessly, looking at him with worried expressions, clearly expecting some sort of explanation.

'I'm off out,' he muttered. Picking up his jacket he left before they could ask him any questions.

Frannie arrived within minutes. The heavy doors were firmly shut and there was no sign of life inside the pub. He paced up and down the pavement, nerves jangling with anticipation. If the pub had been open, he would almost certainly have gone inside for a large shot of something to calm his nerves. The day was still young and the sun still low, yet his body was clammy. As he paced up and down, he wiped the sweat from his palms onto his thighs. He contemplated turning back to his brother's house. He had been panicked into agreeing to go with them and felt angry for being forced into his current predicament. He knew though, that he couldn't let them drive out of their way to pick him up for him to be a no show. He clenched his fists and paced some more.

He heard them before he saw them. He wasn't sure what the noise was at first. A rumbling in the distance of some sort of machine. The noise got louder as the vehicle approached. He suspected some sort of works vehicle—a diesel powered steamroller. If they had been in the country, he would have expected to see a tractor coming round the corner. When the small camper van finally appeared, he was astonished—on a number of levels. Firstly, that the thunderous din was coming from *that*, but also, that anyone would want to be seen driving such a beaconing eyesore. He was so distracted watching the skip of a van drive down the street, that he only noticed the passengers as they were directly opposite him.

'What the…?' He groaned.

Some were gesturing and there seemed to be general chaos inside. There was a bus directly behind the van, and a queue of cars behind the bus. The camper van rumbled past an open-mouthed Frannie and jolted to a halt at the end of the road. The passenger door opened and Rachel jumped out. The bus beeped at the camper van, signalling it to move along, and Frannie watched it bunny hop round the corner.

'Your face has just made my day,' joked Rachel.

'What in God's name was that?' said Frannie, still unsure if what he had just witnessed was actually real, or a figment of his nerve jangled imagination.

'That's Petal's minivan! I tell you what—for someone who is supposedly here to calm our nerves, she's done a pretty good job of scaring the shit out of all of us already! She can't drive the bloody thing. I'm not even sure she has a driving licence!'

'Where's she gone?'

'To try to park round the corner. She couldn't even park in an empty car park this morning, so we'd better go before she takes out half of the street!'

Rachel turned to walk away, but Frannie hesitated. She turned back.

Frannie remained rooted to the spot, his hands trembling. 'I don't think I can, Rachel.'

Rachel looked at the man on the pavement in front of her. The wrinkles under his eyes were darker and more apparent than usual. Any sign of his usual good humour and spark were undetectable. She felt an overwhelming mixture of pity and affection for Frannie—he had made the lessons more bearable for her with his jokes. She walked towards him and embraced him, tightly and genuinely.

'I'm not going to make you do this, Frannie, but I know how you'll feel if you don't do it. The reason I know is because I've had the exact same conversation with myself this morning. We'll be up and down in no time. Think of the others too. They want you to succeed. We all do. You deserve this, Frannie.'

Frannie pulled out of her embrace and wiped traces of tears from his eyes. 'Why did I ever sign up for this bloody thing. Come on, let's go before I change my mind.'

Rachel beamed, hooked her arm through Frannie's and led him to where she hoped the camper would be waiting for them.

Petal had managed to park the van, in a fashion, over half a parking space and half a loading bay, midway down the adjacent street. Rachel climbed in the front, alongside Petal and a rather pale-faced Hugh. Frannie slid open the side door and climbed sheepishly into the back.

He was welcomed in like a hero, which embarrassed him even more.

He was still trying to locate the seatbelt when Petal kangaroo'd the van away from the kerb and onto the road. McKenzie howled with laughter as Frannie jerked forwards in a sudden, whiplash inducing movement.

Petal chose to interpret the stop sign at the end of the road as a give way sign, almost taking out an old man who was crossing the road.

'This is better than *Grand Theft Auto*,' sniggered Jalil.

As they rounded the next corner a small overhead cupboard flew open, scattering a musty smelling jumper, a packet of Rizla cigarette papers, some filters and a porno-dressed-up-as-educational DVD about tantric sex onto the vehicle's floor. McKenzie picked up the DVD and immediately began to read aloud the blurb.

'This DVD lets you explore the spiritual and physical pleasures of one of the most natural acts in the world. Klaus Greening and Beryl Wainright,' he instantly collapsed into fits of laughter. 'Beryl! You have some porno dude called Klaus then a woman called Beryl. Ohmigod man, I have to watch this!'

Everyone in the back, including Will, was unable to contain their laughter. Hugh and Rachel turned around to see what was so funny, unable to hear over the noise of the engine and the volume of the pan pipes which was blaring out of the one tiny speaker that was working. Petal's head swivelled over her shoulder to see what on earth was going on.

A cacophony of voices yelled at her immediately.

'Look out!'

'Watch the road!'

'Jesus Christ, look out!'

'Aaarg!'

Petal turned back to the road and veered the vehicle back onto the main carriageway after clipping the pavement with the front wheel.

All of the passengers exchanged looks of horror. Despite his complete apathy to all forms of religion, McKenzie crossed himself as he had seen done on the television in times of panic. Jalil put his head between his knees and giggled hysterically.

'Anyway, back to Beryl.' McKenzie continued to

read (and improvise) from the back of the DVD. 'Klaus Greening, Porno King, and Bingo Beryl, take you on a spiritual and educational journey, showing you how to channel your sexual energy into positive fuel for both you and your partner. "Usually, all of that energy leaves the body after orgasm," says Beryl, tantric sex convert of thirty years. "We will share with you some techniques to help you to prolong the act of love-making, with the aim of feeding off each other's energy for many hours at a time."'

'Hours!' screamed Rachel. 'Who the hell would want that?'

'Beryl, obviously,' laughed McKenzie. 'She's enough of a minger though—I reckon I could go for quite a while!'

Will shook his head at the turn the conversation was taking.

Jalil was astonished. He had seen a few bits and pieces of porn but had yet to do the deed himself. He had been worried about not being able to last more than a couple of minutes, so the news that some women expected hours, or even days of sex was a blow! He hoped that Holly wasn't a secret 'Beryl'.

'It's just a nasty bout of thrush waiting to happen, that is,' tutted Rachel disapprovingly. 'And I'd get bored. Are you allowed to watch telly at the same time?' she asked. 'Have a look and see if it says,' she instructed McKenzie.

They had just got onto the dual carriageway when Jalil said, 'I'm sorry but I really need a wee.'

The message was relayed to Hugh, who couldn't hear the conversation in the back. 'Can't you hang on?' he asked. 'It's only another twenty minutes or so.'

Jalil frowned. 'Sorry, Hugh, I think it's the nerves.'

'Okay,' sighed Hugh. He leant over and spoke to Petal, who banked left into the hard shoulder, and pulled up to a stop.

Jalil threw open the side door and climbed out, apologising for the unscheduled stop. 'Actually,' said Frannie, 'I might jump out too. Nerves,' he explained apologetically.

'Me too,' said McKenzie, throwing Beryl and Klaus onto the seat and unclipping his seat belt.

'I could do with going too, but I'm not going in the hedge,' moaned Rachel.

Despite being the last out of the van, McKenzie was the first back. 'Can't do it,' he explained. 'Nerves and an audience—ain't happening!'

Hugh, conscious of all of the delays, was becoming more and more impatient. He tapped the dashboard as he waited for his two students to get back in the van.

Fully loaded once again, Petal crunched the van into gear and set off. Within a few minutes they had passed the first signs indicating the direction of the airport. It was Rachel who spotted it first. 'Oh God, we're nearly there. I feel sick.'

McKenzie had also noticed the signs, but his fear had manifested itself in his bladder. 'Guys, I'm really sorry but you're going to have to stop again. I really need to go!'

'We only stopped two minutes ago,' Hugh reprimanded through clenched teeth.

'I know, I know, but if you don't stop I think I might seriously piss myself, man. Sorry!'

Hugh was reminded of family holidays to Wales when his children were infants. The relatively short journey used to take almost twice as long because his wife insisted on stopping at every service station to take the children to the toilet. 'Anyone else?' he roared, mightily miffed now.

'I think I might need some fresh air,' said Rachel, clambering out of the van and onto the embankment.

Hugh heard her shout 'I'm not looking,' presumably to McKenzie. Hugh hoped that McKenzie's piss would be forthcoming this time. He was beginning to worry they might miss their allotted time slot.

A few minutes later the van was rolling again. 'Has anyone else made any final requests?' shouted McKenzie.

'Like what?' asked Frannie.

'I dunno. Like a will or something.'

'You're not going to need anything like that,' protested Hugh irritably.

'I wasn't going to! It's just that I was awake quite a lot last night, and I was just thinking, that if the plane goes down, I've got, like, a shit load of tunes and synthesiser gear that would end up going to my mum, and I was thinking, like, what a waste! So I wrote a little note on one of those little notepads that they keep in the drawers in your hotel room, instructing the police, or whoever the hell's job it is to sort that shit out, that all of my techno gear has to go to my mate Gee.'

Jalil's heart quickened. He knew he had been right about McKenzie. Little Gee was one of the other members of the Urban Phantoms. He had messaged McKenzie the other night to ask him for a favour—a present for Holly.

McKenzie hadn't replied, but Jalil was clever enough not to mention it to him until after the flight.

'I haven't got anything worth leaving,' huffed Frannie. 'Kim spends everything before I've had chance to save it, so unless anyone wants a load of cushions and curtains and coats they're going to be sorely disappointed.'

Will noticed that Frannie had been much quieter than usual, unable to muster the strength required to bring out his usual defence mechanism, he was sitting quietly, focusing only occasionally on the banter in the van.

'I haven't got anything worth leaving either, love,' Rachel sympathised. 'Not yet, anyway. I've got my eye on Charlie's mum's Royal Albert tea set, when her time comes, but I've noticed that his sister has started to make comments about it when she goes round. I blame Mary Berry and that bloody Cath Kidston. I've *always* liked that tea set, and no bugger else was interested until all of this *British Bake-Off* nonsense. Now they all want it! And I wouldn't mind but Charlie's sister is lactose intolerant! What the hell use is a milk jug to her? Bloody greedy, that's what she is!'

'This is the turning,' instructed Hugh to Petal, who had been particularly quiet for the entire journey.

A collection of low buildings surrounded a small airfield. There were a few hangars, some out-buildings and a control tower. The main airport building was tiny in comparison to any airport that the class had experienced in the past. Petal was directed to a parking area reserved for the airport's flying club. She parked in between a Lexus and a BMW, leaving the camper van in gear exactly as JJ had instructed.

Apparently the handbrake had a very temperamental nature. McKenzie dived out first, kissing the ground before Petal appeared round his side of the vehicle.

'Where do we need to go, Hugh?' asked Rachel. 'I'm desperate for the loo.'

'We need to go and sort out the paperwork in the office,' he pointed to a small building next to the clubhouse, 'but the clubhouse is open so you can use the facilities in there.'

Frannie was pleased to get out of the van. The noise of the engine combined with the knackered suspension had made him feel sick. He needed a couple of minutes out in the fresh air before he went inside. As he paced up and down he absent-mindedly checked his mobile phone. He had two missed calls—one from his brother, Gary, and another one from his sister-in-law, Sharon. He had decided that he would call them after the flight, when he noticed a text message from his brother.

If you don't call me back right now I'm telling Kim.

Telling Kim what? he thought. He hadn't mentioned a thing about the course or the flight to his brother. There was nothing he could do except call. He dialled the number. The call was answered within seconds.

'About time,' came an angry voice.

'What was that text message about?' asked Frannie.

'Don't play the dickhead with me, mate. Now I don't know what the hell is going on with you lately—whether it's a mid-life crisis or what, but I never had you down for this!'

Frannie sighed. 'Look, I'm really not in the mood for dealing with this right now, Gary. What's the matter?'

'The affair!' snapped Gary. 'And don't try to deny it because we saw you.'

'Affair?' spluttered Frannie.

'Aye, laugh about it why don't you. I know *we* did when Kim first mentioned it. To be honest with you, we didn't believe her, but we've seen it now and I'm fucked off with you—one, for being a dickhead and cheating on Kim and two, for lying to us!'

'I'm not having a bloody affair!'

'Come off it! You've been taking secret phone calls, screening calls when we're around. We even heard you this morning. Sure enough, it sounded like you were trying to end it, but you went running in the end. We followed you to the pub—saw you together, walking arm in arm down the bloody street. I'm telling you—if you don't get home right now and tell Kim what's going on, then *we* will!'

'Have you finished?' snarled Frannie.

'I'm just doing this for your own good!'

'And I'm doing *this* for my own good. Well not really for *my* own good, but for the good of Kim and the kids. There *is* no affair. I'm on a bloody Fear of Flying course!'

'*What?*'

'I've been going every Wednesday for weeks. I haven't told Kim because you know what she's like—she'd take over—try to organise me! But this is something that I need to do myself! Just me!'

'But,' Gary stalled. 'What about the woman? You were hugging and kissing on the corner—walking off arm in arm.'

'I wasn't bloody kissing her. Her name is Rachel—she's on the course too. I did try to back out today—that must have been what you heard when you were earwigging on my phone call. They convinced me to come. When you saw us Rachel was trying to encourage me to come, because, to be honest Gary, I'm fucking shitting myself here.'

'Where are you?'

'I'm at the bleeding airport—we're about to go on our graduation flight.'

'Jesus Christ mate, I had no idea!'

'Exactly—and that was just the way I wanted it.'

'So why now? You've been scared of flying for years.'

'Why do I do anything? Money! That seems to be my only role in life—I'm a human bloody cash cow. If I can't fly then I can't get this promotion at work. That's why I haven't applied for it yet. And before you say anything, no, I haven't told Kim that either. She'd go bloody mad!'

'I'm sorry, mate,' said Gary. 'Listen, do you want me to come with you? I can be at the airport in twenty minutes.'

'No, it's fine, I'm going to do this on my own. Anyway, it's City airport out in Eccles.' He looked around. 'It looks like the frigging toy-town version of an airport to me. I hope they know what they're doing.'

'Good luck, Frannie. You'll be fine. And hey, mate—sorry about all that.'

Frannie hung up, put his phone back in his pocket and made his way inside.

Inside the building, the others were filling out the necessary paperwork. The hysteria of the minibus ride had evaporated and most of the class were now focussing on their own thoughts. Jalil handed his completed form, along with his previously unused passport to the flying club official to check. As he stood at the desk, he noticed Hugh's open passport. He had a lot more hair on his passport photo than he did now.

'Nice pic,' smiled Jalil. 'Let's see yours,' he asked Will as they were waiting around the desk.

'Mine is awful,' said Will, showing Jalil the pic. 'I was eighteen then. I'm surprised that the picture doesn't stick to your hands, there was that much gel on my hair.'

'I quite like mine,' said Rachel. 'It was taken before I had any kids—back when I was thin and carefree!'

She flashed the picture around for the others to see. Sure enough, she looked about twenty years younger on the photo, rather than the eight years difference there actually was.

All of the passports were passed around for each other to inspect. Frannie looked a bit thinner on his and, like Hugh, had a bit more hair. But it was McKenzie's which displayed the most drastic change from his current image. His hair was braided in cornrows which dangled messily around his shoulders. Several heavy gold chains hung around his neck, and right ear sported a large diamond earring.

Frannie chuckled. 'The mayor of Manchester just called—he wants his bling back.'

McKenzie smiled good naturedly as his picture was passed around the group. When it came to Jalil, he only glanced at the photo for a second. He was more interested in the information underneath the picture. Name: McKenzie Robert Wright. He knew he had been right all along. He passed back the passport without a word.

'Everyone done?' asked Hugh. 'If you could all take a seat, I'd like, very quickly, to brief you on what's going to happen next.'

'Where's Petal?' asked Rachel.

Hugh looked around. 'She's probably just gone to the ladies' room. Anyway, this is for *your* benefit really. So, as you all know, the plane we are flying on today is a Cessna turboprop. It has an excellent safety record, and in my experience, is one of the best small planes you can get. Our pilot for today is a very good friend of mine, Captain Martin Graham. Martin has a CV that any aspiring pilot would be envious of, having flown commercial flights for KLM, Air France, and more recently with Flybe. And if that wasn't enough, Martin has a share in his own plane, which he flies for pleasure! That is the plane we will be using today. I'll be in the cockpit alongside him for our short flight. As you all know, I too, have many years flying experience. As we make our short journey, I shall be talking to you through the speaker system every step of the way, explaining what is going on.'

Hugh paused to consult his notes, aware that the usual interruptions and sarcastic comments were absent. 'It's a lovely little route we're doing today. We've got perfect weather for it too. If you can try your best to relax, then who knows, you might even enjoy it!' he laughed. 'I'll just go and find Martin and see if he's nearly ready for us.'

'I need another piss, man,' said McKenzie.

'Me too,' said Jalil, following McKenzie out of the office and into the clubhouse.

'I just want to get this over and done with now,' said

Rachel, to whoever was listening. She felt herself getting teary again and pulled the soggy, crumpled tissue from her handbag to dab at the tears that had been springing from nowhere all morning.

Will was making notes on each of the students—asking them exactly how they were feeling and what they were thinking.

'It's the kids,' Rachel explained to Will. 'Even if it wasn't for Poppy, I couldn't imagine anyone else looking after them. They'd miss me! But with Poppy's condition—I just wouldn't trust anyone else to do it!'

'Are you feeling any physical signs of your fear?' asked Will.

'I do feel sick, but not here,' she pointed to her stomach. 'It's here,' she pointed to her throat. 'And I can't stop crying. All morning, I've been crying on and off. Is that normal?'

Will laughed. 'There is no *normal* for phobias,' he explained. 'But what you are describing are classic signs of anxiety. How would you rate your fear now on a scale of one to ten?'

'Definitely a ten!' she replied shakily.

'What I would suggest, is for you to take a quiet moment whilst I have a chat with the others. Try to practice some of Petal's breathing techniques.' He smiled encouragingly at her.

'What about you, Frannie?'

Despite the warmth of the day, Frannie's complexion had the hue of porridge. 'I'm not right good, lad, but I've just got to get on with it, haven't I?'

'Physically, how do you feel?'

'Sick! And my hands seem to be leaking.' He managed a weak smile.

'There it is,' smiled Will. 'I knew that *that* sense of humour was still in there somewhere. So, on a scale of one to ten?'

'Twenty!'

Will made some notes and nodded. 'Why don't you try some of those techniques Petal showed you?'

He was just about to go and sit down, when Jalil came racing through the office door. 'Rachel, can you come quick—it's Petal!'

'I thought it was an animal at first,' said McKenzie, 'but then I realised it was someone crying. I shouted through the door, but I didn't want to go in—in case people thought I was some sort of perv!'

'It's okay,' said Rachel, 'I'll go.'

She opened the outer door to the ladies' toilets. Inside it was fairly cramped with only enough room for two cubicles, a single hand-basin and a hand-dryer. She knocked on the closed toilet door. 'Petal? Is that you? Are you okay, love?'

'I-can't-do-it!' came the reply in a strangled voice, punctuated with sobs.

'Do what? Listen love, come out and we can have a chat.'

'I'm not coming,' she cried.

'Whatever it is, we can sort it out,' urged Rachel, who was feeling exceptionally guilty about the collective mocking of her driving. 'If we've done anything to upset you, then we're truly sorry. Come on out.'

There was a moment's silence, then the sound of the sliding metal lock sliced the air. The door creaked open slowly but Petal remained seated on the closed toilet lid, her head in her hands.

'Hey, it's okay,' soothed Rachel.

The main toilet door opened ajar, and Frannie shouted through, 'Is everything okay?'

'We'll be out in a minute,' shouted Rachel brightly, still unaware of the extent of the problem. She lowered her voice again. 'What on earth has got you this upset?'

Petal gulped in big breaths of air. 'I'm not doing it I can't I've never been on a plane before and I didn't know I was actually going to be going up in the air and Hugh never told me that this was part of the deal and I'm just not prepared…'

'Oh fuck!' whispered Rachel under her breath. She then knelt in front of Petal 'Slow down, just take a deep breath and calm down,' she urged.

'I can't, I can't!' Petal gulped. 'If Hugh finds out he'll sack me and I won't have a job or a house or any money or a baby and I'll have to live off skip food and I won't get my garden and I'll be stuck living with Moon and my life will be over before it's even started even though I'd just decided to change everything and…'

Rachel held her hands up to Petal 'shh, shh, shh—just calm down, I'll be back in a second!' She bolted out of the toilets to where McKenzie, Frannie, Jalil and Will were waiting anxiously outside.

'What's the matter? Is she ill?' asked Frannie.

'She's having a full blown panic attack!' cried Rachel.

'You mean she's scared of flying?' said Jalil, in disbelief.

'It turns out that she's never been on a plane in her life,' said Rachel, 'and apparently she's not going to start now!'

'Fucking hell!' said McKenzie, shaking his head.

'Do you want me to go and tell Hugh?' said Jalil.

'No!' said Rachel. 'I think that'll make things worse. She was worrying about losing her job!'

'Poor cow—I know how she feels,' said Frannie.

'Are you sure this is about the flight?' asked Will, looking confused. 'It's just that I never picked up any signals from her over the last few weeks that she might be concerned about anything.'

Rachel shrugged. 'I'm not sure, Will. To be honest she wasn't making much sense. At one point she was talking about going to live on the moon or something. I think she might be delirious!'

'What are we going to do?' asked Frannie.

'Come on, let's all go and talk to her. Try to calm her down.'

All five adults squeezed into the tiny gap between the cubicle door and the opposite wall.

'Look who's here,' said Rachel brightly. 'Everyone's worried about you.'

'Have you told Hugh—is he here—is he going to sack me?' she sobbed.

'No, no—he's busy getting the plane ready, isn't he?' she looked at the others for support.

'Yes,' they all agreed.

Petal looked up at them. Her face was florid and there was snot all over her cheeks and chin. 'I'm not getting on it! I don't want to go! I've messed up everything and now I'm messing this up and I've got no plan! My only plan has gone and now I have no plan…'

'Hey, chill out about your plan, Petal,' said McKenzie. 'I haven't got a plan either—it's shit but there's no point getting all, like, stressy about it.'

'If you're not coming, then that's fine,' said Rachel, 'but we will have to tell Hugh something.'

'No!' cried Petal. 'My job!'

'Well, what then?' said Rachel. 'If you don't calm down then you won't be able to come.' She looked to the others to help her out. 'Do you think you might be able to just calm down enough to think about coming with us?'

Petal began to hyperventilate.

'Jesus Christ,' said Rachel. 'Deep breaths, Petal. In for one,' she glared at the others to help. Scared of Rachel, they all joined in, doing the breathing exercises that Petal had taught them, complete with hand actions. A collective gasp of breath could be heard with a whooshing of hands. 'And out for seven,' instructed Rachel. Again, the breaths of four men and one woman could be heard exhaling audibly for the benefit of Petal. 'And again—in for one—out for seven.'

Petal still remained inconsolable. Rachel looked at the others.

'I've got some valium?' shrugged McKenzie. Immediately, the others eyed him with horror and envy.

'What?' he asked defensively. 'I haven't taken any. Not after the last time I used them for flying and ended up hammering them with a load of vodka. I noticed this morning that they were still in my jacket pocket.'

Frannie looked uncomfortable. 'I'm not sure about this. My recent experience of drugs is that they're bad news.'

'Up to you, man,' shrugged McKenzie.

Will looked at his watch. 'We really must get going. Petal,' he said in a loud but gentle voice 'we need you to decide whether you want to come with us or not. It's entirely your choice.'

'I need to come, but I can't I'm going to lose my job,' she took a couple of gulps then started waving her arms in front of her face 'oh no I can't breathe I can't breathe.'

'SLOW DOWN!' ordered Rachel. She turned to Jalil 'Go and get some water—quick!'

Jalil disappeared into the clubhouse whilst the group tried desperately to calm Petal down.

'What should we do?' asked McKenzie.

Frannie looked torn. 'Those tablets. Are they genuine valium?'

'Yes,' said McKenzie.

'Not some shite knocked up on someone's kitchen table?'

'They're the genuine article, man—I promise.'

Frannie put his head in his hands before saying, 'Go on then—she needs something!'

McKenzie squeezed into the doorway of the toilet and showed Petal the tablets. 'Petal, I've got some diazepam here—valium. It will help to calm you down if you want some help. I'm not forcing you—this is ONLY if you feel you need some hel—'

Petal snatched the tablets out of his hands. Her own

hands shaking she tore at the foil before throwing two of them into her mouth.

'Steady on!' warned McKenzie. 'They're not bloody smarties.'

At that moment the toilet door burst open and Jalil came running in with a pint of water. He pushed past Frannie, Will and Rachel, staggered to the open door where McKenzie was still squatting in front of Petal and threw the entire pint of water over Petal's head.

Time momentarily stood still. Rachel gave a little squeal of horror. Frannie and Will watched open-mouthed and McKenzie fell backwards onto his arse. Petal gave a sharp intake of breath before looking up in shock at the panting Jalil.

McKenzie looked at Jalil, then at Petal, then back at Jalil, who was still panting—empty glass in hand. 'What the hell are you doing, man?' he asked, eyes wide, voice teetering between shock and hysteria.

Jalil looked around him, suddenly aware that all eyes were on him. 'Rachel told me to,' he gasped. 'To calm her down!'

'I didn't mean to chuck it at her—I meant for you to get her a drink!' squealed Rachel.

Everyone turned to look at the sodden Petal. She looked like she was still in shock. She had stopped crying and was looking out at all of them, wide eyes, hair still dripping onto her shoulders.

McKenzie was the first to laugh. It started as a burst of illicit giggles that he desperately tried to restrain. At the sound of this, Frannie joined in, this time with a huge belly laugh. Rachel, still slightly horrified, turned to look at Petal's reaction. She was petrified that this might just tip her over the edge. It took a few seconds before Petal's shoulders started to jerk. Once, then again a few seconds later, until her head and shoulders were shaking uncontrollably. Rachel watched in desperation now, completely out of ideas to calm her down, until she realised that Petal, too, was laughing. It started out as a half-laugh, half-cry—tears still streaming down her face, until it gradually morphed into pure laughter.

Jalil, who had stood mortified with his head in his hands for the endless seconds which preceded that moment, cracked a broad smile of relief. Frannie laughed as he put his arm round him. 'Good job, lad!' he laughed.

Just then, the main toilet door creaked open. It was Hugh. He eyed them all suspiciously. 'What on earth's going on in here? I've been looking everywhere for you!'

Petal chose that moment to emerge from her cubicle. She waved at him coyly.

Hugh's face wrinkled at the sight of his assistant, seemingly soaked to the skin. He asked the obvious question, using only his hands and face.

'There's a problem with the plumbing,' explained Frannie, quickly. 'Petal turned the tap and it came on full blast. Poor thing couldn't turn it off. She got soaked. She tried to stop the flow but had to call for help. That's why we're here.'

'Yeah,' nodded McKenzie. 'You wanna tell them to sort that shit out, man.' He winked at Petal.

Hugh clapped his hands. 'Well, as long as I've found

you, that's the main thing. Come on, we've got a plane to catch!'

Hugh strode ahead, leading the group across the tarmac to where some planes were parked up. The others followed in a tight, slow-moving group. Rachel had a firm hold of Petal's arm, talking to her in a gentle, calming voice all the way.

'Tell me that's not our plane,' said McKenzie. 'It's like a toy!'

They had all been told that the Cessna turboprop was a small plane, but none of them had been truly prepared for the scale of it.

Frannie felt a new sheen of sweat appear on his brow. 'Is this thing going to take our weight?' he asked Will, urgently. He patted his large stomach. 'I'm not exactly Mr Slim. For the first time in my life I wish I'd listened to Kim and stuck to that frigging diet.'

'It's fine,' reassured Will. 'Do I look worried?'

A hatch door hung open vertically off a hinge halfway down the body of the small aircraft. Two small aluminium steps provided access for the passengers.

'Seating is single inside this aircraft,' explained Hugh, 'so feel free to sit wherever you feel most comfortable. One of you will have to sit next to the emergency exit, right here, so just have a think about that before you get in. If you'd prefer not to, then I'm sure that Will or Petal will do the honours.'

'I'll do it,' said McKenzie, immediately, wanting to retain at least one element of control.

Rachel climbed in first, walking to the back of the aircraft. She held her hand out to Petal, leading her to the opposite seat—as far away from Hugh as they could manage.

Next came Frannie, then Will, followed finally by Jalil and McKenzie. Hugh appeared after everyone had boarded and gave McKenzie his instructions for operating the emergency exit.

After everyone was seated correctly, Hugh and Captain Graham were chatting happily in the cockpit, pulling on headphones and consulting charts. The engine was started. Plane checks complete, Hugh switched on the plane's intercom to address his passengers.

'So, we're almost ready to go!' he shouted over the noise of the engine. 'Weather conditions are perfect—hopefully there'll be plenty to see on the way. We're just waiting for the final go ahead from control and we shall be on our way. I'm obliged to give you all a safety announcement, NOT that we'll be needing it,' he laughed. 'I imagine that you've all got your seatbelts securely fastened, but if you haven't yet done so could you please fasten them now. You are welcome to unfasten them when we reach cruising altitude, but we're not going to be up for long, so it might be an idea to just keep them loosely fastened. Keep your tray tables upright and armrests down. Lifejackets can be found under your seat. They are fitted with a light and a whistle for attracting attention. That's the official bit done. What I'd like you to concentrate on now is remembering all of the work we've covered in our lessons—the theory and the practical. The fact that you're here, on this plane right now is a huge achievement. You've come a long way, each and every one of you. It's time to go now, so I'd like you all to sit back and enjoy the flight.'

The plane taxied towards the runway. Rachel caught sight of an orange windsock, lifting up and down in the breeze. She leant forward and tapped Will on the shoulder. 'It looks a bit windy to me. Are you sure we're going to be okay?'

Will smiled at her. 'You heard them—perfect weather conditions!'

'But that thing is blowing like mad. Do you think they've seen it? Do you think we should tell them? A bit of wind under this diddy little wing and it could be game over!'

'Rachel—do I look worried?' said Will once again.

The plane came to a halt at the end of the runway. The engine revved up to what seemed like maximum throttle. The whole plane was shaking with the sheer power.

Frannie wiped his wet palms onto his trousers, then mopped his brow with a cloth handkerchief. McKenzie repeated the instructions for the operation of the emergency exit over and over in his head—turn, pull and kick, turn, pull and kick. Jalil closed his eyes tight and visualised the beach in Kavos. In his mind he was sunbathing next to Holly, their hands loosely touching on the hot sand. Rachel was trying to concentrate on keeping her own breathing level, but was distracted by Petal who was beginning to look jittery again.

'We've been cleared for take-off,' shouted Hugh. 'We're taking off from the westerly runway today.'

The plane began to accelerate, building up more and

more speed as it went.

'Those small bumps are just the runway lights,' explained Hugh as a thudding sensation could be felt throughout the cabin.

Frannie, Jalil and McKenzie all closed their eyes tight.

Rachel daren't take her eyes off Petal who looked confused and was tugging at her seatbelt.

The nose of the plane lifted and within seconds the group could feel that they were airborne.

The plane bumped ever so slightly a couple of times as they ascended to their cruising altitude. Frannie and Jalil both cried out in fright, but were immediately informed by Hugh that this was perfectly normal, and that everything was absolutely fine.

'In a moment the engine noise will reduce. This is because we will have reached our cruising altitude and we can reduce the power,' explained Hugh.

Rachel reached over to Petal who was now whimpering in her seat. 'I don't like it, I want to get down,' cried Petal.

'We're all right, Petal. Hugh is looking after us,' soothed Rachel.

'It's too small, I can't breathe,' she flapped.

'Big, deep breaths. Look at me Petal. Look at me!' Rachel ordered. 'In for one, out for seven. In for one, out for seven.'

'It doesn't bloody work!' screeched Petal. 'I need some more of those tablets. Where's McKenzie?' Petal scrambled with her seatbelt again.

'We are now cruising at 3000 feet,' came Hugh's voice over the tannoy. 'If you look out of your window you'll see that we are just passing over the M62. I defy you all not to feel at least a little bit of satisfaction that you're up here on this glorious day instead of stuck down there amongst that traffic,' he said, oblivious to the stress that was unravelling in the back seats.

'Look at me,' said Rachel. 'LOOK at me!' she ordered. 'It *does* work, and you *know* it does. Now just calm down and concentrate on your breathing. In for one, out for seven.'

Petal tried to follow Rachel's instructions, but her breathing was rushed and she was gabbling away to Rachel at the same time which wasn't helping.

'I need to get off!'

'Well we bloody can't, so just listen to what I'm telling you and you'll be fine,' said Rachel, losing patience.

'My life! It's running along without me. I need to stop it. I need to change things, but it's too late,' Petal groaned. 'What if it's really too late—my life is over already!' she cried.

Frannie turned around, aware of a commotion behind his seat. 'What's going on?' he asked Rachel before catching sight of Petal. 'Oh, bloody hell,' he uttered. 'She's off again! Do your breathing, love.'

'I've tried that!' replied Rachel. 'She's not having it!'

Frannie unclipped his seatbelt and maneuvered himself around to help. 'What about the other stuff—the singing? Have you tried that?'

Rachel raised an eyebrow. 'Be my guest,' she replied sarcastically.

'We're now just east of Warrington. Those of you on the right-hand side might just be able to make out the

Runcorn Bridge in the distance.'

'Petal, love, I need you to concentrate for me. We're going to sing a song.' He glared at Rachel. 'Aren't we?'

Rachel rolled her eyes and agreed reluctantly. 'Well go on then,' she prompted.

Frannie shrugged. 'I don't know?'

Rachel huffed and started them off. 'Row row row your boat, gently down the stream.' She paused for a moment. 'Well bloody join in then!' she snapped.

Frannie grudgingly joined in the song. 'Merrily, merrily, merrily, merrily, life is but a dream.'

As they repeated the song, Petal began to slowly join in, nodding her head in time to the rhythm.

On the third refrain, Frannie asked 'Is there any more to this song? It's a bit, you know, repetitive.'

'That's the whole point,' explained Rachel.

'How about *Twinkle Twinkle*?' he asked. 'Just for some variety?'

They began the new song, but Petal immediately started to get skittish again, mumbling something about leaving Moon.

'Oh heck, she's starting to get deluded again—all of that talk about stars has got her thinking about living on the moon again. We're going to have to go back to *Row Your Boat*.'

'Row, row, row your boat,' they began again.

'We're now approaching the Wirral Peninsula. We're going to take a path across the River Dee before turning back to the airfield. Halfway there folks—you're doing well. I hope you're enjoying it.'

Jalil finally plucked up the courage to open his eyes. He was struck immediately by the deep blue of the sky pierced by a dazzling white sun. He took a deep breath in and regulated his outward breaths. He looked at the ground beneath them. Roads cut through the surrounding fields like arteries pumping sanguine cars in a steady flow. He didn't know what he had been expecting, but he felt remarkably calm. It was almost as if the turmoil of the previous weeks had numbed his ability to feel fear. He'd gone through the worst of it already—the humiliation, the fear of the drug scare and the train line incident. Compared to all of that, this was a walk in the park. He looked around him to see how everyone else was faring. He noticed some sort of commotion at the back of the plane. He tapped McKenzie's arm across the aisle.

McKenzie had been concentrating on a new song. It started as a mindless, repetitive tune as they were taking off. Something to take his mind off what was about to happen, as Petal had advised them in class. After a couple of minutes he started to add some lyrics.

Forget the past, mistakes are for making, get your vibe back, life's for the taking. Eagleheart; Eagleheart.

He looked at Jalil, who was pointing to the back of the plane. They both unclipped their seatbelts and walked back to where Frannie and Rachel were gathered round Petal.

'We're now crossing the Dee estuary,' explained Hugh. 'It's remarkable in that for such a large estuary, there is relatively little water. Some people believe that as well as the river Dee, the river Severn or the river Mersey once entered the sea here, which explains the large opening.'

'Is she okay?' asked Jalil.

'Merrily, merrily, merrily, merrily…' sang Rachel.

'She's fine as long as we keep singing this song,' explained Frannie. 'We must've sung it at least fifty times!'

Rachel used her hand to gesture that he should continue to sing. Frannie dutifully took over.

'I haven't even had time to think about being on this flipping plane,' explained Rachel.

'Do you know what—it's actually all right,' said Jalil with surprise. 'Do you want us to take over here for a bit, so you can have a look outside?'

McKenzie nodded his agreement. 'Go on—your turn to listen to Hugh's history lesson!'

'Only if you're sure!'

'Course.'

'If you keep singing she'll be fine. If she starts jabbering on about going to live on the moon again, you're losing her. Sing faster!' suggested Rachel. She squeezed past the lads and took Jalil's seat at the front of the aircraft.

Frannie settled himself back into his original place. He chanced a look out of the window. They were heading back towards Manchester now. Down below he recognised the path of the M56. One of his first jobs as a chartered accountant had been for the large chemical manufacturer ICI near Runcorn. It was in the early 1980s and his pride and joy had been his Ford Cortina in Dragon Red. He smiled to himself as he remembered the amount of miles he had racked up in that old thing.

Jalil and McKenzie took over the singing. After the eighth rendition McKenzie suggested changing the song.

'Petal, do you know any other songs? Chris Brown? Will.i.am?'

Petal began to look panicked.

'Okay, take it easy,' said Jalil. 'What about that CD you had on in the car? The funny owl one.'

McKenzie looked at him quizzically. 'You mean the pan pipes?'

'Dunno—whatever!'

'There were no words, you goon! It has to have words, innit.'

'Okay,' huffed Jalil. 'You pick one then.'

'Okay man, let's go with Pharrell. Ticks all the boxes— repetitive and annoying!'

'Fine,' shrugged Jalil.

McKenzie started off with the chorus of Pharell William's song, *Happy*.

Petal recognised the song immediately. It was ubiquitous. On the second rendition of the chorus Petal started to join in with the refrain. McKenzie, encouraged by this, began using his fingers on Petal's armrest to drum in some additional percussion. Jalil, smiling now, drummed a complimentary bassline using his hands on the back of Frannie's seat.

Turning round to see what was going on, Frannie watched as Petal vacantly joined in with the repetition that came in on every alternative line.

McKenzie was beginning to enjoy himself now, and conducted Frannie and Will to join in by clapping twice on the word 'happy', singing that word only until it appeared again in the song, when they were instructed to do the same.

Rachel, glad to hear anything that wasn't *Row, Row, Row Your Boat*, turned round too. She had watched the film *Despicable Me* hundreds of times with her children, and recognised the song from that. McKenzie, loving the attention, gave Rachel a different harmony—singing the word 'happy' over and over again four times over every beat of eight.

When Hugh came on the intercom to tell them that they were approaching Manchester, they were all in such full voice that no one heard him. It was Will who noticed Hugh waving through the cockpit to get their attention. Will gestured to McKenzie to sit back down again and fasten his seatbelt. Not to be deterred, McKenzie continued conducting the strangest version of Pharrel Williams' song that would likely ever be heard—all the way back to the airfield. The singing was only broken as the wheels touched down on the runway at City airport, triggering a euphoric outburst of cheering and laughing.

'I can't believe I did it!' cried Rachel, bursting into tears as everyone congratulated one another on their momentous achievement.

'Well done each and every one of you,' said Hugh through the intercom. 'Now I don't know about you lot, but I think that calls for a drink! See you all in the clubhouse.'

They were still high on adrenaline when they burst through the clubhouse doors, each talking over the others. Frannie was halfway to the bar before he noticed a familiar figure seated at a small round table with a dimpled metal surface.

'Kim? I...I...' He looked around at Rachel. 'This isn't what you think.'

She stood up. 'Come here you silly sod!' she said, opening her arms to receive him in an embrace.

'What are you doing here? How did you…?'

'Gary told me everything.' She sighed. 'Why didn't you tell me? I could have helped! I wouldn't have worried that you were up to no good.'

'I wasn't, Kim—I told you…'

She shushed him. 'I know now! But you shouldn't have shut me out, Frannie. Shut us all out. We could have helped you.'

He shook his head. 'I needed to do this myself,' he said.

'Well? How was it?' she asked, tentatively.

'You know what—it was okay. The worst part was the anticipation.' He jerked a thumb towards the others who were ordering their drinks at the bar. 'This lot were a big help. Just having other people there who knew what it felt like. I couldn't have done it without them.'

Kim smiled. 'So are you going to introduce me, or what?'

He took her arm and grinned. 'Come on.'

'What are you having, Frannie?' asked Hugh.

'I could murder a pint,' he replied. 'Hugh, everyone, this is my wife, Kim. She's come to get me to sign on the dotted line for an exotic holiday now that I'm a flyer!'

'Hey!' she protested, nudging him in the ribs. 'The thought hadn't even crossed my mind! But now you come to mention it.' She smiled. 'Nice to meet you all,' she said. 'You've all done *so* well!'

'Do you know what—I'm bloody starving!' said Frannie.

'Me too,' chorused the others.

'I haven't eaten a thing all day,' said Jalil. 'Hardly anything all week actually.'

'I'd assumed that would be the case,' said Will. 'I asked Hugh to sort out some food—should be ready soon!'

Hugh smiled bashfully, slightly ashamed that he hadn't even considered this himself as course leader.

'I'll bring it out now,' said the volunteer behind the bar.

They picked up their drinks and moved tables about so they could sit together.

Hugh held up his glass. 'To hard work, perseverance, self-belief and bravery! To my team!'

'To the team,' they echoed, clinking glasses and beaming with pride.

The party suddenly got bigger as two little faces, followed by a bigger one appeared in the clubhouse.

'Charlie! What are you doing here?' Rachel's face was a picture of pleasant surprise.

'These are for you, Mummy,' said Jasmine, holding out a small bunch of flowers which Rachel accepted with squeals of delight.

'Thought we'd better come and make sure you hadn't brought air traffic control to a standstill,' he smiled before kissing her with pride. 'How was it?'

'I did it!' she enthused. 'Come and sit down and I'll tell you all about it. Everyone, this is Charlie, Jasmine and Poppy.'

The rest of the group greeted them with genuine warmth. 'I'll get some drinks first,' said Charlie. 'Anyone ready for another?'

Frannie stood up. 'Aye, but I'll get it. That last one went

down too quick! Anyone else?'

Petal raised her hand. 'Yes please,' she said, offering her empty glass to Frannie.

'What was it?'

Petal shrugged and looked at Jalil who had ordered Petal the same as his the first time round when she didn't know what to get.

'That was a snakebite with a Jägerbomb chaser. Are you sure you want another one of those?'

Petal nodded cheerfully.

McKenzie got up and followed Frannie to the bar. After his recent experience in mixing diazepam and alcohol he was concerned for Petal's well-being. 'I'm not sure that snakebite chaser is such a good idea for Petal. She had at least two valiums earlier. Just get her half a lager shandy and she'll be none the wiser!'

'Righto,' nodded Frannie.

Back at the table the food had arrived. Rachel decided to have a chat with Petal. The poor woman had calmed down, but Rachel was still worried about her.

'How are you feeling now, love?' she asked. 'Is there anything you want to talk about?'

Petal had a glazed look about her. She was systematically picking up the warm cocktail sausages and pushing them into her mouth.

'I feel okay at the moment,' explained Petal. 'I'm not sure what's going to happen when I get home though.'

'Is there anyone you would like me to call?' asked Rachel, sympathetically.

'No.'

Rachel didn't want to press any further, so was about to change the conversation completely when Petal suddenly poured her heart out. She told Rachel everything. About Moon, about the tiny flat, about living in practical poverty for the sake of their beliefs, about her recent birthday and about the baby. Rachel listened as Petal opened up to her about her desire to be a mother, saying nothing, her heart aching for this stranger who had now become a friend.

'I think you need to leave him,' Rachel advised, when Petal had finished. 'You're still young enough to start again.'

'I can't. We can barely get by together—we just wouldn't be able to afford to live alone.'

'But you can't stay with someone just because you can't afford to leave!'

'I have to. I'm stuck!'

'Could you get a new job? Maybe do your yoga teaching as an extra?'

Petal shrugged. 'I didn't really have a conventional upbringing. I was home educated. I don't have all of the qualifications and experience that you need to get a 'proper' job. My parents didn't think I'd need one.' For a moment she seemed distracted by her own thoughts. 'Neither did I.'

Frannie and Charlie remained chatting at the bar. McKenzie sat next to Jalil, who was occupying Poppy with his earbuds, placing the music into her ear and watching her smile, then taking it out again like a little game. Rachel watched on, delighted and relieved that Poppy was provoking such a positive reaction.

'She's great,' smiled Jalil, whose experience with young children was extremely limited.

'How old is she?' asked McKenzie, who had a young nephew to compare her to.

'Five,' said Rachel proudly. 'But some of her development skills are more like a two or three-year-old,' she added with a tinge of sadness.

'There was a kid in my class at school who had learning difficulties. He struggled for years and years. Then they discovered he had some sort of dyslexia. They gave him these special glasses and he had to do his work on coloured paper—the difference was unbelievable, man!'

Rachel smiled, thankful for his kind encouragement. 'Unfortunately, we know what Poppy has and there is no cure for it. It's likely that she will struggle for the rest of her life.'

McKenzie looked crestfallen. 'That shouldn't be happening in this day and age!' he said. 'I mean, if they can put a man on the moon, surely they should be able to find cures for all these illnesses.'

'You never know, Rachel,' added Jalil kindly. 'With a bit of research they might just find the magic cure.'

'Yeah,' nodded McKenzie. 'Have you done any fundraising? Get some cash—give it to the best science dudes you can find!'

Rachel shook her head. 'Nah! What could I do? And anyway, nobody would come. The other parents at Poppy's school aren't interested in her unless she's done something naughty.'

'We'd come!' said McKenzie.

'Thanks boys,' said Rachel, gulping down a rather large lump in her throat.

'So, did you get my message?' asked Jalil, after Rachel got up to take Poppy to the toilet.

McKenzie tapped his fingers on the table and nodded.

'Listen, I know it's you. I saw your passport earlier.'

McKenzie closed his eyes as he realised beyond doubt that he had been rumbled. 'Jalil—I really, and I mean *really* don't want anyone finding out about this course.'

Jalil held up his hands to protest his innocence. 'I'm not going to say a single word to anyone. I just thought, you know, since you were at a loose end at the moment…'

'…That I'd DJ a party for you?'

Jalil nodded, only now feeling that his request was slightly forward. 'It's not actually for me.'

'Oh yeah?'

'There's this girl…'

Jalil told McKenzie all about Holly, and how she was a massive Urban Phantoms fan, about his unrequited love for her, and about how thanks to his friends she now believed he was a Class A dickhead.

'If I could just do this for her…'

McKenzie sighed. 'It sounds to me like you're too good for this girl.'

'No, no, she's not like that. She's great.'

'All right all right. When is it?' He took out his iPhone and tapped in the details.

When Rachel returned to the table she looked concerned. 'Something's just dawned on me.' She looked at Petal. 'She's in no fit state to drive us home.'

McKenzie laughed. 'To be fair, she wasn't in a fit state this morning.'

Jalil spluttered into his drink.

'We can't have Hugh finding out about what's gone on. I'll see if Charlie will drive the camper van back. I'll take our car. I'd offer to drive it but I think I've had enough drama for one day!'

After the adrenaline had settled, the euphoria wore off and was replaced with exhaustion. Saying goodbye to each other was harder than they had imagined. In the few short weeks that had passed they had formed a tight little bond. Suddenly they were all to go their separate ways. They exchanged phone numbers, promising to stay in touch.

Hugh was pleased and relieved—probably more relieved than pleased. The course had been, in his eyes, a success. Rescued from the verge of disaster on a number of occasions, he had done what he intended to do, and got a group of aerophobes into the air. It may not have always gone to plan, but they had got there in the end. He looked forward to spending the fruits of his labour with his mistress. After that, he would decide whether to put himself through all of this again.

Will boarded the camper van clutching the last of his notes which would form the basis of his PhD. He had collected far more material than he had ever expected and was eager to start writing it up.

Rachel explained to Hugh that Charlie had agreed to drive so that Petal could have a celebratory drink with them. Watching Petal's head bounce back and forth against the camper van window as they chugged away from the airfield, she hoped that Petal would make the right choice.

FRANNIE

Frannie wasn't in the mood for a 'talk'. Elated, exhausted and still pleasantly tipsy from the post-flight drinks, the sofa and television beckoned. When they arrived home, it was clear that Kim had other ideas.

'We need to talk,' she informed him.

'Kim,' he moaned. 'I'm shattered.'

'I know and I'm sorry, it's just that the children will be home soon.'

Frannie sighed. 'How are they? What have they made of all of this?'

Kim squirmed. 'Well…'

'Well what?'

'To be honest, Frannie, I'm not sure they noticed that you'd gone.'

Frannie felt like he'd been slapped in the face. 'Well that's just bloody marvellous, isn't it? Says a lot, that does!'

'You know what teenagers are like, Frannie…'

'Do you know what, Kim? I don't. I don't know what

they're like because I rarely get to see them or spend any time with them. This was what I was trying to tell you last week! I feel like a bloody spare part in this family. All I'm good for is providing the cash and taxiing folk around. If I died tomorrow I could be replaced by a Barclaycard and a frigging Ford Fiesta!'

'I think you're over-reacting, Frannie.'

'It's okay for you—you get to spend some time with them. To be honest with you, I'm not sure it's even worth me unpacking my bags. I might as well just get a bedsit next to the office so I can be on call 24/7.'

Kim shook her head. 'Now you're being completely ridiculous!'

'Am I?'

'You're not being serious, Francis? You mean to tell me that you would actually walk out on us?'

'You don't need me!' he cried.

'Of course we do,' she protested feebly. 'I was devastated when I thought you were seeing someone else.'

'Oh aye, worried about what I might be buying for her were you?'

'Will you stop going on about money!' she snapped.

'Why? It seems to be at the heart of our bloody misery. Money and time. The man that can get the right balance in life is a smarter man than me!'

Kim stood up and paced around the living room, pinching the bridge of her nose. 'So what, *exactly*, would you like to change? Hmm? Are you saying that I need to get a job? Do you want me working the tills at Marksies like Sharon?'

'You don't have to say it like it's something degrading, Kim! Honestly, I think you sometimes forget where you grew up! And, to be fair to Sharon, she seems to enjoy her work! She sees people, has a good social life, brings home a good few quid. What's wrong with that? You never know, you might actually enjoy a little part-time job!'

Kim visibly shuddered. 'If you think I'm going to humiliate myself by getting a job in a supermarket…'

'How the hell would it be humiliating yourself? Humiliating in front of who? I really think you have an inflated idea of who actually gives a shit, Kim! And I wasn't even thinking about the money, I was thinking about you!'

'Okay, so let me get this straight—you would want me to get a job so you can spend more time with the children?'

'You know I didn't say that! That was you putting words into my mouth! I *would* like to see more of the kids though—is there something wrong with that?'

'Of course not. They're just very busy. They don't have a lot of spare time.'

'Yes, about that too! These exams that Simon's doing. The audition for the National Youth Orchestra. Does he actually *want* to do it?'

Kim brushed the comment aside with her hand. 'Of *course* he does.'

'Have you actually *asked* him?'

'I don't need to ask him—he's been working hard for years and years towards this.'

Frannie sighed and lowered his voice. 'I'm going to ask you the question again, Kim. Have you *asked* Simon if that's what he wants?'

'It's a ridiculous question!'

'So, can *I* ask him when he gets in?'

Kim fluffed her response.

'What I would like,' said Frannie, 'is for us all to sit down together, and have a family meeting.'

Kim rolled her eyes. 'I think that's totally unnecessary!'

'Well if you're right, which you seem convinced you are, then you've got nothing to worry about, have you?'

'Fine!' she spat.

Frannie made a pot of tea and arranged a selection of biscuits onto a plate which he placed in the centre of the small round dining table. He was aware of Kim snorting in the background about the formality of the meeting, but chose to stand his ground and ignore her.

'Hannah, Simon, can you come here please,' he shouted.

A few seconds later, Hannah appeared in the kitchen, tapping away at her mobile phone.

'Come and sit down, love. We're having a family meeting.'

This got her attention. She looked up from her screen, frowning. 'What? Why?'

'I'll explain when we sit down. Where's Simon?'

'Dunno. Upstairs?'

'Would you go and get him please?'

Hannah returned her gaze to her phone and continued tapping away.

'Hannah?' repeated Frannie.

'I'm doing it!' she snapped. 'I'm Facebooking him! You don't expect me to actually go upstairs do you?' she laughed.

'Silly me,' Frannie huffed under his breath.

'Kim, are you coming?' he shouted.

Simon could be heard thudding slowly down the stairs before he could be seen.

'What's going on?' he mumbled.

'Family meeting,' said Frannie, brightly.

'Why?' asked Simon, with the negligible level of enthusiasm that only a teenager can convey.

Frannie began to get frustrated. 'If you'll all sit down then we can get started!'

'Ooooo, biccies,' said Hannah, rushing to the table and grabbing three chocolate chip cookies from the plate.

'Hey!' complained Simon. 'You're such a pig! Give me one of those.'

Hannah crammed the second biscuit into her mouth, laughing and pointing at the remaining biscuits on the plate.

'Dad, she's scoffed all the chocolate ones and left the Ginger Nuts and the HobNobs. I hate HobNobs. She's such a spoilt little brat!'

Frannie marched over to the table, picked up the plate of biscuits and emptied them into the bin. 'Can we forget about the bloody biscuits and just sit down. Please!'

'This is going well,' said Kim smugly as she breezed into the kitchen and poured herself a glass of water.

'Can you get me a drink, Mum? Orange juice.'

'Me too!' said Hannah. 'Actually, have we got any J2O left in the fridge?'

'Can we all just bloody well sit down?' bellowed Frannie, banging his hands on the table.

'Oooh, okay Dad. Chillax!' said Hannah.

Frannie waited until everyone had taken their places before he began. 'I called this meeting because I felt that you two were old enough to make some decisions for yourselves, but now I'm wondering whether I made a big mistake!'

Kim smirked.

'Do you know that Gemma's mum and dad let her decide what time she goes to bed? They say that it's up to her to manage her time, and that if she's too tired for school the next day then it serves her right!'

'Hannah, that's just bad parenting! I don't think that's what Dad had in mind. Is it?' Kim contributed quickly.

'No, of course not. We're not giving you the keys to the asylum or anything. I just think that you need to start taking a bit more control of your own time. I've noticed that I have been seeing you both less and less lately—I don't know whether you have noticed that too?' He looked at each of them for confirmation but found two blank faces staring back at him. 'Well, anyway, I thought we should have a chat about all of these extra-curricular activities and see if there's anything we could cut out to free up a bit more family time.'

'How about we start with the Manchester City matches that seem to be on television more and more lately!' said Kim.

'I get to see about one match a month, Kim, and usually it's just half a match because I'm due to taxi someone around in the middle of it. But on the subject of football, it would be great for me to take Simon to the match from time to time.'

'He's not interested in watching football, Frannie!' replied Kim.

'This is what I mean—you are putting words into his mouth! Let him have his own voice. Simon?'

Simon looked stumped, like this could be some sort of trick question. He looked from one parent to the other. 'Well, yeah, it'd be good to go, but like Mum says, I don't really have time.'

Kim nodded her head as if she'd won the first point.

Frannie persisted with the line of questioning. 'But if time wasn't an issue, Simon. Would you like to come to watch City with me?'

'Well, yeah, of course!'

It was Frannie's turn to nod his head.

'Hannah? What about you? Loads of girls go to the footy now. Would you be up for it?'

Hannah thought about the question. 'If I said no, could I get the equivalent value to spend in Top Shop?' she asked.

'There's no arguing that you're your mother's daughter,' said Frannie. 'Listen, this is not about money. It's about us spending more time together as a family.'

'You mean like the Kardashians?' asked Hannah.

'I've no idea who they are! Kardashians, Waltons, The bloody Partridge Family, whoever you like! I'd like us all to just slow down a bit.'

Simon looked at his dad suspiciously. 'You haven't found God have you?' He started to look very worried. 'You know Chris Greggory—his dad found God after his motorbike accident. He started randomly turning up at Chris' football matches and going to parents' evenings for, like, the first time ever. Chris was *well* embarrassed—his dad actually asked Miss Hyland why Chris was doing GCSEs and not O levels. He thought GCSEs were for the remedials or something—'

'I haven't found bloody religion! I'd just like to spend a bit more time with you all—is there really something wrong with that? So, Simon, your violin lessons. Are you still enjoying them?'

Simon frowned. 'Eh?'

'All of this extra practice you're putting in for the audition for the National Youth Orchestra. Do you actually want to do it?'

Simon looked at him mum for guidance.

'Don't look at your mother—I'm asking you!'

'Err, I dunno what you mean.'

Frannie began to get exasperated. 'The National Youth Orchestra. Is this something you really want to do?'

Simon thought for a moment. 'Well, it's kind of the next step.'

'That wasn't the question. I asked you whether you wanted to do it. Not just the audition—do you want to spend the next few years of your life practising the violin?'

Kim couldn't contain herself any longer. 'Of course he does, Frannie. What a stupid question. As if he's going to throw away all those years of practice.'

'Kim, I was asking Simon, not you!'

All eyes returned to Simon who was now looking completely confused and uncomfortable, and darting glances from one parent to the other for guidance. 'Well... like Mum says, I should probably do it so I don't waste all my talent.'

Frannie sighed. Seeing little Poppy had clarified family matters in his own mind. He wanted his children to have some fun, to run free whilst they still could. One thing he had learnt in the past few weeks was that you never knew what hand life might deal you next. He wasn't about to squander the hand he had been dealt. 'Simon, you've just told me that you 'probably should do it.' Now I'm not sure that's a good enough reason for you to spend the next few years locked in your bedroom every night, practising away when you could be doing other things with your time.'

'So you're happy for him to just squander his talent, are you?' interrupted Kim.

'It's not squandered. He obviously has a good ear for music. He can read music as well as anyone. He can get the strings to make a tune. I don't know Kim—maybe he could take up the guitar or something instead? Something a bit more sociable, and more importantly, on a casual basis, without all the exams!'

Kim looked horrified at this, however, Simon's face began to light up.

'Yeah, the guitar sounds cool,' he nodded.

'Simon?' pleaded Kim. 'Are you telling me that you would honestly give up the opportunity to play in the National Youth Orchestra?'

Simon shifted about in his seat. 'Well, I had never actually thought about *not* doing it before. I just kind of assumed that I had to. But I really like the idea of learning the guitar, Mum. And it would be nice not to have to practice every single day. I hate practising!'

'Simon! Why have you never told me this before?'

Simon gave a guilty shrug of the shoulders. 'I dunno—suppose cos you've never asked me.'

Kim put her head in her hands before looking over to Hannah. 'And what about you?'

Taking the lead from Simon, but more confidently, Hannah answered, 'well, I hate my piano lessons. I could quit that. You know you'd probably get a load of money for our piano, Mum. And I still like dancing, but maybe I could give up ballet and start something else like ballroom dancing. I'd have to have spray tans, like, every week to be good at it—that's what they do on *Strictly*. All the best ones are like, mega-tanned!'

'Okay, okay,' said Kim, holding her hands up in defeat. 'Looks like we need to make some changes.'

'Listen, love. I'm not saying that they need to give up everything—just not do everything with such intensity that they miss out on everything else. All of the workshops you book them into in their holidays—are they really necessary?'

'I just did that to fill their holidays because you bloody well refused to travel anywhere decent!'

'Okay, well that might change from now on. It's not just you and the kids who need to change—I do too. If you want to book a holiday then go ahead. It's fine.'

'Really? Can we afford it?'

'Ha! It's not like you to ask first, but yes, I don't see why not. And I'm going to apply for the Finance Director's job now I know I can get on a plane if I have to.'

Kim's face crumpled. 'You mean you haven't even applied for it yet?'

Frannie shook his head. 'I couldn't, Kim! But I'll email

them later tonight.'

'What if it's too late?' she panicked.

'If it's too late it's too late.' He thought again about Poppy and her future. 'It's not all about money, Kim.'

After the meeting closed, Frannie remained at the kitchen table, took out his Blackberry and logged into his work email. He found his CV and attached it to an email to head office, apologising for the delay in his application. He hovered over the send button only for a second before pressing it. For the first time in months his head felt clear and his heart light.

RACHEL

Rachel sat on the low school bench next to her mother, only half listening to Jean's story about her neighbour's new car.

'She can't park the bloody thing. It's quite entertaining to watch. It took her three attempts to parallel park it in the street yesterday. Then Ken had to go out and move it because it was about two feet away from the kerb. Honest to God, why she had to trade in the little Panda I'll never know.'

'Hmm?' said Rachel, who was distracted by Poppy's clumsy attempts to offer some freshly picked daisies to her classmates for them to smell.

'The Panda!' repeated her mum.

'Oh, is it pregnant again?'

'Mary? Pregnant? She's fifty-three!'

'What? Hang on…Poppy!' she shouted across the eight lanes of running track which separated the parents from the children. 'Don't do that.' She waggled her fingers at Poppy who was ramming a handful of flowers into the faces of her nearest classmates. 'Where's Miss Koslowska?' she muttered despairingly. 'This is exactly the sort of situation where Poppy needs a one-to-one watching her before it escalates into a situation.'

'Isn't that her over there?' Jean pointed over to where the only male teacher, Mr York, was flipping through a set of papers on a clipboard. Miss Koslowska, dressed in tiny summer shorts, a vest top and flip flops was hovering over his shoulder, flicking her long dark hair over her slender bronzed shoulders. She was stunning, and if she ever changed her mind about being a teaching assistant she could easily walk into any modelling office in the country and sign a contract on the spot.

'She needs to stop flirting with Mr York and do something bloody useful,' snapped Rachel, who was anxiously trying to parent Poppy long distance.

'Is this Jasmine's class?' asked Jean, noticing that a group of girls had lined up at the start of the fifty metre sprint line.

'Oh, yes,' said Rachel, feeling guilty for almost missing her eldest daughter's race because she was too busy trying to keep an eye on her youngest.

'Come on Jasmine!' shouted Jean as the girls sped away from the start line.

'Come on Jas!' yelled Rachel as they shot past her.

Jasmine crossed the finish line in seventh place.

'Ooo, did you see how big those other girls were?' commented Jean. 'Big gangly legs on some of them—she didn't stand a chance.'

'Shhh, Mum,' said Rachel, mortified that some of the other parents had heard. 'She's just not that sporty.'

The truth of the matter was that Jasmine might have been good at some sort of sport, but unlike lots of her classmates she had never been given the opportunity to try out at any of the local clubs due to the time and energy Rachel expended looking after Poppy. Rachel constantly felt guilty that Jasmine missed out on these things, even more so because Jasmine never complained.

'Anyway,' continued Rachel, 'you'd better get used to supporting the back-markers—Poppy's class will be on in a minute. Speaking of which, can you see her?'

Both women shielded their eyes from the afternoon sun to look for Poppy, who had vanished from the place she had previously occupied at the front of the big blue mat. Rachel stood up to investigate. Scanning the school field, she caught sight of a little red shape crouched over in the corner of the field where the gardening club held their lunchtime sessions. Rachel set off at a quick walk, until she realised what Poppy was doing, then she changed gear to a run. 'Damn you child for making me run in front of all the other parents,' she cursed under her breath, aware that her bra had been chosen that morning for comfort rather than support.

'Poppy, stop!' she shouted, hoping she could save at least one of the pots of tulips before Poppy beheaded them all.

Poppy turned around, beaming with delight at her finds.

'Oh, Poppy, you're not helping our situation here,' Rachel whined, aware that this was a perfectly unreasonable and futile complaint to put onto a five year old child.

'Flowers,' beamed Poppy. 'Smell!' she urged, pushing the purple and orange petals into Rachel's face as she bent down to pick her up.

'Poppy, these flowers are not supposed to be picked. That's very naughty. The other children will be upset when they find out what you've done.'

'Nice flowers,' she smiled. 'One for Nina, one for Mia, one for Harry…'

'No, love. You have to leave them here. Come on, it's nearly time for your race. You know what you have to do? When the teacher says on your marks, get set, go, you have to run to the end, down to Mr York. Understand?'

She deposited Poppy at the start line and took her seat, ignoring any filthy or pitying looks she might be receiving from the other parents.

'What was she doing?' asked Jean.

'I'll tell you later,' mumbled Rachel in reply.

Rachel heard the teacher call on your marks, get set, go. Poppy had been put in the third heat of eight children, having missed her original slot. As the other children left the start line, Rachel was amazed to see that Poppy followed them. She wasn't distracted by flowers, or water tables, or dolphins—she actually ran away from the start line with the other children. Within a matter of seconds she had been left behind, but she continued to run, in her own fashion, both arms folded up to her chest, fists clenched tightly together. Usually when Poppy tried to run she fell over, her inability to judge depth making her prone to accidents. Almost a quarter of the way down the track, she was still on her feet. Her gait was slightly off centre, giving the impression of a limp, and her body leaned forward in a fashion which almost defied gravity. As Poppy approached the halfway line, all of the other children had finished, but she was grinning from ear to ear. Suddenly Rachel heard some of the other parents shouting Poppy's name, encouraging her to make it to the finish. Children from the older classes began chanting her name, urging her on. Suddenly Rachel's eyes filled with tears. She was usually an expert at containing her emotions in front of anyone other than her family, but this was too powerful. The sound of dozens of parents shouting Poppy's name was choking her and within seconds tears were streaming down her face. As Poppy finally crossed the line, on her own, but beaming with pride, a huge cheer erupted from the school field. Instead of hearing it as a cheer of pity, Rachel drew comfort from it. For the first time in a long time she didn't feel quite so alone.

Less than an hour later, Rachel was waiting for the children to finish their tea so that she could go onto the computer. The old PC had been a hand-me-down from Charlie's sister, and, whilst it was rather slow to come to life, it did the job and they were grateful for it. Rachel had set it up on a small desk in the corner of the living room. As the girls ploughed their way through their potato waffles and fish fingers, Rachel contemplated going through to switch the computer on. Dinner was often selected on what Poppy was least likely to choke on, and whilst fish fingers and potato waffles were usually a safe bet, Rachel decided not to take the risk of leaving her alone even for a moment.

She was desperate to go onto the Dravet forum and see if she had any messages from other parents. She had been spending a lot of time on the website recently, chatting to other parents and swapping information on medication, education, behaviour management and all sorts of other things. She had been delighted to find that there were other mothers just like her—other parents who understood exactly what it was like to have a child like Poppy. Charlie had told her that he thought she was spending too much time on the website, but she found it comforting to know that she was not alone, so he left her to it—often chatting late into the night.

This particular evening she was waiting to see if she had any responses to her enquiries about the benefits of a ketogenic diet for Poppy. At the original diagnosis, the doctor had mentioned this, along with a million other things which Rachel had been struggling to take in. She knew that it involved limiting the calorie intake of the child to a state of near starvation so that the brain would produce ketones, which could apparently re-boot the brain—a bit like re-starting a computer when it had a problem. Rachel had been fairly cynical about the whole thing, after all, Poppy had been taking a cocktail of powerful drugs all her life and they hadn't managed to make her much better. She wondered how simple food could possibly make a difference. That was until she had discovered the forum and noticed that some parents were reporting miraculous results. She was still unsure as to whether to go ahead with it. It felt cruel—depriving a sick child of one of the things they took pleasure from. She wasn't sure if she was able to do that to Poppy, even if it might improve her health.

She watched Poppy methodically eat her fish fingers—one hand full of fish finger, one big dip into the tomato ketchup, and then slowly towards her mouth, concentrating on getting the food in her mouth with her limited co-ordination. Rachel sat next to her with some kitchen roll, wiping her mouth after every few bites, wondering how she could possibly begin to explain to Poppy that fish fingers and ketchup may be off the menu permanently.

As soon as the kids had finished eating, Rachel gave Poppy the iPad so she could watch an episode of *Flipper*. Jasmine was lying on the rug in the living room, glued to the Disney Channel. She turned on the computer and waited impatiently as it groaned, whirred and thumped its way to life. Eventually she got onto the Dravet website and carefully used two fingers to enter her login. The home page looked different—there was a long stream of messages and conversations, with new messages popping up as she stood and watched. She scanned the messages and took a massive gulp of air. Suddenly all of the words on the page began to swim together, dancing across the screen like a swarm of bees. They appeared to be messages of condolence. With a shaky hand she took the mouse and hesitantly scrolled down the page so that she could see the beginning of the conversation. The trembling effect coursing through her entire body was making it difficult to control the cursor. More and more messages swam past, until she saw the one name that she had prayed not to see—Daisy. She leapt from the chair and bolted upstairs to the bathroom, making it to the toilet just in time. She threw her head down the toilet bowl and vomited violently.

She remained on the bathroom floor for an unaccountable length of time. She held her head in her hands and sobbed as she tried to imagine what Daisy's parents must be going through. Although she had never met Daisy, the pretty looking teenager had made a big impression on Rachel. She bit her knuckles and sobbed for the little girl with the sparkly eyes and pretty face. She sobbed for Daisy's family and friends—for her brothers and sisters. She sobbed for her grandparents, then she sobbed for any family who had ever lost a child. She pictured her own family—Charlie, Jean, Jasmine—all the aunties and uncles and grandparents, and she imagined something like this happening to them. She picked herself up off the floor and made her way to the bedroom. Her head was throbbing. She picked up the phone and called Charlie. 'I need you to come home, right now,' she wept.

When Charlie looked at the website himself, later that evening, he appeared visibly shaken by the news. They had both been made aware of the statistics regarding the life expectancy of children with Dravet syndrome, but to see evidence of a little life being cut so tragically short was still utterly shocking.

'I feel like I should do something,' she whispered as they sat quietly on the sofa together. Rachel's eyes were red raw and her head lay limp on Charlie's shoulder.

'What do you mean? Send some flowers?'

'I don't know,' sighed Rachel. 'I felt like I knew her, but the reality is I'd never met the girl. I don't know if sending flowers would be a bit weird.'

'I wish there was something we could do for all of them,' said Charlie. 'This thing with Daisy—it could have happened to any one of our kids. One bad fit, and that's it—they're gone! That's what we have to live with every day. Every time we put them to bed we have to wonder if it'll be for the last time.'

Rachel broke down again. 'Oh Charlie, I can't bear it.'

'I know, love. But that's why you're right. We should do something. A charity event—*anything* that will raise a bit of money for more research into this condition. At least we'll feel like we're *doing* something. Not just sitting round waiting for fate to decide their future.'

'I don't know, Charlie. I mean, I'd like to, but what could we possibly do? And who would come?'

Charlie shrugged. 'Family? Friends? Poppy's school friends and their parents?'

Rachel raised an eyebrow. 'I'm not sure, Charlie. I don't really know any of them. I can't see them turning up.'

'Well even if it's just our family. We have to do something. Maybe you could ask your friends from the Fear of Flying Club—they seemed a nice bunch.'

Rachel thought again of the picture of Daisy, smiling for the camera outside the pop concert. She knew that Charlie was right. 'Yes, let's do something. Let me have a think about it.'

Rachel lay in bed next to her soundly slumbering husband and willed sleep to come. She kept thinking of different ideas for her charity event. A mental list of events—jumble sale, music and hotpot evening, bingo, sponsored sports activity re-arranged themselves constantly in her mind. She had never done anything like this before and the thought of it was slightly overwhelming. Nevertheless, she felt a quiet determination to achieve something—even if she only raised a hundred quid. After lying awake for over an hour she decided to get up and write down all her ideas.

She switched the kettle on, then fired up the computer. She needed some feedback to reassure her that her ideas would work. She couldn't think of anything more humiliating than standing in an empty room because nobody had turned up. She logged on to her email and sent a message to her friends from the Fear of Flying Club. They had all been really supportive when it came to the flight, and even if one of them said they would turn up it would be a start.

She drafted a message stating what she was planning to do and why. The message was hesitant, and showed her lack of confidence in herself, but she was hoping that if there were any major flaws in her plan her friends would spot them.

She remembered meeting Frannie's wife at the aerodrome—she seemed to be a very self-assured woman. She was the sort of person who Rachel imagined would be on the school PTA. Just the sort of person she needed for advice. She asked Frannie if he wouldn't mind asking Kim to look at it too. She listed all of her ideas and asked them which one they thought would work, and if any of them would be interested in attending.

She was surprised to receive a reply within minutes. It

was from McKenzie. She looked at the clock and wondered briefly what he was doing up so late, then she remembered that he was a young man in his early twenties living in London—he was probably out partying. She immediately felt grateful to him for replying to a frumpy old mother like herself about a silly little fundraiser. Obviously she didn't expect him to travel up from London for her event. She should have removed him from the mailing list before she sent it to avoid embarrassment. She opened the message. It was brief and written in a shorthand that it took her a moment to understand.

Sounds gd Rch. I'm coming up to Manch to do a gig for Jalil 4 July. If it's same wknd count me in. If you need a dj I'll have my decks and synth with me. Lt me know. Gd luck!

Rachel gasped. It was that easy! She didn't even know what she was planning yet but she already had a DJ. She wondered whether to do some sort of disco. She smiled, closed the computer down and went to bed.

In the following days she received messages from Frannie, Petal, Jalil and Hugh. All agreed to support her event, but much more than that, they all offered to help in whatever way they could. Frannie's wife had replied on his behalf, asking her if she required any music as her son's orchestra sometimes did charity events. She continued by offering to provide some baked goods, and suggested a number of ideas she had previously tried out at school fundraisers. She also offered the services of Frannie on whichever station Rachel needed help with, adding that they could always use his stomach as a bouncy castle if necessary.

Hugh thanked her for her email and said that he would try to make it, offering to speak to his friends at the aerodrome if she wanted to use the clubhouse.

Petal very sweetly agreed to come, adding that she didn't have much to offer but that she was happy to do some yoga and meditation sessions if Rachel wanted her to.

Rachel was overwhelmed by the support she was receiving from the people around her. However, the emails hadn't helped her to decide what sort of event she should do. One minute she was thinking about a sponsored yoga session, the next, an orchestra recital, the next minute she decided that she should do the disco as McKenzie had been the first to offer.

'I just don't want to offend anyone now they've offered to help,' she whined to Charlie when he returned home from work.

'Well don't.'

'What do you mean—I can't do all of these things.'

'Why not? We could make it a family fun-day, have a bit of variety. I'm fairly sure there was a big garden area outside the clubhouse at the aerodrome. I reckon we could fit a bouncy castle on there. Get a barbecue going too. Sod it, let's just do a bit of everything. If it's a disaster then who cares—at least we've tried.'

'Do you know what Charlie, you're right. I love you!'

JALIL AND McKENZIE

Jalil watched McKenzie in awe as he set up the most amazing sound equipment that he'd ever seen. He had told himself that he was going to act cool and just watch casually as McKenzie set up some synthesisers, speakers and a set of decks, but he couldn't help picking things up and asking for a detailed description of their function.

'I'd love to be a sound engineer,' he told McKenzie, who had a single headphone pressed to his ear as he tested a particular loop.

'You could do it, man. You're smart enough. I mean, *I* think I know a lot about this gear, but this is only half of it. The proper sound engineers are like, geniuses. You should get yourself on a course. Who knows, if I ever get a second chance I could hire you!'

'Yeah,' grinned Jalil, his smile reflecting the general state of his well-being since he had taken the flight weeks earlier. 'Hey, I didn't tell you I'd booked a holiday. I'm doing it— I'm going to Kavos with the boys.'

McKenzie gave his apprentice a high five. 'Awesome! The clubs out there are wicked! Maybe I should get myself out there too. Earn a few quid. Anything's gotta be better than working at the call centre.' He put on a bored, monotone voice. 'Hello, Instant Finance, How can I help you?'

Jalil felt sorry for McKenzie. 'Is it really that bad?'

'Bad? It's so boring I actually offer to make the tea at least five times a day. I don't even drink tea but it saves me from wanting to hang myself with my headset. You know, even if I did that, I reckon my robot colleagues would just look up at me dangling from the ceiling and say "Hello, How-Can-I-Help-You?"'

Jalil laughed. McKenzie did a great robot impression.

'So where is the birthday girl?' asked McKenzie, looking towards the kitchen area of the social club where women were relaying plates of food covered in tin foil from behind the heavy double doors.

'She's not arriving until later. Apparently all the girls have booked into a hotel to get ready together.'

'Jesus Christ, I hope it's not my hotel,' he laughed.

'Doubt it,' shrugged Jalil. 'You know you could have stayed at mine.'

McKenzie nodded. 'Yeah, I know—cheers. It's just easier, with all my gear, you know.'

They both nodded.

'So, have you got any further with Holly?' asked McKenzie as he slid dials up and down to get the perfect sound.

'This has helped,' smiled Jalil gesturing towards

McKenzie. 'I know I keep saying it, but thanks, man. She was so hyper when I told her. She didn't believe me at first. She didn't believe that I knew you. But once she got over that and realised I wasn't bluffing she has been, like, my best friend.'

'Hmmm,' laughed McKenzie. 'That wasn't really what we were aiming for, was it!'

'No, but it's fine. We chat a lot at school, mainly about music. Then in the evenings we Facebook each other all the time. We talk about other stuff then. More personal things. Things it's harder to talk about face-to-face. So that's it really. I still fancy her, but if I get to stay friends with her then that's cool too.'

'Don't give up yet, mate.'

A dance track began to play from somewhere under the decks. Jalil looked around for the source of the music.

'That's my phone,' explained McKenzie. 'Here—have a listen to this and see what you think.' He handed Jalil the headphones with a sample of one of his new tracks before turning away to take the phone call.

'McKenzie, it's Alfie.'

McKenzie's heart sank. He knew exactly what his former manager was calling for. He would be demanding the return of the contract that McKenzie had failed to return, terminating their working relationship.

'Hello,' he said flatly.

'You are one lucky little bastard,' he said without further introduction. 'It's not often that you get second chances in this industry, but this, sunshine, is your lucky day.'

McKenzie's heart raced. 'I'm back in the band?'

'It's looking that way.'

'But why? What made you change your mind?'

'Two words—your mum!'

McKenzie groaned. 'You what? Oh my God—I had no idea Alfie, I didn't send her, oh Jesus Christ what the hell has she said?' Even without knowing the details, McKenzie felt like crawling under the table to hide from the mortification of what his mum might have said or done.

'…Well actually, it wasn't just your mum. The new kid we auditioned—Chime Boy—the others can't work with him, and if the whole band goes tits up then my arse is on the line. Plus I won't get my bonus this year, which my girlfriend will not be happy about. So, the bottom line kid, is that you're back in.'

McKenzie raised his eyes skywards and mouthed a silent thank you. 'Thank you, thank you so much Alfie, you won't regret it…'

'Hang on, there are some conditions.'

'Ok. If you think I'm going to fuck up again I won't, Alfie, I promise…'

'Your fear of flying!'

McKenzie gulped. 'It wasn't my mum's business to tell you about that,' he replied defensively.

'You should have told me yourself. It could have saved your arse—and mine! To be honest it seemed so far-fetched that I didn't even believe it at first, but when Little Gee backed it up I realised that it was fucking true!'

'Little Gee told you as well?' McKenzie felt betrayed by the two people in his life who were the closest to him.

'They were doing you a favour kid—you should be

thanking them! Luckily at Dark Star Records we don't see problems—we see opportunities. And this is a perfect marketing opportunity. We'll stick out some press releases. A story like this should get us at least a few columns in *NME* and the other industry rags. You, in the meantime, need to get back to rehearsals. The arena tour is weeks away and you need to get yourself back up to speed. Phone Little Gee and get yourself over there pronto.'

'What, now? I can't, Alfie. I'm in Manchester.'

'Manchester? What the fuck are you doing up there?'

'I'm doing a favour for a mate.'

'Tomorrow then?'

'The gig is tomorrow. It's a charity event for a sick kid.' McKenzie wondered whether Alfie's patience was thinning. 'Alfie, I've promised! I said I'd play a few records, that's all—I can't let them down. The little girl and her family are all going to be there. I'll come back straight afterwards and be back in London on Saturday night if you like.'

The line went quiet.

'Alfie? I'm sorry, I…'

'What charity? Where?'

'It's for Dravet Syndrome—it's a rare neurological disorder. I think it affects one in 40,000 kids or something. It's kinda like really bad epilepsy, only worse. The parents have hired the clubhouse at the airfield.'

'Can you text me all that—my spelling is shit.'

'Err—yeah, ok,' replied McKenzie, wondering why on earth Alfie was interested. He signed off and glanced over to Jalil who seemed to be enjoying the new tracks that McKenzie had written.

'These are great,' smiled Jalil when McKenzie returned to the small stage where the equipment was installed.

'Thanks. Hey, you'll never guess who that was!'

The whole of the sixth form plus a number of other people had turned up at Holly's party, mainly to get a glimpse of McKenzie. Jalil was feeling the full effect of McKenzie's reflected glory, and, as a friend of the star, was the person everyone wanted to be seen with. He had made an effort with his hair and his clothes, and spent a lot of the evening wandering back and forth between the dance floor and the equipment decks. On a number of occasions he caught himself beaming with self-satisfaction and consciously had to remind himself to look cool. He almost burst with pride when McKenzie handed him the headphones and asked him to mix a record whilst he concentrated on the synths.

Every time he looked at Holly his heart jumped. She looked amazing. Too good! She wore a tight pink dress with a set of heels that made her legs look like a supermodel's. She told him that her hair had been professionally done. As she leant in to tell him this over the sound of the music, he inhaled deeply. Her long, teased locks of hair smelt delicious. He vowed to remember that smell for the rest of his life!

There was a bar in the social club which was only serving people who could produce the correct ID, but, for the kids who had not yet reached eighteen there were plenty of others willing to buy alcopops on their behalf. Jalil, however, was on such a natural high that he didn't need alcohol. McKenzie only drank water when he worked, and

Jalil, as his assistant for the evening, was happy to follow McKenzie's example. As the music continued, Jalil noticed some of his friends getting worse and worse for wear.

He was glad to see that Robbo and Zain were enjoying themselves. They seemed to be getting friendly with a couple of the girls from the lower sixth. Ever since the incident on the railway line, things had changed between them—for the better. The teasing had stopped, and not a single word had been spoken about Jalil's fear of flying. They had only spoken about the incident itself once, days after it happened. They had been shocked by Jalil's actions, and without having to be told, they understood why the little switch in his brain had suddenly flipped. It had been awkward at first. He had seen the little glances that Robbo and Zain gave each other each time someone made a joke, as if they were worried that Jalil had completely lost his sense of humour and might do something stupid again in reaction. But slowly, gradually, the status quo was restored. When Jalil announced that he would be joining them in Kavos they had seemed genuinely delighted. With the holiday only weeks away, things were definitely looking up for Jalil.

McKenzie continued his set. It was a good test run for the new tunes he had written. It was always interesting to see how they were received, and the first indications were all good! He played a mixture of Urban Phantoms tracks and popular dance music. This kind of party was what he had been brought up on—it had been his bread and butter. The gig the following day, however, was more concerning to him. He had no idea what the fuck he should play at a family fun-day. They would have been better off just hooking up someone's iTunes account to a speaker, but since had made the offer he felt that he couldn't back out. In any case—he could always do that if the grannies and the kids weren't getting into his usual vibe.

The set was due to finish at one a.m., and by 12.30, only a few of the teenagers had drifted off to either have sex or vomit. Jalil discovered that Becca had fallen into the latter category.

'She promised she'd stay until the end,' complained Holly to Jalil, who was listening intently to her as she slurred her words slightly. 'She was supposed to be sharing a room with me at the hotel.'

Jalil smiled. 'I saw the state of her when she was dragged out of here by her dad and, believe me, you wouldn't want to be sharing a room with her tonight!'

Holly looked him directly in the eyes and twisted a long lock of her hair round her index finger. 'But I'll be all on my own,' she pouted, her thick black eyelashes waving up and down like miniature fans.

Jalil felt his boxer shorts tighten. 'Err—would you like me to walk you back to your hotel later?'

She smiled coyly. 'Yes please! I'd like that a lot.' She leant in and gave him a single, gentle, kiss on the lips, before turning briskly away and joining a group of her friends on the dance floor.

Jalil stood rooted to the spot for a few seconds before he realised that he looked like a dick. He scurried back to where McKenzie was working up to the end of his set.

'I clocked that, mate!' smirked McKenzie.

Jalil didn't reply. He just touched his lips gently.

'Looks like you've pulled!'

Jalil smiled cautiously for a moment, before his admission. 'She's drunk! She'd never have done that if she'd been sober.'

'I dunno, Jalil. Lots of people show their true feelings after they've had a few.'

Jalil thought about it. 'I can't do it. I'd be a complete twat to take advantage of her when she's drunk.'

McKenzie shrugged. 'Your call, mate.'

Jalil couldn't believe he was travelling in a taxi, on his way to a hotel room where he had been invited to spend the night with Holly. It had been close enough to walk, but given the late hour, they had decided to go by cab. She had her head on his shoulder and was holding his hand. Her hair smelt as delicious as it had done hours earlier. Her high heels were on his lap—she had removed them as soon as they had got in the taxi. When they reached the Travelodge, he took her hand and led her through the maze of corridors to her room. He slid the card in the lock and opened the door.

'Bloody hell! I thought girls were supposed to be tidy!' he exclaimed in genuine shock at the carnage that awaited him when he entered the room. Items of clothing were strewn across the two beds, towels had been dropped on the floor and left there. Make-up, hairspray cans, glasses—some empty, some still half full of not so sparkly wine—and electrical gadgets littered every available surface. The smell of perfume and hairspray still lingered heavily.

Holly stumbled in and flopped backwards on the double bed.

'Hey, let me move these for you,' offered Jalil.

She sighed heavily as he rolled her gently off a pile of clothes that were getting crumpled beneath her.

'Come here,' she whispered in a baby voice. She held her arms out to receive him on the bed.

He tried to slow down the racing of his heart. This was what he wanted. This was what he had been waiting for. He'd got to know Holly so well over the last few weeks, it had only made him want this moment even more. But it was for that reason that he knew he couldn't have sex with her. If he took advantage of her tonight then the friendship might be over forever. He felt like kicking his own arse for what he was about to do, but instead of falling on the bed with her he disappeared into the bathroom to get her a drink of water.

'Drink that, otherwise you'll feel rough tomorrow.'

'Are you getting in?' she asked.

'Holly—you're drunk. I can't.'

'Just a cuddle?' she pleaded.

He looked at her—the ultimate image of gorgeousness. Lying in front of him. He was aware that a certain part of his body was giving her a different message than the one coming out of his mouth. He wondered what it would be like to fall asleep with that sweet smelling hair on the same pillow. Surely a cuddle wouldn't hurt. 'Okay, let's have a cuddle.'

He lay on the bed next to her and wrapped his arms around her gently. He leant over and kissed her on the cheek. 'Happy birthday, Holly,' he whispered.

Within minutes Holly was fast asleep, snoring in a very

unladylike fashion. Jalil pressed his face into her hair and took a deep breath. Whatever happened in the future— right now he felt like the luckiest boy in the world.

FAMILY FUN-DAY

RACHEL

Rachel had been awake since five a.m. Her sleep had been broken with cold sweats and nightmares where she was standing alone in the aerodrome clubhouse, waiting for someone to come and attend her fundraiser, knowing that no one was going to turn up—not even Charlie or her mum. In one of the dreams she had been standing in her underwear, having been in so much of a hurry that she had forgotten to get dressed. It wasn't even nice matching underwear either! She felt sick with nerves. She hadn't even felt this anxious about her wedding!

At seven a.m. her mobile phone rang. Rachel felt her stomach lurch even further. No one ever called at this time of the morning. She immediately concluded that something dreadful had happened to one of their parents, and by the time she answered the call her heart was pounding in her ribcage.

'Hello,' she cried urgently.

'Hello, is that Rachel?'

'Speaking,' she replied.

'Rachel, my name is Alfie Diamond. I work for Dark Star Records. I'm so sorry to call you so early but I wanted to talk to you about the fundraising event you are holding at City airport this afternoon. I wanted to catch you before you left.'

'Ok,' said Rachel, struggling to understand who this person was and why he was interested in her fundraiser.

'I believe that my client, Big Mac, is volunteering to help at your event.'

'Err—I'm sorry?' questioned Rachel.

'I beg your pardon, *you* might know him as McKenzie. I'm the manager of his band—the Urban Phantoms.'

Rachel began to make some sense of the conversation through her sleep-deprived brain. 'Oh, yes. McKenzie is going to be our DJ for the day. Lovely boy—do you know he's come all the way up from London just to help us out!'

'Yes, yes. Indeed. Which is why I'm calling. Now, you may not be aware of this but the Urban Phantoms are a very popular breakthrough band. They have a lot of followers already and after they do their arena tour in a couple of months we are hoping they'll hit the big time.'

'Oh, really?' said Rachel. She was surprised to hear that McKenzie's band were important enough to have a manager, never mind having fans, although she was hoping that this Alfie bloke would get to the point of the conversation. She eyed up the pile of bread rolls that needed cutting for the barbecue. Her mum was coming round at eight a.m. to help her prepare the rest of the food, but she needed to make a start if she was going to be ready to leave at ten-thirty in order to set things up at the clubhouse.

'Yes. I understand that McKenzie didn't want to make a big fuss or draw any attention to himself, but when we heard about what he was offering to do for little Poppy, we felt that he could do more for the charity with a bit of publicity behind him.'

'Oh, ok,' said Rachel, feeling a little nervous. 'You *do* realise that it's just a little event? We're having a family fun-day. Just a barbecue, some music, some demonstrations, and a bouncy castle for the kids, a few stalls, that sort of thing.' She was hoping that he wasn't going to send someone from the newspaper along who would turn up and be disappointed at the low scale of the event.

'And a parachute jump,' laughed Alfie.

'What? I'm really sorry but I think you've made a mistake. I haven't organised anything like…'

'I know Rachel—I have! It was too good an opportunity to miss!' he bellowed gleefully. 'I had a little chat with the marketing team at the office and we wondered what we could do to generate some interest in one of our hottest talents, who just so happens to have a fear of flying, and then—bingo! We came up with it.'

Rachel was confused. 'With what?'

'McKenzie is not only going to get himself *into* an aeroplane in support of your charity—he's going to jump out of one!'

'He's going to do what?'

'Don't worry—it's all organised. I had my team on it last night. You don't need to do another thing. I just wanted to let you know that there's a chance you might get an influx of Urban Phantoms fans turning up to support the event. Oh and the press of course. *NME* have confirmed. A couple of the other industry papers have said they might come if they can get someone up to Manchester in time. *The Daily Mirror* seemed pretty interested in the story too. Oh and of course we've got the regional news on the case. I thought I'd better ring you early in case you needed to increase the catering order.'

Rachel placed a hand on the top of her head and cursed herself for putting off her hair appointment for the last few weeks. She was going to be in the national newspaper with split ends and grey roots! Then she looked over at the ten packets of Tesco value buns she had bought the previous evening and blanched.

'Of course, we are promoting this all via social media. All of the Twitter and Facebook feeds for the band have links to an electronic payment site where people can donate to your Dravet Syndrome Charity. I've just received an email from my secretary saying that we've got over a thousand pounds already—and we only got it live late last night.'

'Ohmigod!' whispered Rachel in disbelief.

'And Dark Star Records will obviously match any amount that is raised through the website.'

At that moment Charlie appeared in the kitchen wearing his old blue dressing gown, bed hair sticking up at odd angles from his head. He looked at her with a worried expression through his bleary eyes.'

'I don't know what to say,' she stammered. 'Thank you.'

'Good luck—I'm leaving shortly so I'm hoping to be

there by lunchtime. The rest of the band will be there too. Bye, Rachel.'

Rachel ended the call and looked at Charlie with wide-eyed shock. 'I think we're going to need more bread rolls!'

FRANNIE

The round dining table in Frannie's kitchen was covered in piles of paper. He had been putting off the recruitment issue for several weeks now, preferring to concentrate on the side of the job that he felt more comfortable with— the technical responsibilities of his new role as Finance Director of Manchester Aerospace Engineering. Knowing that he could no longer delay the job of recruiting a new PA, he decided to bring the work home with him. Which was how he now found himself studying a pile of CVs over his Saturday morning tea and toast.

'I thought you'd decided on one?' said Kim curtly as she eyed the pile of papers that were messing up her immaculately tidy kitchen.

'I'm not sure about that one now,' answered Frannie who was distractedly scrutinising another CV whilst scratching his chin.

'Why not? She had plenty of experience didn't she?'

'Hmm,' he muttered. 'I'm just not sure I trust anyone

who lists their main hobby as "Collecting Pink Things.""

'I'm sure there's no harm in her.'

'Exactly! She'd turn up on the first day on a bloody unicorn and wouldn't last the week with the lads at our place. No, I'm just not entirely happy with any of these. I need someone who I know I'm going to get along with. Someone I can trust.'

'Don't frigging look at me!' cried Kim.

Frannie scoffed. 'Don't flatter yourself! It's bad enough that I have to listen to you bossing me about at home. The only peace I get from you is when I'm at work. I wouldn't give you the job if you were the last person on earth.'

'Well that's good cos I wouldn't bloody take it if it was the only job on earth,' she laughed. 'So what are you going to do? You need an assistant. That I *do* know. You've always had me organising things for you at home—you've never had to do a thing. You'll get snowed under in no time if you don't sort something out soon.'

'I need someone who is organised and who I know I'll be able to get along with. But also someone who would be prepared to travel out to this side of Manchester and who's prepared to work for the poxy salary that they've budgeted.' He gestured to the pile of CVs on the table. 'Most of this lot will piss off as soon as something better comes along.'

PETAL

Petal chewed unenthusiastically at a corner of her triangular shaped piece of toast, trying to force down some breakfast ahead of her busy day. Her appetite had been waning recently in correlation with her general state of happiness. She sipped at her cup of herbal tea as she brushed loose tobacco debris off the kitchen table where Moon and Ash had been rolling their joints the night before.

After the fiasco of the graduation flight, Petal had felt herself falling deeper and deeper into a black despair at the state of her life. She should have been mortified at what happened in front of Hugh and the students from the Fear of Flying Club, but the truth was she felt very little anymore. It was as if someone had anesthetised her to life itself. Life had continued, of course. She went through the motions of doing her yoga classes, and feigning enthusiasm for the food that Moon brought back from his skip raiding, but since the realisation finally dawned on her that she would be stuck in this life forever, with no chance of becoming a mother or getting out of Jubilee House, she was numb to everything around her.

She had been pleased to receive the email from Rachel, not only inviting her to the event, but asking for her help. That must mean that she didn't think Petal was a complete waste of space. She knew that there wasn't much she could do to help, but Rachel had seemed pleased with her idea of an outdoor yoga session, which was what she was preparing herself for as she ate her meagre breakfast. She looked at the clock on the kitchen wall and realised that she had absolutely nothing to do until Frannie and his family picked her up in a couple of hours' time. Her life was hollow and pointless. She put her toast down and stared into space.

JALIL

When Jalil opened his eyes it took him a moment to get his bearings. The room was dark, but before his optic senses had time to wake up, a familiar smell made him jolt awake with the sudden realisation of where he was. He turned his head very slowly and gently to avoid disturbing the sleeping beauty to his left. Piles of fragrant hair trailed across the pillow from where she lay sleeping. He watched her for a moment, too scared almost to breathe in case he woke her up. He knew that when she woke the spell of last night would be over, and she would go back to being just his friend.

He took one final deep breath, savouring her perfume, before transferring his weight slowly and carefully onto his right arm so that he could prise himself out of the bed without waking her. He had almost managed it when she began to stir. He froze, willing her to go back to sleep. Moments later her eyes fluttered and she gazed at him with a confused look on her face.

'Hey?' she said.

'Hey. Listen, I just want you to know that nothing happened. I didn't even get undressed—look.' He gestured to his crumpled shirt and trousers that he had slept in.

'That's ok,' she said grimacing. 'My head is a bit sore. Did I have a good night?'

'It was awesome,' he replied. 'The best party ever. Everyone was saying that.'

Holly made an attempt to sit up in the bed.

'Stay there—I'll get you a drink of water.'

'Are you sure?'

'Of course.' Jalil scurried into the bathroom and looked at his reflection in the mirror as he ran the tap and filled the small plastic cup from the bathroom shelf with tepid water. *Ohmigod*, he thought. This is going to be really awkward. He took a deep breath and walked back into the bedroom where Holly was sitting up in the double bed, her hair tousled, dress slightly twisted and make up still in place. 'Sorry, it's not very cold,' he apologised.

She took the small cup and drank the contents in one go. 'It's fine,' she said. 'Thank you—I needed that.'

'So…' said Jalil, struggling to find a way out of this excruciating situation. 'I'd better go.'

'Really?' she said.

'Yeah—I'd better let you get ready. I'm sure you've got loads on today.'

She shook her head. 'Nothing.'

Jalil shifted from one foot to the other. 'Oh, right. Well, errr…'

'Would you like to stay a bit longer?' she asked,

maintaining a cool eye contact which Jalil struggled to return.

'Well, erm, yes. I mean, of course. As long as you want me to.'

Holly threw the covers back and patted the empty space in the bed next to her. 'Get back in,' she smiled.

Jalil struggled to contain the look of shock on his face. He tentatively got back into the bed fully clothed and pulled the covers back over him. Before he knew what was happening, Holly had thrown her arms around him. He rolled over to face her and she kissed him, slowly and deeply on the lips. It was the most mind blowing kiss he had ever had. He returned the kiss gently. Holly responded by kissing him more urgently. He pulled her closer to him and she began to tug at his clothes.

'Wait I haven't got a...'

'In my bag,' she whispered.

Jalil flew out of bed and began to ransack the room in search of Holly's bag. She giggled as he held up shopping bags, make up bags, and spare handbags until he found the right one. He jumped back in with the condom in his hand. 'I think I should warn you, this is all kind of new to me,' he explained shyly.

'Don't worry—you're doing just fine,' she replied before pulling the sheets over both of their heads and disappearing underneath.

McKENZIE

McKenzie woke up in the overheated hotel room and kicked the covers off. His alarm had not yet gone off. He automatically reached for his phone to see what time it was. It was only eight-thirty. Overnight he had received more than twenty messages and eight missed calls. Confused, he rubbed his eyes and sat up in bed. His smartphone also indicated that he had over forty Facebook notifications and hundreds of tweets on his Twitter feed.

'What the fuck?' he muttered sleepily to himself.

He started with the text messages, but what he read didn't make any sense to him. Lots of people were wishing him luck for today. He scrolled down and saw more of the same. Then he saw two words which made his jaw drop to his chest—parachute jump. Before he had a chance to compute any of the information he had read, his phone erupted into life.

'Hello?' he said, still shaking his head in total and utter confusion.

'Big Mac, it's Alfie.'

'Alfie—what the hell…?'

'No need to thank me boy, no need to thank me. You're trending on all the major social networks as we speak. Now where are you?'

'I'm in bed—I've just woken up. Now can you tell me what the actual fuck is going on?'

'You, young man, are going to go from media villain to media hero in a matter of hours.'

'A parachute jump?' said McKenzie incredulously.

'Correct. Fucking genius idea that was. One of my finer moments.'

'A fucking parachute jump!' repeated McKenzie. 'Are you out of your fucking mind!' he squealed.

'I'm perfectly sane thank you. Now listen—this is just marketing *gold*. Young pop star, afraid of flying throws himself out of a plane for charity. I've even got the TV interested!'

'Can I stop you right there and tell you that there is no way, not even in the realms of your tiny, warped fucking imagination that this is happening!'

'Too late, Kenz, it's all sorted. I've just checked your fundraising page again and you've already got nearly three grand in sponsorship.'

'My what?' snapped McKenzie.

'Your fundraising page. Again, no need to thank me kid. Now listen—you need to get yourself over to the airfield for ten a.m. A fella called Liam is going to meet you there and do all of the health and safety nonsense with you before you do the jump at three p.m.'

'Hang on—you can't just do this without consulting me. Even if I had agreed to do this, which I quite fucking clearly haven't, you seem to be forgetting one minor detail. I don't do planes!'

'Yes you do, kid! And anyway—your mum told me that you've been on a course to sort it out.'

'The course was shite!' he screamed. 'Yes, I managed to do one small flight without getting off my tits on valium and vodka, but I don't think it means I'm ready to go chucking myself out of the sky for your fucking entertainment!'

'Well I'm very sorry you feel like that,' said Alfie gravely. 'I'm sure that that little girl's mum will completely understand when I phone her back and tell her that she's not going to get the thousands of pounds for her kids charity that I promised her earlier.'

'You rang Rachel?' shouted McKenzie.

'Oh yes. Dead pleased she was too, thinking that all those kiddies could be helped with your sponsorship money.'

McKenzie moaned and tugged at his hair. 'For fuck's sake, Alfie.'

'So shall I phone her back then—tell her you've bottled it?'

At that moment, McKenzie knew that he had no choice but to go through with Alfie's stupid, selfish publicity stunt.

'You are one ruthless cunt, Alfie,' groaned McKenzie.

'Why thank you, young man. That's the best compliment I've had all morning. Now check your mail—I've sent you the details!'

RACHEL

Rachel flitted round her kitchen in a complete fluster. Charlie had been sent out to buy more burgers before he had even had his first mouthful of morning tea and her mum, who had arrived with her next door neighbour in tow, seemed more interested in discussing the television coverage than in providing butter coverage on the bread.

'I wish I'd known, Rachel,' complained Jean. 'I would have brought my hair appointment forward. And look at the state of me,' she gestured to her beige trousers and cotton top. 'I would have worn my new dress.' She sighed. 'Or at the very least put a decent bra on.' Jean looked down at her breasts in dismay.

'I really don't think they are interested in your chest, Mum,' replied Rachel irritably as she slammed the fridge door closed whilst simultaneously opening a cupboard door in search of the two large bottles of ketchup she knew she had bought the day before. 'Where the fuck are they?' she muttered.

'Err, language!' reprimanded Jean. 'We can't have any swearing in front of the television people. And I don't just mean Fs. That goes for Bs and Ss and...?' Jean racked her brain for her anthology of swear words.

'Peas!' cried Rachel, suddenly remembering that she had forgotten to ask Charlie to pick up some frozen peas for the pasta salad.

Jean and her neighbour gave each other a quizzical look. 'Prick?' Jean mouthed curiously.

Jasmine wandered into the kitchen in her pyjamas and began picking up the large bags of crisps. 'Mmmmm,' she said.

'Jasmine—I told you to get dressed half an hour ago. Can you please go and do it,' said Rachel, far more sharply than she had intended.

'You didn't put any clean knickers out for me,' said Jasmine by way of explanation.

Rachel's stress levels were reaching capacity. Organising the fun-day had taken her completely out of her comfort zone to begin with. Now it had grown out of control, and even worse, they were going to be late if they didn't hurry.

'You know where your clean knickers are kept,' she yelled. 'Go and get a pair! Now!'

'*So-ree*,' huffed Jasmine, marching back upstairs to get dressed.

'Mum, do you think we've got time to bake some more cakes? I'm worried that we might not have enough.'

Jean looked at the clock and then glanced around at the bombsite of a kitchen. 'We've baked four dozen between us, that'll have to do. If we run out, then so be it. Calm down, love. It will all be fine.'

'Will it?' said Rachel. At that moment in time she was beginning to think that she might have made a huge mistake.

PETAL AND FRANNIE

Moon was just getting out of bed as Petal was getting ready to leave. She had been ready for hours.

'What's for breakfast?' asked Moon, scratching his scalp through his long matted hair.

'It's nearly lunchtime, Moon,' she replied. 'You'll have to have a look for yourself—I'm going out now.'

Moon looked confused. 'Where to?'

She replied with one word. 'Yoga.'

She felt less and less inclined to elaborate on anything lately, choosing to provide Moon with only skeleton information. It just took too much of her energy. She picked up her roll of yoga mats and her bottle of water and headed for the front door. 'I'm not sure what time I'll be back. I'll see you later.'

She walked towards the main road where she had arranged for Frannie to pick her up. The summer sun warmed her shoulders as she travelled. She didn't even notice the group of teenagers who now sniggered at her every time she passed them.

Frannie arrived exactly on schedule in his tidy people carrier. Petal put her yoga mats in the space in the back of the car next to Frannie's daughter, Hannah. There were already some bags in there, as well as Simon's violin case. She climbed into the middle row of seats next to Simon.

'Hello everyone. Thank you so much for this—it would have taken me hours on public transport.'

'No problem, love,' replied Frannie and Kim.

The car was cool and clean. Petal listened as Frannie's family chatted easily amongst themselves. A One Direction song came on the radio.

'Listen, Hannah—it's your favourite band,' teased Simon.

Hannah took the bait. 'No it isn't. You know I hate them. They're for kids.'

'Oh, and you're not a kid?' laughed Simon.

'No, I'm not a kid, I'm a tween,' retorted Hannah with absolute conviction.

'Remember when you used to be in love with Harry?' laughed Simon, pleased that he was getting such a quick reaction from her.

'I was not,' squealed Hannah. 'Mu-uum. Tell him. Tell him to stop telling lies.'

'Alright you two—that's enough,' shouted Frannie flatly. He looked at Petal. 'Teenagers hey—who'd have em?'

'I think you're all so lucky to have each other!' said Petal, genuinely.

Hannah and Simon looked at each other and pulled a horrified face.

JALIL

Jalil was waiting at the bus stop with Holly. They had two suitcases between them, both of which Jalil felt were completely ridiculous for a single night's stay.

'Do we need to drop Becca's stuff off at her house?' he asked.

'No, she said she'll come and get it later, when she's feeling better.'

Jalil laughed. 'Feeling rough is she?'

Holly smiled and nodded. 'She's been throwing up all night apparently. She says she can't remember a thing past ten o'clock.'

'I'm not surprised,' said Jalil. 'She was battered!'

The bus approached and they struggled on board with their cases. They found a double seat and sat down. They held hands shyly as the bus pulled away.

'Do you have any plans for later on?' asked Holly.

Jalil thought about Rachel's charity event. He had promised that he would go and support it, but was fairly sure that whatever Holly was about to propose would be a zillion times preferable.

'Err—I've kind of promised a friend I'd go to a charity gig.'

'Oh, ok,' replied Holly, sounding slightly disappointed.

'But, you know, I suppose I don't have to,' he stuttered.

'No, if you've said you'll go then you should go,' she replied.

The bus chugged along through the busy streets of the Manchester city outskirts. They both looked out of the window in silence.

'You could always come along?' Jalil suggested tentatively after the silence was becoming awkward.

'Really?'

'Well, only if you want to. I mean—don't feel like you have to or anything. It's just a family fun-day for a kid's charity. But McKenzie will be there, so the music might be ok.'

'I'd love to,' she beamed. 'Let's drop this stuff off at mine. I'll quickly get changed and we'll go from there.'

Jalil was suddenly struck with terror. 'Will your mum and dad be okay with me turning up with you? What will you tell them?'

Holly laughed. 'I'll tell them that you stayed and looked after me last night.'

'Fucking hell,' said Jalil. 'Won't your dad, like, kill me or something?'

'Well I'm not going to broadcast the fact that we had sex. Twice!' she laughed. 'Although I'm sure they will have worked that part out themselves.'

'Shit,' mumbled Jalil.

Holly nudged him playfully on the arm. 'Don't worry—they really like you! They're just relieved that I'm not hanging out with that other idiot anymore.'

'Who? The drug dealer?'

'Hmm,' she nodded. 'He was Becca's mate really, not mine. I never actually liked him to be honest. Anyway, my mum and dad will be so pleased when they see you that you won't need to worry about a thing.'

'I bloody hope not!'

McKENZIE

McKenzie was lying face down on a padded table in a dish position, arms stretched out in front, ankles crossed, wondering how the fuck this had happened to him. The skydiving instructor was teaching him the various positions that his body needed to be in during the different stages of the skydive. He kept telling himself not to worry, because clearly he was going to wake at any moment. That this had to be a terrible nightmare.

He was aware of a flow of words coming from the instructor's mouth, but his brain had defaulted to a state of stunned inertia and so the messages were not being received properly.

After a period of time—he had no idea how long—he was led from the training room out to the airfield so that he could look at the plane which would be taking him to jumping altitude.

As he walked out into the blinding sunshine in his royal blue jumpsuit, he heard some familiar cries from across the field.

'Looks like you've got some fans,' laughed the instructor.

'It's my band,' replied McKenzie, stunned to see the familiar profiles of Little Gee, Kitty and The Prof in the distance. 'I didn't know they were coming. Could you give me, like, one minute to go and say hello?'

'Certainly,' said the instructor.

McKenzie started to jog towards the band, who had turned up in The Prof's van, but found that his legs weren't working properly. As he approached he heard a cacophony of cheers, whistles and whooping.

'What are you lot doing here?' he asked.

'We couldn't miss this! Not for anything,' laughed the Prof. 'Hey, you're looking a bit pale. Are you ok?'

'Err, do I look ok? There's a reason these trousers are elasticated at the bottom and it's fuck all to do with aerodynamics!'

'You'll be fine,' laughed Kitty. 'People do these all the time. You're lucky to get the chance to do it!'

'You bloody do it then,' he snapped.

'I can't—we're in charge of music now that you're doing your stunt.'

McKenzie looked at Little Gee pleadingly. Surely his oldest friend would understand. 'Come on, man. You've got to help me get out of this. I can't do it—you know I can't.'

Little Gee laughed. 'What exactly do you want me to do?'

McKenzie glanced desperately at the van. 'Have you unloaded yet? We could just do a runner.'

Little Gee raised his eyebrows. 'Oh, yeah, Alfie would

love that wouldn't he? That's exactly the sort of publicity he wants.'

McKenzie looked pained. 'So you're all saying that you're not going to help me. You're seriously all just going to let them force me onto one of the smallest planes in the world and then stand back and watch as they chuck me out of it?'

'Oh, we're not going to stand back and watch,' laughed The Prof. 'We'll all be recording it on our phones too.'

The others fell about laughing.

'You won't be laughing when I die, either splattered on the ground, or of fucking stress. When you've got to work with Chime Boy because none of you would step in and save me. I'll come back and fucking haunt all of you! I'm serious!'

'Go on, your instructor's waiting,' laughed Little Gee.

McKenzie looked at them in disbelief, before turning and making the dead man's walk back to his instructor.

FRIENDS REUNITED

Rachel arrived at the airfield only slightly later than she had planned. She had a lot to prepare and knew it would be difficult trying to set everything up and keep an eye on Poppy at the same time. She waited impatiently for her mum to set up the small cake stall, knowing that she could then hand responsibility for Poppy over to her, allowing Rachel to get on with other things.

She had brought some things for the kids to play with—some hula-hoops, the small inflatable ball pit which both her girls had loved when they were younger and the little plastic water and sand table from her back garden. As Poppy played in the water, she only looked up momentarily at the sound of the bouncy castle being inflated, before turning her attention back to the water toys.

'Do you think people will pay 50p for a cake?' shouted Jean, frowning slightly.

'Yes, Mum, it's all for charity. Are you nearly finished? I need to go and start getting the food ready.'

Jean ignored the question. 'I don't want folk thinking we're ripping them off.'

'Mum—50p is fine. I've already laminated the price signs so they're staying at 50p. Now can you come and look after Poppy for me?'

Jean made a move away from the table, took a quick look back at the display, and began re-arranging the cakes on the cake stand.

'Mum! They're fine.'

'Okay, okay. It's just that if I'm responsible for cakes I want to make sure it's done right. You know—I'm wondering now whether we've got enough.'

'I asked you that this morning, but you said it would be fine,' whined Rachel. 'Oh God—it's going to be a disaster isn't it!'

'Girls. Everything will be fine—will you stop worrying,' shouted Charlie from his position alongside the clubhouse wall where the barbeque was being set up.

McKenzie's friends were setting up lots of sound equipment, and every so often a blast of noise was emitted through a speaker. Rachel had been surprised to find them at the clubhouse when she arrived. They had seemed a nice bunch, and hadn't flinched when she had asked them if they could play some mainstream pop music and some kids' tunes as well as their own music (which she was completely unfamiliar with). She had given them a pile of children's CDs, and Kitty had very sweetly gone through each of the discs with Jasmine and Poppy asking them to pick out their favourite tunes. Rachel had also expressed her astonishment at McKenzie's parachute jump, telling them that it was the last thing on earth she thought McKenzie would be willing to do. They all just laughed.

Rachel hadn't yet had the opportunity to speak to McKenzie as he was in training for his jump. She would make sure that she got to speak to him before the stunt which was scheduled for three p.m.

Frannie had told Rachel that he would be there around noon to allow Simon and the others from the orchestra a chance to set up and tune their instruments. She was surprised then, that the next car to approach was not Frannie's people carrier. She assumed that it must be one of the other kids from the orchestra, and was on her way over to say hello when she recognised two familiar faces.

'Miss Koslowska? Miss Myers? What are you doing here?'

'We've come to support our lovely Poppy, of course,' smiled Miss Koslowska.

Miss Myers beamed at Rachel. 'I hope you don't mind us turning up early, but we thought that we might be able to help by looking after Poppy for you. We know how much effort goes into these fundraisers and we also know that you can't leave little Poppy alone either.'

Rachel was speechless. She had given Miss Myers a set of flyers to give to the children in Poppy's class, but she wasn't really expecting any of them to turn up, never mind the teacher and the teaching assistant. She couldn't believe that they had actually considered how difficult the day would be for her with Poppy there to look after. She couldn't believe that someone finally 'got it.' She felt like hugging them. Instead, she said a genuine and grateful 'thank you' and led them to where Poppy was playing at the water table with her mum.

The next to arrive was Frannie, along with his wife, children and Petal. They all piled out of the people carrier, arms laden with paraphernalia. Kim seemed to be taking charge.

'Hello, Rachel,' said Kim, kissing her on both cheeks. 'Now, if you just tell me where you want the orchestra I'll sort them all out when they get here. I've done a fruit cake for guess the weight of the cake, which Hannah will run, and Frannie is going to do Guess the Name of the Teddy.'

Frannie poked his head out from behind the giant teddy bear that he was carrying with great difficulty. 'Hi, Rachel,' he said.

'Wow—thank you. I don't know what to say,' said Rachel, looking at the beautifully decorated cake that Kim had made which wouldn't have looked out of place on *The Great British Bake-Off*.

'Oh, and there are a couple of dozen cupcakes in there too,' added Kim. 'Frannie—can you get them out of the car please, I don't want them melting.'

'Yes dear,' nodded Frannie obediently.

'Come on, I'll show you where to set up,' replied Rachel, utterly grateful for Kim's assertiveness on every level.

Rachel returned to greet Petal, who had been unloading her yoga mats from the car. She hadn't seen her since the flight day and had been worried about her state of mind. She would have to make sure she took the time to speak to Petal later on, but for now, she pointed over to an area of grass where she thought Petal could do her yoga demonstration and left her to set up.

As one p.m. approached, Rachel felt a familiar sensation of butterflies in her stomach. Almost as severe as the last time she found herself at City aerodrome, but not quite. A gentle breeze rustled the lines of bunting which Charlie had strung around the buildings and gazebos. The barbecue was emitting a delicious smell of hot dogs. Jasmine was dancing to *Gangnam Style* with Kitty in front of the record decks.

'Oh God, someone's coming,' cried Rachel.

Charlie looked up and saw two cars driving down the single track road towards the clubhouse.

'Don't panic!' he laughed. 'That's what we want.'

Within fifteen minutes a steady stream of cars had filed down the track, with others walking down towards the clubhouse from the main parking area of the airport.

'Look—Mia!' cried Poppy.

Rachel looked over to where Poppy was pointing and saw Mia, one of the children from Poppy's class, running towards the bouncy castle. Her mum, dad and older sisters were there too. Rachel immediately went over to say hello. She had never really spoken to Mia's mum before, and was astonished that she had turned up.

'Hi. Thank you so much for coming,' said Rachel, genuinely.

'No problem at all,' said Mia's mum. 'Mia was looking forward to coming, and for us, well, it's nice to be able to do something to help. Here!' she said, holding out a Tupperware box. 'I'm not great at cakes, but I'm pretty good at gingerbread. The girls helped me to decorate them this morning.'

Rachel opened the tin and saw a pile of colourful

gingerbread people, separated with greaseproof paper. 'I don't know what to say,' she gulped.

'Oh, it was nothing! And wait until you see what Lisa has made.'

'Lisa?'

'Harry's mum. She's the cupcake queen! She's made violet frosting for the topping. I've had them before—they are amazing. They taste just like those sweets we used to have when we were kids—Parma Violets. Did you try any of the ones she did for the Christmas fair?'

'No,' muttered Rachel, feeling humbled at the effort these mums who she had dismissed so easily in the past had made for her child. 'I'll go and put these on the cake stall. And thank you again.' She wiped a tear from her eye as she handed the gingerbread men to her mum.

Rachel took a brief step back to survey the scene. Families stood in groups around the bouncy castle, the adults chatting whilst the kids bounced up and down. Rugs had been spread on the grass where people were eating their barbecue lunch and enjoying a drink from the bar. A small group of kids had now joined Kitty and Poppy on the grass in front of the record decks and were dancing to some chart hits. The orchestra were arranging seats and music stands whilst Kim chatted to the conductor about the format for the afternoon. It was then that Rachel noticed McKenzie for the first time. He was heading towards his bandmates dressed in a set of blue overalls. She hurried over to thank him for what he was about to do.

McKenzie had completed his training and was now free

until he was required to board the small plane at ten minutes to three. The instructor had told him to go and get some lunch, but there was no way that he could even consider eating anything. He made his way over to his bandmates, still hoping for a get-out-clause.

'Is he here yet?' McKenzie asked Little Gee.

'I assume you mean our great leader, Alfie!'

'Yeah. If he's not coming then I might be able to get out of it. If we all tell him I did it then who is to know?'

'Too late,' said The Prof, glancing towards the top-of-the-range glossy black Range Rover which was pulling up right in front of the clubhouse.

'Fuck!' said McKenzie.

It was then that Rachel appeared. 'McKenzie. I can't believe what you're going to do for Poppy. I just *cannot* believe it,' she repeated, shaking her head violently. 'When I got that phone call this morning, I thought it must have been some sort of a joke, but then when we looked at the website and saw all that money that had come in already...'

'It's over eight thousand pounds now,' added The Prof with a delighted smile at both McKenzie and Rachel.

'Eight thousand pounds!' gasped Rachel. 'And to think—if it wasn't for you we would just have had a few cakes to sell and the proceeds from the bouncy castle. Honestly, McKenzie, I don't know how I can ever thank you!'

'We're running a little sweepstake on how many times he goes to the toilet before the jump,' laughed Little Gee. 'That's got to be worth another tenner!'

Rachel rubbed McKenzie's shoulder. 'Are you absolutely

sure that you want to go through with it, love?' she asked. 'Being scared of flying and all that…I mean—it can't be easy.'

McKenzie felt all eyes burning in his direction. What other answer could he possibly give other than the one which stumbled automatically out of his parched mouth? 'Of course, Rachel.'

At that moment the music from the speakers faded right down and the orchestra officially opened the event with their first tune—*Those Magnificent Men in their Flying Machines*.

McKenzie blanched. 'I need to go to the loo,' he shouted as he scurried off in the direction of the clubhouse.

'That's three already,' laughed Little Gee.

As three p.m. approached, the field had filled with people. Local radio had picked up on the piece about McKenzie's parachute jump, and a swathe of teenage Phantoms fans had turned up to get a glimpse of the band. Alfie occupied himself with sweet-talking the press, but did ask Rachel to come and speak to them briefly, which she was pretty horrified about.

'I hope they don't use that on the radio,' she complained to her mum. 'My voice was shaking! I was so nervous.'

'It doesn't matter, love,' said Jean. 'Look around you. Look what you've done! All this is down to you, Rachel.'

'I had a lot of help!' laughed Rachel.

'Even so. I know I don't tell you this very often, because, you know us, we don't do the whole affection thing. Too American for me, but I'm bloody proud of you!' Jean's voice began to quiver.

'Don't!' ordered Rachel. 'I can't do any more tears this week,' she laughed, allowing a couple of salty drops to fall from her eyes before she took control of herself. 'Anyway, it's nearly time for him to jump. Where are Frannie and Petal?' she asked, looking around to alert them so they didn't miss it.

At that moment a small plane took off from the runway. People began to congregate in the middle of the field, eager to get a glance of McKenzie—Big Mac—jumping to raise money for Dravet Syndrome.

Rachel was pleased to see Frannie and Petal heading in her direction. They had been joined by Jalil, who was walking with his arms around the waist of a stunning looking girl. Rachel felt a stab of maternal pride for Jalil— the shy eighteen-year-old who had barely said a word at the first Fear of Flying meeting. Their little team huddled together on the dry, crunchy grass, their faces turned skywards, eyes scrunched tightly.

'Do you think he's actually going to do it?' asked Jalil.

'I can't believe they've even got him this far!' marvelled Frannie. 'And to think…it's all down to Hugh and his Fear of Flying course!'

Rachel laughed. 'Hapless Hugh! I think we got each other through that course, in spite of Hugh. Err—no offence, Petal!'

Petal just nodded and shrugged. Rachel and Frannie exchanged a concerned glance.

'Three minutes to go,' said Jalil.

'Do you know, I feel sick for him,' moaned Rachel.

'Me too! I can't think of a single thing worse than what

that lad's about to do,' said Frannie.

'Come on, love. You can do it,' whispered Rachel, crossing her fingers and waving them at the tiny dot in the sky.

McKenzie sat in a state of trance on the floor of the small aeroplane. The noise of the engine droned pleasantly through his head, blocking out any lucid thoughts his brain might be trying to process. His whole body vibrated gently, as if the plane was soothing him with a sedatory lullaby. He still believed that at any moment he was going to wake up in his own bed. He now knew what people meant when they described out of body experiences. He had not uttered a single word of his own accord in the last hour. He had somehow, automatically trotted out the responses that the instructor had required in the final briefing before they boarded the plane. He was just drifting pleasantly into a deeper void of nothingness when the plane door was heaved open and a gust of cold wind began battering his body. It was like someone had roused him from a deep and peaceful sleep by dousing him with a bucket of ice cold water. He was suddenly, acutely aware of the traumatic event which he was about to undertake. Before he could stop himself, a scream of terror came from the depths of his soul.

'Aaaarrggh!'

His instructor shouted at him with a smile on his face. 'Don't worry—this is the worst part. It always gets people.'

McKenzie spluttered urgently. 'But I'm not most people. You don't understand—I don't like heights or planes or...'

'Everyone thinks that at the moment the doors open,' shouted the instructor. 'If you just remember everything we did in training you will be absolutely fine.'

'I can't remember—I don't know,' he gasped aware that his breathing reflex didn't seem to be working properly.

The instructor made the final checks to the harness. 'Now you need to shuffle across to the exit.'

McKenzie felt himself being pushed gently from behind.

'I don't think I can…'

'Come on now—nearly there.'

McKenzie tried to understand how he had gone from his cocooned oblivion to the raw, exposed state of terrified reality he now found himself in, in a matter of mere minutes. As the instructor shuffled him along he felt his feet lose contact with solid matter. The sensation travelled up the back of his calves, until his entire lower legs, all the way to the back of his knees, dangled helplessly in the air. He gripped onto the doorway of the plane, his fingernails bending against the cold metal.

'Ready?' asked the instructor.

'I…'

And then they were gone—hurtling towards the earth at a death defying speed.

'Aaaaarrrrrgggg!'

'Look!' shouted Jalil, pointing to a tiny black dot in the sky.

A cheer rippled around the airfield as spectators caught their first glance of the plummeting pop star. The Prof had chosen the *Mission Impossible* theme tune to play as

McKenzie descended. As soon as the dramatic music began, Rachel began to get nervous.

'Is this safe?' she asked, suddenly worried that if the parachute failed to deploy, it would be her name splattered across the newspapers too.

'It's a bit late to ask that now,' laughed Charlie.

'Unbelievable,' gasped Frannie.

'Ohmigod—look at the tiny parachute!' cried Rachel. 'That's never going to hold the two of them.' She buried her face in Charlie's chest.

'That's just the guide chute,' Jalil told her.

'Is there going to be another one? Why hasn't it opened yet?'

'Don't panic, Rachel, they know what they are doing,' said Charlie. 'I'm sure McKenzie is loving it.'

'Aaaarrgh, aaaaarrrgghh, aaaarrrgghh.' McKenzie repeated the same sequence of screams the entire way through the free-fall. The pressure of the air was battering his face, taking away his breath and contorting his face. He fought the urge to be sick, and desperately tried to regain control of his bowels. After what seemed like an age, the instructor pulled the cord to deploy the main parachute. Suddenly, it felt like the brakes had been applied. Everything slowed down. It no longer felt like he was being fired towards earth like a bullet. He felt himself being tossed from side to side as the huge silk canopy fought to tame the velocity of the descent. Moments later, the volatility eased, and he opened his eyes for the first time since he had been forced from the plane.

He saw what seemed to be a tiny crowd of ant-like people in the field below. He could make out the square outline of the bouncy castle. The only noise he could hear was the wind whistling past his ears. Everything was suddenly very peaceful. As he floated towards the earth below, he knew that the worst was over. He remembered how to breathe properly, and for the first time that day, he felt a huge sense of relief.

By the time the crowd of people had magnified enough for him to make out individual shapes he was smiling broadly. With fifty feet to go his hearing picked up the first sounds of terra firma. People were clapping and cheering. Mobile phones were being held above heads as the fans tried to capture the moment on camera. He couldn't believe he had actually done it. He began to laugh, loud and uncontrollably.

The instructions from the morning's lesson came back to him, and as the ground came towards him he lifted his legs out in front of him, before taking a few steps and stumbling back onto his bottom. The instructor busied himself unclipping the harness whilst McKenzie sat on the warm ground, laughing to himself. He stood up, and felt the heat of the day overwhelm him. He unzipped his blue jumpsuit and pulled it down to his waist. A smart-suited figure in designer sunglasses approached, grinning sadistically.

'Well done, Big Mac! You've passed your re-initiation!'

McKenzie shook his head. 'You're still a first class twat, Alfie. Consider this quits! Well and truly quits. In fact, no— not quits, you owe me!'

Alfie chuckled. 'Now, now, play nice! The press are recording this. You need to get up, smile, tell them all you fucking loved it, then go and play some music and mingle.'

Rachel had burst into tears the second McKenzie had touched down.

'Hey,' smiled Charlie. 'It's ok.'

'I j-j-just can't b-b-believe he did that for us,' she sobbed.

'I know! He's a true star.'

Jalil had removed his arms from Holly's waist to applaud enthusiastically. 'What a legend!' he beamed.

Even Petal had snapped out of her low mood and was smiling at the waving figure in the blue jumpsuit.

'I'm going to get that lad a beer,' said Frannie, shaking his head in admiration before turning towards the clubhouse.

A camera crew, who had been filming the descent approached Rachel and Charlie. 'Could we do a quick interview?' asked the reporter.

Rachel's eyes widened in horror. 'Go on!' urged Charlie. 'If McKenzie had the guts to jump out of a plane, then the least you can do is give an interview to thank him publicly.'

Rachel knew he was right. 'Has my make-up run?' she asked, wiping beneath her eyes in a futile attempt to clean away the mascara streaks.

'Yes, and you still look beautiful,' said Charlie, kissing her on the lips. 'Come on, we'll do it together.'

Another camera crew were interviewing McKenzie, whilst rival reporters from the press stood by taking notes and photographs. When Rachel had finished her short piece, she hurried over to McKenzie, interrupting him mid-interview to throw her arms around him in a hug of pure gratitude.

'Thank you,' she gasped, tears dripping down her face once again.

Within moments, Kitty, Little Gee and The Prof joined the huddle, slapping their bandmate on the back and shouting words of congratulations. Alfie stood amongst the reporters, pleased with his day's work.

Frannie pushed his way through the media scrum. 'Here you go, lad,' he said, offering McKenzie a cool pint of lager.

Once they had secured their interviews, the reporters disappeared, leaving those gathered on the field to enjoy the rest of the fun-day. The orchestra began their second set of pieces and Petal tasked herself with setting out mats for her final yoga session of the day. Rachel, finally able to relax, grabbed the chance to speak to her before the demonstration.

'Petal, thank you so much for coming today. It really means a lot to all of us.'

'It's no problem at all. I'm glad to help. It's nice to feel useful.'

'Petal,' Rachel stalled. She was unsure how to broach the subject of Petal's breakdown at the graduation flight, but she knew that if she didn't speak to her about it now, she might not get another opportunity. 'Is everything alright? With you, I mean.'

Petal nodded. 'I'm fine.'

Rachel sighed. 'I've been worried about you, love.' She reached out and tentatively stroked Petal's arm. 'I've been thinking about that fella of yours, and, I just think you deserve better.'

That was it—she'd said it. Perhaps a little blunter than she had intended, but it was out there now and there was nothing she could do to take it back.

Petal nodded and after a few moments of silence, replied. 'I did think about leaving him. After that flight. For a moment everything made sense. I'd move on with my life, find love, have a baby...'

'So what happened?' asked Rachel.

'Circumstance!' replied Petal. 'There's no way that either of us could manage financially on our own. I did have a mad moment where I thought we might be able to get ourselves a job, but then I woke up. Who in their right mind would want to employ a couple of ageing hippies?'

'You're still young, love! And it's not your responsibility to take care of your boyfriend. He has to do that for himself. And you can't throw away the chance of having a baby. I mean, I know I'm not the best person to talk to about the joys of motherhood—to be fair, we got the shitty end of the stick when it came to luck. But do you know what, I still wouldn't change one single thing. Even when I'm sick with tiredness or sitting at a hospital bed with my heart in pieces, I still thank God for my two beautiful little girls. They are what make me get out of bed every morning and they are who I will continue to breathe for every day for the rest of my life. Please don't throw that chance away because of circumstance, Petal. You deserve far more.'

Petal bit her top lip and stared into the distance. She took a deep breath. 'I'd better get on with the demonstration.'

Rachel trudged back across the field, slightly deflated. She re-joined her friends from the Fear of Flying Club. 'I'm worried about Petal,' she told them.

'Aye, she didn't seem herself in the car this morning,' said Frannie.

Rachel repeated the conversation she had had with Petal to the others, who listened with concern. They changed the subject when Frannie's son, Simon joined them, his violin now packed away in its case.

'Well done, son—that was actually really good!' said Frannie, genuinely surprised at the quality of the music that the orchestra had provided.

'Cheers,' mumbled Simon.

'I only heard your last set,' said McKenzie, 'but it sounded top quality! I was thinking—I could actually do with someone to lay down some strings for some tracks to go on the next album. You interested?'

Simon's face lit up. 'Are you being serious?'

'Totally!' nodded McKenzie.

'Awesome,' grinned Simon.

Frannie excused himself from the conversation. The heat was beginning to fade from the sun. He strode across to the small area behind the clubhouse where Petal was setting up her yoga class. He cleared his throat with a small cough before addressing her. 'Alright, Petal?'

'Hi, Frannie. Have you come to have a go at the class?' she asked.

Frannie looked terrified. 'God, no!' he spluttered. He patted his round stomach. 'I don't think I'm built for yoga somehow! I've actually come to put a proposition to you.'

'Oh yes?' said Petal, placing the last of the mats on the grass and looking at him with interest.

'I believe you're looking for a job.'

Petal frowned. 'If Rachel has put you up to this then…'

Frannie interrupted her mid protest. 'Nobody's bloody put me up to anything,' he said, holding up his palm to stop her from continuing with her complaint. 'I've spent most of this weekend searching through a pile of CVs trying to find someone who I can work with. That person needs to be reliable, trustworthy, and most of all, it needs to be someone I can get along with. Now it seems to me that you would fit the bill nicely.'

'But, I don't understand? What's the job?' she asked.

'My PA.' He blushed slightly. 'I've been offered the job of Finance Director, but I need an assistant.'

'Oh, Frannie, I'm sorry, but I don't know the first thing about accounts.'

He shook his head. 'You don't have to—that's my job. I've got accounts assistants for that, too. What I need is someone to organise appointments, arrange travel, do a bit of filing and typing. From what I can see, the main thing you need to be able to do the job properly is organisation. And I know you're good at that.'

Petal's mouth hung open for a moment. 'Are you being serious?' she asked.

'Of course I'm bloody serious! Come on, love. You'd be really helping me out. What do you say?'

The colour that had long ago disappeared from Petal's face, returned in front of Frannie. Her eyes sparkled with hope, and he could see a glimmer of the old Petal back at last.

'Yes, boss!' she grinned. 'I'd love to.'

'Before we go on, I have to tell you that the money might not be great…'

'I don't care—I'll take it!' she smiled, before he had chance to finish.

He held his hand out for her to shake. 'When can you start?' he laughed.

She returned the handshake, then pulled him in for a hug. 'Thank you!' she cried joyfully, before pulling away from him as she heard her name being called out on the Public Address system.

Little Gee had been approached with a request. He faded the music, then introduced the song over the PA system. 'This next track is for a very special group of people. Can we please have McKenzie, Rachel, Jalil, Frannie and Petal to the dancefloor. That's McKenzie, Rachel, Jalil, Frannie and Petal. This one's for you!'

Smiles spread across all five faces as the unmistakeable first bars of Pharrell Williams' song, *Happy*, blared out across the airfield.

EPILOGUE

FRANNIE

Frannie walked along the picturesque harbour wall, his short-sleeved flower-print shirt billowing gently in the warm evening breeze. He had been unsure about taking a holiday so soon into his new tenure as Finance Director, but had caved into pressure from Kim and his colleagues to have a break.

He stopped and leaned over to examine a freshly landed catch of shellfish being hauled in a large net from a small blue fishing boat. The air smelled of salt and fish. It took him back to his childhood holidays in Scarborough. He had been stunned when Kim had presented him with the details of their holiday. He had left her in charge of arranging the whole thing. He had been expecting to be presented with a bill for transatlantic flights, or at the very least a substantial sum owing on his credit card for a Spanish villa, but the first summer after his graduation flight from the Fear of Flying course had seen Frannie holidaying in Cornwall.

The family meeting had hit Kim hard. As much as

she tried in the days that followed to pretend that the children were perfectly happy with their micro-managed lives, she could not un-hear the words they had spoken. The following week, after having polished off the majority of a bottle of Cabernet Sauvignon, Kim had emailed the National Youth Orchestra to cancel Simon's audition, and had paid the violin teacher the balance of what they owed for Simon's lessons, cancelling them with immediate effect.

In a matter of weeks, Kim saw a change in both her children as they developed into young adults. Having been given the freedom to do what they wanted with their own time, their personalities shone through.

Simon decided to sign himself up for some guitar lessons, but they were purely recreational, and the best part was that Frannie had decided to give it a go too. Every Wednesday, they both travelled to a flat in Salford where they learned lead and rhythm versions of their favourite songs. The most difficult part was deciding what to learn. Frannie was horrified to know that Simon had never even heard of his favourite band Squeeze, and similarly, he had *no* desire to play a lot of the modern crap that Simon suggested. Various other suggestions Frannie had made had been met with derision—until they bonded over Bowie. Frannie had suggested him one evening whilst flicking through the music channels on TV for inspiration. He discovered that Bowie was one of the few artists whose credibility had travelled with them into the new millennium. Simon was familiar with *Space Oddity* after seeing the Canadian astronaut Chris Hadfield transmit his version of the hit from the International Space Station. Which is how Frannie and his son found themselves spending their evenings singing about a spaceman, and arguing over who got to play the lead (given the fact that Simon was a natural musician and Frannie wasn't, the lead usually went to Simon).

Frannie's new job was going as well as could be expected. It had taken a bit of getting used to—sitting on the inside of the glass cube looking out instead of the other way round, but Frannie was finding his feet, taking time to talk to his colleagues to ensure that the transition was as easy as possible. Petal had helped enormously. He had experienced a moment of last minute panic in the days before she started—wondering whether he had let his heart rule his head when it came to giving the young lady a chance to start again. Manchester Aerospace Engineering had never really experienced anyone like Petal before. It was a very male dominated environment, and the women who had worked there before tended to be either old and matronly, or trendy young things. It turned out that he need not have worried. Petal's organisational skills were second to none, and, after a few tutorials on the computer she was flying. Some days he pondered whether she knew his job better than he did!

As for his fear of flying—that hadn't disappeared completely. He still lost sleep on the nights before he was due to fly to head office, but he was always able to get on board, get the job done and get back. He found that it acted as an additional motivational factor for his job, in that he endeavoured to cover as much ground as he could with head office during every trip, to avoid having to come back again in the near future. They were so pleased with him that they had already discussed a pay rise in the New Year.

And then there was Kim. He hadn't realised how far apart they had grown until they had started to spend more time together. She still nagged him to lose weight, and told him what he had to wear when they went out, but he could live with that. He no longer felt like a spare part in his own family, and that had to be the best feeling in the world.

PETAL

The PA job at Manchester Aerospace Engineering might have been a minor opportunity for many people, but for Petal, it had literally been life changing. She had returned home after the fun-day, and told Moon that she could no longer be a part of his life. He had been stunned, and when he unbelievably claimed that he hadn't seen it coming, Petal knew she had done the right thing.

Moon moved out the same week, and as far as Petal knew, he was living with Ash and Dawn in their squat a few blocks away. Out of guilt, she let him take whatever he wanted from the flat. She noticed that the tea-pot with their measly savings had been emptied by him, but she didn't care. For the first time in a long time she felt truly free. Ironic really, since free living was the epitome of their chosen lifestyle.

She had used the money which she made from her first couple of yoga classes after the fun-day to scour the charity shops for some suitable work gear. Even Petal knew that turning up at Frannie's office wearing a tie dye skirt and sandals was not the correct thing to do. She found some lovely summery tunics which she could wear with either leggings or coloured tights, and bought a pair of boots and her very first pair of heels, which she donated straight back to the charity shop after her initial disastrous attempt to wear them.

She had been sick with nerves on her first day. The office environment was completely alien to her, and, more than not wanting to embarrass herself by her naivety, she was determined not to let Frannie down. She struggled with the technology at first, but Frannie and one of the younger accounts assistants, Nathan, had helped to show her the basics. Frannie had even let her take a laptop home to practice, which she did with every free moment she had. Within weeks she was up to speed.

The discovery of the internet had been a complete revelation to Petal. Obviously she had known about it, but it was only when she found herself dipping in and out of search engines did she realise what a powerful and all-encompassing resource she had at her fingertips. She realised that she could use it to track down her dad—last seen heading east. After a couple of weeks she had located some of his old friends. She hadn't managed to track down her father as yet, but his friend had reported that he had been last seen living on a communal farm in Sofia, Bulgaria. An overwhelming feeling of happiness had enveloped her. He was on the right road—she hoped that he would eventually achieve his dream of reaching Istanbul.

As for her biological clock, it was still ticking away,

just not as loudly as it had been before. Petal's new job had managed to fill a huge void in her life. There was also the matter of her new boyfriend: Nathan, the accounts assistant, whose mentoring had gone beyond his initial remit of showing Petal how to use the computer.

She hadn't 'sold-out', as Moon had accused her. She still held the same principles and beliefs as she had always done. She had actually introduced some greener practices in the office within a couple of weeks of her arrival. And she still taught yoga, which she enjoyed, but more than anything Petal had found herself again. She had been given a chance to start over, and it had all been down to a group of people who were scared of flying. She would never forget them.

JALIL

Jalil knew that whatever was going to happen in the future, it was never going to get better than this. It was just past lunchtime and the beach was beginning to fill up with teenagers, fresh from their beds (or from the beds of others). Jalil had left Holly in her hotel room to get ready whilst he found his mates—eager to hear about their fortunes the night before. He lay on his stomach and tried, for reasons of public decency, not to think too much about what he had got up to hours earlier. Now that he was no longer wracked with terror every time he had sex with Holly, he felt like he was getting quite good at it. She hadn't *complained* about anything yet, which was a big relief.

The holiday was going to mark the end of an era. Jalil, Zain, Robbo and Holly would all be moving on to a new chapter in their lives. Colleges and universities beckoned, but for now, it was still their tight little group. He knew that they would always be friends—no matter what. Anyway, he had the backstage tickets for the Urban Phantom's gig at the O2 Arena in London which was happening in a couple of months' time, so he knew that they would be friends until *then* at least!

He was still basking in the reflected glory of McKenzie's appearance at Holly's party. It had gone down in St Mary's school's history as one of the most legendary parties ever—suddenly everyone wanted to be his friend. He was clever enough to realise that most of the attention was superficial, but still, he was enjoying it.

His exam results had arrived the week before they had departed for Kavos. He had got three Bs and an A in Computer Science, which he had been thrilled with. Zain and Robbo had also done well, and so far the holiday had been one massive celebration. Encouraged by McKenzie's comments at the party, he had decided that he was going to train to be a sound engineer. He had made some enquiries and had been accepted onto a course starting in September in central Manchester.

The flight out to Kavos had been a challenge on his nerves. He had wondered whether the boys would start taking the piss again at the airport, but they had just left him to his own devices. He plugged in his headphones as soon as he was permitted to after boarding the plane, and tried to remember Petal's advice. He had been distracted by Zain and Robbo's attempts to chat up a group of girls from Derby who had been on the same flight. No matter how disinterested the girls had seemed, the boys continued their heroic efforts to pull. Jalil had wondered whether his friends would get lucky at all during the holiday with efforts like that, but he needn't have worried. There were plenty of alcopop-fuelled girls who had been willing to jump into bed with his friends at the end of the night. It was great, as it meant Jalil no longer had to tactfully dodge their virginal questions on shagging.

In the space of a year, Jalil had gone from being the outsider, to one of the most popular boys in the sixth form. He could never have imagined—even six months ago— that anything positive could have come out of his fear, but Jalil was finding out that life can be surprising. He was anxious about the months ahead. Everything was going to change, and he was probably going to find himself fighting at the bottom of the pile again, but for now, he had Kavos, and that was more than he could wish for.

McKENZIE

McKenzie was back doing what he did best—making music. He was never cut out to work in a call centre (he wondered if *anyone* was), and had taken great delight in quitting via email the same day that Alfie had signed all of the paperwork confirming he was back in the band.

The publicity that Alfie had generated from the parachute jump had given them a huge exposure boost, and they had collected a significant number of new fans in the weeks that followed.

Once his bandmates had realised the reasons behind his previous strange behaviour, they welcomed him back with open arms (and a fair amount of piss-taking!). It felt good to be back, playing music with his friends. The fact that he was actually being paid to do this was still beyond his comprehension.

Alfie had kept his side of the bargain and was no longer being a complete twat. On the contrary, he had given instructions to his PA to arrange all of McKenzie's travel by *train,* whenever possible. Obviously he was keen not to undo any of his good work by having another incident like the one in Sweden.

McKenzie also found, as much to his surprise as anyone's, that he was no longer single. He had a stunning girlfriend who went by the name of Eva Koslowska. He had met the girl, who looked like a supermodel, at Rachel's fun-day. Eva had been a teaching assistant at Poppy's school. To an outsider it would have seemed inevitable—the hero of the hour getting together with the most beautiful woman in the vicinity, but to McKenzie it had been a total surprise. She had travelled to London the following weekend to see him, and within weeks had handed in her notice in Manchester and moved to East London, where she found a job in a local school.

Living in the east of the city had been something that McKenzie had never found particularly extraordinary, however, as the date of the arena tour approached, McKenzie couldn't help but feel an explosion of butterflies in his stomach every time he caught sight of the Millennium Dome. Knowing that in a very short period of time he would be performing there, instilled a newfound pride in his heritage.

As he ambled around Greenwich market with Eva one Sunday morning, he caught his breath as the roar of a plane taking off from City airport rumbled overhead. This was the calm before the storm. If Alfie was right, his career was about to go stratospheric. He squeezed Eva's hand and laughed to himself. What a lucky boy he was.

HUGH

Hugh sat on the villa patio with Margueritte and reflected on his golfing performance that day. He was one shot over on the last hole and was annoyed with himself for making a poor choice of iron.

He tried not to let it spoil his evening. After all, he had Margueritte all to himself for a whole four days. He would have liked to have booked a full week, but the Fear of Flying course hadn't been as profitable as he had hoped. Still—at least the students had got something out of it. Hugh had felt both immense relief and pride on the day of the graduation flight. He had felt certain that one of them would make an almighty scene and show him up in from of his old friend Captain Graham. Thank God he had taken some back up with Will and Petal, otherwise who knows what might have happened.

Now that he was confident in his ability to cure aerophobia, he considered running the course again. If he could get more students he would be able to afford a whole week in the sun next year. As he sipped his G&T he picked up a pen and drafted the beginnings of his new advert on the back of a serviette. 'Are you scared of flying?'

RACHEL

Rachel sat back in her business class seat and closed her eyes. The stress of the last few days had completely exhausted her. If anyone was ready for this holiday, she was! As well as the usual packing stress, she had had to ensure that she had two weeks' worth of every possible medication that Poppy might need, all labelled, packed, and then duplicated in various bags in case any luggage went missing in transit, and cleared in advance by US customs. She had to contact the airlines to give them warning of Poppy's medical condition, and get directions and contact details for the nearest hospital in Florida in case anything went wrong. The airline had been fabulous, and had upgraded them to business class after hearing about Poppy's epilepsy. As a stewardess offered them a glass of champagne for the third time, Rachel couldn't help but notice that this journey was a lot different from the last plane ride she had taken.

She refused the champagne politely, knowing that she, as always, had to keep a completely clear head. She smiled to herself—even refusing the stuff made her feel glamorous! She looked at the seat to her left. Poppy seemed tiny, curled up in the large armchair style seat, eyes fixed on the episode of *Flipper* she was watching on her iPad. She felt sick with excitement when she thought about how delighted Poppy would be when she realised she would be swimming with a real dolphin. They had decided to keep this part of the trip a surprise for both of the girls.

Rachel took a moment to mentally thank everyone who had made this trip possible. She thought back to how it had all began. She had been furious at the nurses for suggesting that Poppy was some sort of charity case, in need of a trip to Disneyland. At the time, Rachel had considered the word 'charity' a dirty word, despising it almost as much as the pitying looks she regularly got in the playground at school from the other parents. Now, she was an ambassador for the Dravet Syndrome Foundation—a fundraising charity to which she had contributed nearly twenty thousand pounds by way of her first ever fundraising event.

Then there had been Hugh, whose advert she had answered in the local newspaper, signing up for his course which she had hoped would cure her fear of flying. Of course, what direct part Hugh had played in getting her on board this flight today was debatable. What she could be sure of was that if she had never gone to that first meeting of the Fear of Flying Club back in April, then she would never have met some of the people who she now counted amongst her closest friends.

Friends—it was a funny thing, but Rachel had never considered her lack of friends unusual or problematic.

Any support she needed came from her husband and her mum. Self-preservation had created a spiky shield between herself and any well-meaning, pity-wielding outsiders. All of that changed after the fun-day at the aerodrome. Over half of the parents in Poppy's class turned up to support the event, and not, it seemed, purely out of pity. It turned out that the other kids genuinely enjoyed Poppy's company too! Unlike the run-ins that Rachel witnessed in parks and playgrounds, the children in Poppy's class had got to know her. They were understanding when it came to her lack of social skills, but what Rachel hadn't realised, was that they adored Poppy's sense of humour! When Poppy mimicked Miss Koslowska's accent, the other children in the class squealed with laughter, not daring to do this themselves. When Poppy shouted 'fart' when she passed wind, often in the middle of quiet story time, the other children giggled uncontrollably. Rachel had learned a lot about her daughter that day, because she had finally taken the time to listen.

Since that day she had been on a couple of nights out with the other mums from school. The first time she had expected it to be awful, but Charlie had convinced her to go and it had turned out to be a pleasant enough evening. It was after the second night out that she made the decision to go and have a look at the special school that Miss Myers had suggested. Finally being accepted as part of the class had given her permission to make the best decision for Poppy from a balanced perspective. She no longer had to dig in and hold on out of spite.

It had been a wrench, moving Poppy away from her old friends, but she still got to see them, with Rachel finally getting round to inviting them round for tea. The facilities at Poppy's new school were unbelievable. There was a multi-sensory room, which Poppy loved; a swimming pool; one-to-one supervision at all times and a medic on-site who was fully trained to deal with Poppy's seizures. Rachel had felt like a huge burden had been shared the moment she signed Poppy's papers.

She still thought about Daisy and her family. She had written a heartfelt letter to Daisy's parents, expressing her absolute sympathy over the loss of their daughter. They had replied, thanking her for her touching letter, and had given her a piece of advice that she would treasure forever. They had told her never to compare what she had with what others had, but to celebrate what she had for what it was. She had suddenly realised how much of her energy she had wasted in the past worrying about how Poppy matched up to other children, and worrying about how other people would react to her. Now, when Poppy passed a new milestone, like eating an entire meal using a fork, she shared her joy with her new friends. When Poppy did something funny, which amused the class, she too took delight in it instead of being embarrassed. It felt good to be able to share all the wonderful parts of her youngest daughter with other people.

She was just beginning to feel slightly smug about her two beautiful, funny, perfect little girls when Poppy's voice filled the business class section of the plane.

'Fart!' shouted the tiny girl with the angelic face.

Two loud giggles, followed by a foul smell, filled the area.

ABOUT THE AUTHOR

Angela Roberts was born and educated on the Isle of Man before gaining a degree in French and business studies. After an eight year career in marketing, she swapped the glitz and glamour of international travel for a keyboard and a classroom, dividing her time between teaching French and writing novels.

Her island upbringing has influenced her writing in many ways, none more so than with her first published novel The Fear of Flying Club (apparently being an aerophobe when you live on a tiny rock in the middle of the Irish Sea is not particularly convenient).

In addition to writing novels, Angela enjoys writing lifestyle articles and short stories (one of which ironically won her two return flights to Paris).

kk

Also Available from
Pillar International Publishing

Sour
by
Alan Walsh

Oothangbart
by
Rebecca Lloyd

The Young Dictator
by
Rhys Hughes

Pinhead Duffy
by
Helena Close

The Essential Stephen Leacock
Compiled by
Thaddeus Lovecraft

Books available on Amazon.com
and
in all decent bookshops